Unbreak
My Heart

Khalil Murray

The Equal Team Publications, LLC
Philadelphia, PA

The Equal Team Publications, LLC

Copyright 2015

Library of Congress Control Number: 2015910783

ISBN: 978-0-692-53460-1
First Edition: October 2015

10 9 8 7 6 5 4 3 2 1

City of Secrets
10-book Series

Great Acclaim for
Khalil Murray's
Mr. and Mrs. Gunplay

"Khalil Murray, you're one of the best storytellers of our time. Mr. and Mrs. Gunplay was one of the best novels I've ever read. I cant wait until you release 'Unbreak My Heart."
—Abdus Shaakir AKA Ty; 31st and Tasker . . . S.P.

". . . one of the best 'wife and husband' books that I read in a long time. It was real intense, compelling, captivating . . . keeps you reading from the beginning to the end. Your work is raw Khalil Murray. Can't wait for your second book."
—M.I.; Westside, Pittsburgh

"Two thumbs up Bro., this book is amazing, and a thorough way to start a journey. Mr. and Mrs. Gunplay has taken me to another world. If your next book 'Unbreak My Heart', is anything like your 1st book, you'll be a best-seller in no time.
—Hollywood Pooch; North Philly, H Street

"It's great to have a novel with such infectious swagger, incisive and provoking characters, as Splash and Tia. In Mr. and Mrs. Gunplay, there are so many undeterred, and unapologetic depictions . . . Khalil Murray has responded sympathetically with his characterization of life as a death-dealer."
—P.E.W. Author/Publisher;
Crooket Justice, My Son's father . . . Lu'ap International

"As you can see, the urban novel writers are back with more original and raw writing. Mr. and Mrs. Gunplay set the stan-

dard even higher for other authors out here. In Mr. and Mrs. Gunplay, you can expect the unexpected. The militant mindset of Splash, and Tia's loyalty to him is undescribable. They had me locked and loaded in this book from start to finish. Everything about this novel is outside the box, in a (Kyzer Sozay), sort of way . . . vivid picture painting, and mind blowing events. You haven't read a well thought, and put together urban novel, until you've read Mr. and Mrs. Gunplay."

—Cook Bundy; founder and CEO of
Alayshion Aldori fashion line

"Mr. and Mrs. Gunplay . . . far from typical, but yet, easy to relate to. An eventful story that I would never hesitate to spend money on. As I read this story, it definitely spoke volumes in my mind, and not many authors that I read from were capable of giving me that feeling. I had the pleasure and privilege of getting a sneak peak of (Unbreak My Heart). That joint was crazy! The streets gon' love it. They gon' think they are watching a movie. Khalil Murray, I applaud your skills, and I really look forward to reading anything else you produce. Continue to drop that fire!"

—Mell AKA Kapo; Crown Heights, Brooklyn/Reading

"Mr. and Mrs. Gunplay was real genuine material. When you pick up this novel, you won't want to put it down. It's a page-turner, and will leave you thirsty for more. If every novel from this 10-book series (City of Secrets), is equipped with this much intensity, Khalil Murray will have established himself as a new author to be reckoned with. That's my word."

—Twin; 24th and Tasker . . . South Philly

". . . If I had a wife like Tia, from Mr. and Mrs. Gunplay, I'd be unstoppable anywhere in the world. Her cousin, Rock 'n Roll Rhonda is one of my new favorite characters of all time. I heard 'Unbreak My Heart' is a classic. Khalil Murray, you

got me wanting to visit Philly. Mark my word, your 10-book series is going to be legendary, and I'm feeling how your bookcovers got that movie vibe, too. The book game is yours."

—Jazz; Orlando, Florida . . . the duffel bag boy

"Just when the urban book world became recycled and monotonous, due to weak storytellers, Mr. and Mrs. Gunplay pumped new life into, and resuscitated the game.. Tia and Splash is the quintessence of what death before dishonor really is; Bonnie and Clyde to the 10th power. I was glued from the beginning to end. Never a dull moment, and no weak spots, and airtight with no leaks. Mr. and Mrs. Gunplay has raised the bar too high. All authors are now on notice to turn it up . . . if this was rap, everything else would be the Takeover, while Mr. and Mrs. Gunplay is Ether . . . Flex should drop a bomb to this."

—Bryant 'Tha S-Man' Davis; 17th and Jefferson
Author of the upcoming novel
'The Devil's Den' Due out 2014

". . . Tia and Splash put a new meaning to an age-old saying 'Love ain't what it says, it's what it does'. I haven't come across characters this real, since the HBO drama 'The Wire' . . . if murder for hire was a team sport, I'd have front row, season tickets, to see every game starting Mr. and Mrs. Gunplay. This book has alley-oops, slam dunks, and behind the back, no-look passes, that even Blake Griffin, Michael Jordan, or Magic Johnson, couldn't even perform. If you're looking for a book that is capable of reaching every human emotion imaginable, then you need to look no further, this is it."

—Talib AKA Smitty the Barber; West Philly

"Astonishingly good. I give Bro. Khalil the best on this profound book 'Mr. and Mrs. Gunplay', and I'm sure it'll become a top seller. I also hope that more books on the urban level reaches the platform of how this literary work was done."
—A. Baseer Muhammed; West Philly, 52nd and 60th St.
Co-author of 'Man of Respect" Due out 2015–16

"Mr. and Mrs. Gunplay is a delicacy of deception. Talking about food for thought . . . the beef in this book is well cooked. Enjoy the meal."
—Raheem Pugh; Brownsville, Brooklyn, New York

"Reading this book was literally like watching a movie. The book lived up to its name . . . crazy gunplay throughout the whole book. I personally will be buying all 10 books of this mini-series."
—D.D.; Pittsburgh (Wilkinsburgh)

"Mr. and Mrs. Gunplay is a hood classic. It draws you emotionally. It's one of those books that remind you of every day realities, that we deal with in the streets. This body of work is one of the best books thus far. Keep giving them that straight drop, Big Homie!!"
—Ern; South Philly . . . Dream Chasers

*This novel is dedicated to the lasting memory of my
grandfather, Louis 'Gabby' Williams.
Death hasn't separated us G-Pop.
Every step I take, you also take.
I'm going to continue building our legacy,
and instill the importance of family structure
with my own grandchildren, so that our dreams
can survive for centuries, Insha Allah.
I miss you severely.*

How can love be so kind and so gentle, and then turn and be so cold/
And why must my arms feel so empty for what my heart still holds/

Musiq Soulchild . . .

Chapter One

"Ay, won't 'chu tell me a secret, you never told nobody else."

"Boy, you crazy."

"It ain't like we ever gon' meet. We both up at two-somethin' in the mornin', talkin' on the party-line."

"I met people I talked to on the party-line before."

"Earlier, you told me you didn't."

"That was earlier."

Silence.

"You probably did somethin' typical that most chicks do, and fucked one of ya best friend's dudes, or some shit like that, didn't chu?"

"Wrong."

"You got the wrong nigga thinkin' he ya daughter father?"

"Wrong again."

"You strippin' on the low somewhere?"

"Nope."

"Alright, well, what's one of ya secrets nobody else know, then?"

"You go first."

"I'm locked up."

"You are not."

"I am so."

"Where at, then?"

"On State Road, at the 'F'."

"How you been talkin' to me on the phone for all this time, then?"

"I gotta cell phone."

Silence.

"Ya turn."

"My turn for what?"

"Yo, stop the nut shit, Shay."

"My name not Shay."

"Naw?"

"It's Gabrielle, but everybody call me Gabby."

"Gabrielle?"

"Yup."

"Hold up, hold up. Wait a minute . . . so, you was lyin' about how you look, and how old you really is, too?"

"No . . . not about how I look. I did add three years to my age, though."

Silence.

"So , you only nineteen?"

"Yup."

"Why you lie?"

"The same reason why you said you lived on City Line Avenue in a condo."

"That wasn't no lie."

"Thought 'chu was locked up?"

"I am. I been locked up for a month and a half."

"And I'm really-Boy, do you really expect me to believe that?"

"I wouldn't care, if you did, or didn't."

"So, why you locked up?"

"It's a long story."

Silence.

"Yo, you owe me a secret, Gabrielle."

"Is Hakeem your real name?"

2

"Absolutely."

"Oh."

"And I'm really locked up. I really gotta condo on City Line Avenue. And I'm really twenty-two."

"Okay, okay."

"Alright, now, go 'head."

"You can't hang up on me, after I say what I'm about to say."

"I'm not."

"You promise?"

"Promise."

Silence.

"Okay, um, all my, um, friends, and everybody in my family, think that all the scratches I got on my wrist come from tryna kill myself, but they don't."

"So, where they come from then?"

Silence.

"Hello?"

"They come from my daughter," Gabrielle confessed, as her watery eyes rested on her daughter's sleeping face. Her child's face was the spitting image of the man that had molested her four years earlier. "She be-She be tryna stop me when I be chokin' her, Hakeem. I, um, I been tryna kill my daughter, since she was two. Her father raped me. He, um, He raped me when I was fifteen-years-old. Hello?"

"I'm still here."

"You about to hang up, ain't 'chu?"

"You want me to?"

"No."

"I just got quiet, 'cause what 'chu just told me wasn't easy for me to process."

"It wasn't easy to say."

"I can imagine."

"Hakeem, I'm not crazy."

"Look, for me to believe that, you gon' have to finish

3

where you left off, 'cause only somebody crazy would be tryna out their own four-year-old daughter. I'm just bein' real wit'chu."

"My daughter's father is my foster father."

"What?"

"My foster father is the man that raped me," Gabrielle explained, becoming choked up with revealing the painful memory that had left her with unhealable, mental, and emotional scars. Her hazel eyes were overflowing with justified tears. "My foster mom don't know. Neither do my foster sister. Nobody do. That's who I was talkin' to when I told you to hold on earlier. Hakeem, I'm an orphan. Well, I used to be. My, um, foster parents adopted me when I was six. I'm originally from Miami. Some Haitian guys killed my real parents, 'cause they supposed to had found out that my dad was snitchin' on them. Hello?"

"I'm still here."

"Oh . . . why you keep gettin' so quiet?"

"'Cause, it ain't my turn to talk, yet."

"Don't hang up on me, okay?"

Silence.

"Okay, Hakeem?"

"I'm not gon' hang up."

For the first time in her life, Gabrielle Epps felt like God was paying attention to her. Finally to her, it actually seemed as if she was being allowed the opportunity to share all of her misfortunes, without the threat of being judged by someone. All of her experiences in life had stains of bad karma on them. Enjoyable moments was a stranger to her; a ghost even. Not one teardrop of honest joy had ever managed to escape her beautiful eyes. Her heart was black as a panther. Her eyes and unsmiling face mirrored this darkness effortlessly.

"Do you want my cell phone number, so we can get off the party-line and talk to each other regular?"

"Alright, what is it?"

After giving Hakeem her cell phone number, Gabrielle laid across her bed in the darkness of her bedroom, silently regretting that she had ended their call. In all of her countless times of being on the party-line, coupled with all of the different men that she had met off of it, by far, none of these men came as close to being nearly as intriguing to her as Hakeem. Something about him was oddly different. Something about this strange man had her believing that maybe some form of normalcy could actually exist in her life, which was why when her cell phone began to ring in her hand, she anxiously answered it and pressed it against her ear, and then did something that was highly unusual for her, she smiled.

"Hakeem?"

"Hakeem?! Who the fuck is Hakeem?!"

Gabrielle's smile disappeared.

"Bitch what'chu deaf, now?!"

Gabrielle let out a long, disappointed sigh, and switched her cell phone to her other ear. To her, the father of her child was a merciless tyrant, who just seemed to thrive off of abusing her. Her right eye was black and swollen because of him. He was the devil to her. Because of him, her death, at least in her eyes, was her only way to achieve some salvation.

"So, did you give that conversation we had earlier some thought?"

"I'm not doin' it."

"Excuse me?"

"Mr. Dave, I'm not lettin' ya boss fuck me."

"Don't make-Bitch, do I gotta come over there and put my size ten in . . . "

Removing her cell phone from her ear, Gabrielle turned back over onto her side and stared at her sleeping daughter. Their faces were only inches apart.

Between the two of them, there was enough suffering to bring tears to the eyes of the angel of death.

At nineteen, Gabrielle was wise beyond her years. Hard times had fashioned her into a pessimist. This only added a darker shade to her personality, which stumped the intelligence of everyone that knew her, because she was actually a gorgeous, young woman. Gabrielle stood an even six feet tall, and she had the physical sculpture of a ballerina. Her skin was the color of chestnuts, and her face, at any moment, could produce a smile that could easily make the angriest man on earth blush. Growing up, Gabrielle's aspirations were to become a model, or a fashion designer for someone famous in the music industry. She had such a good eye when it came to clothes, and she didn't have a problem with buying an item out of a thrift store, if it met her stylish taste.

Gabrielle had integrity, but she just lacked self-worth. She was a whirlwind of conflicted values, and the owner of selfless standards, that sometimes made her a fierce opponent to her very own creative thinking.

"Mr. Dave?"

"Bitch, I'm on my mother fuckin' way."

"Mr. Dave, don't 'chu ever get tired of puttin' ya hands on me all the time?"

"Not in this goddamn life, I won't. I got somethin' for that ass tonight."

David Epps was psychologically damaged. The first Iraq war had ruined him. He wasn't even a fraction of the man he had once been. In a North Philadelphia hospital, his wife was confined to her death bed, dying from cervical cancer, and he hadn't visited her once. Their daughter went by the hospital to see her daily, accompanied by Gabrielle, who would spend most of these visits, sitting in a chair, crying her eyes out.

David Epps couldn't wait for his wife to die.

He couldn't wait.

David Epps was fifty-two, and he was a monster. By day, he was an auto mechanic. At night, he posed as an undercover police officer, with his black, Mercury Marauder, and he drove all around Philadelphia, robbing drug dealers, wherever he was able to find them. Mr. Dave was a sick man. So sick was he, that after his wife's death, his plan was to force Gabrielle into marrying him.

To live . . .

is to suffer.

Gabrielle woke up each day, hoping for some type of miracle, or relief, from life as she knew it. Some days, she absolutely craved for an escape. Mr. Dave had a death-hold on her life, and its ever-tightening embrace, was gradually pushing her to the territory of suicidal thoughts.

"I'm so tired of this shit."

In tears, Gabrielle slowly walked out of her bedroom and went into her small, living room. She lived in a one-bedroom apartment, above a check cashing place, on the corner of Randolph and Girard, in North Philadelphia. Mr. Dave paid her rent. Her foster mother, Mrs. Tammy, before falling ill, used to give her a hundred and fifty dollars as a weekly allowance. That money went to her bills, food, clothes, and her weed habit.

"It's two days before Christmas, and I gotta be goin'" through this shit," Gabrielle complained, while turning on a few of the lights in her living room. She continued to let her teardrops fall from her eyes uninterrupted. "Mrs. Tammy can die any day, and he more worried about what it is I'm doin', and who he think I'm fuckin', then spendin' time with her. Asshole. She the only person that love this crazy—"

When Gabrielle's cell phone began to ring at the edge of her coffee table, she frowned as the vile taste of vomit crept up her throat and tainted her tastebuds. She felt lightheaded, so she inched her way over to her couch and sat

down. All at once, she had the shakes, gas, and felt nause-ated.

Mr. Dave was coming.

Still crying, Gabrielle reached out for her cell phone. It was on its seventh ring. Suddenly, it dawned on Gabrielle that the ring tone emitting from her cell phone didn't match the ring tone that she had stored for Mr. Dave's incoming calls. It was someone else.

"Hello?"

"Gabrielle?"

"Hakeem?"

"You still was woke?"

"Um, Ha—Hakeem, why you—Why you took so long to—"

"I was prayin'."

"Prayin'? Prayin' for what?"

"For ya daughter. For you."

"Why?"

God was listening.

"Gabrielle, my dad always told me that, if you need help, no matter what kind it is, to go to God for it."

"Well, I hope he was listenin'."

"Gabrielle, he always listenin'."

"Speakin' of listenin'," Gabrielle sighed, rising to her feet. The sound of a car door slamming outside had reached her ears, instantly causing her heartbeat to accelerate. "I want 'chu to listen to how horrible my life is. Hakeem, I'd be one of the first people to say that I'm not perfect. But I know I don't deserve what I gotta deal with everyday. It's like, its never no end to my pain, Hakeem. Never. My foster father—Hakeem, my foster father mad at me, 'cause he want me to let his boss fuck me tomorrow. Since, I don't wanna do it, he 'bout to come over here and beat me up. I already gotta black eye, from the last time he hit me. My foster mom in the hospital, dyin' from cancer, and now, I can't even go and see her, 'cause she gon' wanna know what happened to my face. Ha-

keem, my foster father don't care about nothin', or nobody. He be hittin' me in front of my daughter and everything. I just want'chu to listen to him, okay? Here he come now. You seem smart, and, like, maybe you can give—Maybe, you can gimme some advice, or somethin'. Hakeem, I don't wanna live like this no more. Don't hang up okay? Pray for me again. Pray for me, Hakeem."

With a trembling hand, and multitudes of fearful emotions, backing her heart into a corner, Gabrielle went and hid her cell phone on the floor, behind her couch. She was just beginning to curl herself into a protective-ball, when her apartment door came crashing open. Gabrielle couldn't help but to wonder if her body was going to be able to survive what it was Mr. Dave was about to inflict upon her.

"Whore, by now, your rabbit ass should know I don't compromise! It's my way, or the fuckin'-Bitch on ya mother fuckin' feet!!"

When Gabrielle didn't budge, Mr. Dave unclenched his hand from around the collar of his pit bull, whose name was Sammy Davis. The brindle-colored dog bolted for Gabrielle's prone body like she was his favorite meal. Once he was upon her, he attacked Gabrielle, sinking his teeth into the flesh of her thigh. The large-headed dog started shaking Gabrielle savagely. A wide smile crept across Mr. Dave's face as Gabrielle's hysterical screams echoed off the walls of her tiny apartment.

To.

Live.

Is.

To.

Suffer.

"Sammy Davis?!!!"

With Mr. Dave's shout, came an end to his dog's mauling of Gabrielle. The powerfully built canine obediently backed away from Gabrielle, snarling and growling. Sammy Davis

her neck became tighter and tighter, nearly cutting off her ability to exhale. Mr. Dave's thrusts were rough and violent. All of her fighting had been spent on not allowing Mr. Dave's dog to get a grip on her neck. Physically, Gabrielle was exhausted. Mentally, she felt depreciated.

Emotionally, she was no longer alive.

On the other end of Gabrielle's cell phone, Hakeem Smith was down on the floor of his jail cell, crying on his knees, as feelings of heartache, rage, and absolute shock, trampled his consciousness. Being helpless was an unfamiliar feeling to Hakeem. However, in the past month and a half, all things sacred, and meaningful to him, had all been stripped from his life.

Hakeem had more than enough reasons to wake up an angry and upset man. It was his forbearance with reality that permitted him to appreciate every new day that he was blessed to see. His father had wanted him to become a doctor, or even a lawyer, but sadly, Hakeem had went against all of the morals that had been taught to him, and he had become one of the most successful drug dealers his neighborhood had ever seen. It was Hakeem's gift at appeasing people that had won him more friends, than enemies. Sadly, it was Hakeem's closest friend, who had crossed him, putting him in a position that was not only testing his intellect, but it had also left Hakeem questioning his reasons for not leaving the United States, and moving overseas, with his father and older brothers, years earlier. With a month and a half of ample time to reflect in his jail cell, it was now a decision that Hakeem wished he had never let get away.

To relieve his own sanity, Hakeem desperately wanted to stop himself from listening to the torture that Gabrielle was experiencing on the other end of his cell phone. He wanted to hang up, but it wasn't in him to abandon anyone; especially, now that it was made painfully clear to him that Gabrielle was actually a victim of such an unimaginable

11

lifestyle. Gabrielle's screams were resonating deep down in his soul. The sounds of her daughter crying was peeling away layers from his heart. Hakeem's conscious was forcing his mind to paint images of what the small child could possibly be witnessing.

There came a moment when Hakeem's exhale paused inside of his chest. This happened when Gabrielle's screaming suddenly had stopped, and the noises on the other end of his cell phone had become eerily silent.

"Hakeem?"

"Yo, you cool?"

"He—He took my daughter. He took Macy."

Hakeem stood up, relieved to hear Gabrielle's voice, but sad to hear the revelation about her daughter. His heart went out to the child taken, and the mother left behind.

"Hold on, okay?"

"Where you goin'? Gabrielle, what'chu 'bout to do?"

"I'm—I need to—Hakeem, I'm—I'm bleedin' real bad. Can you hold on, while I—"

"You alright?"

"No."

Silence.

"Hold on, okay?"

"Alright."

"Thank you."

With a sigh, Hakeem lowered his cell phone down to his side and walked to the front of his jail cell, and stopped at the door. He had the entire cell to himself. He was administrated to the hole for fighting another inmate upon his initial commitment to the county prison. It had been the decision of the Hearing Examiner at his misconduct hearing, that Hakeem be restricted from going into the county jail's general population, because Hakeem had spit at him, during his misconduct hearing. As Hakeem stood silently at the door of his jail cell, he looked out at his cell block's empty dayroom area

in deep thought. Discreetly, he thumbed the tiny button on his cell phone, activating its speaker, which would now allow him to hear Gabrielle's voice when she returned to hers. He couldn't shake the deep concern he felt for Gabrielle and her daughter. Although Gabrielle was a complete, and total stranger to him, Hakeem was intrigued by her personality, which caused him to begin to reflect on why he had even called the party-line in the first place. His reasons for doing so were complexed.

"Hello? Hakeem?"

"I'm still here," Hakeem spoke, backing away from his cell door.

"Sorry for making you wait so long."

Hakeem laid down on his bunk. After crossing his legs, he put his cell phone on his chest and sighed, thinking of the man he only knew as Mr. Dave.

"Hakeem, what'chu doin'?"

"Yo, why don't'chu let'cha foster mother know what's goin' on?"

Silence.

"Gabrielle, that nigga can be doin' anything to ya daughter right now."

"He won't hurt her. She the only person he nice to."

"That don't make that shit cool, though. I heard what the fuck he said he gon' do to her when she get bigger. He a fuckin' nut."

"Hakeem, when you gettin' outta jail?"

Silence.

"You not really locked up, are you?"

"Gabrielle, I ain't wit' the fraudin' shit," Hakeem clarified, as he unsnapped the top, two buttons, on his orange jumpsuit. After readjusting his cell phone on the center of his chest, he placed both of his hands behind his head and decided it was time to come clean with Gabrielle. "Listen, if I was home, ain't no way I would've been able to listen to all

that shit that just happened to you, and not move. Gabrielle, I would've asked you where the fuck you lived, and showed up. Plus, we'd be goin' to find ya daughter, if I got there, after he rolled out. Like, I ain't feelin' that at all. I'm locked up, 'cause my old chick brother crossed me. That's why I'm here. Gabrielle, I ain't never been locked up before. My bail only five stacks, and I can't pay that shit, 'cause I can't send no-body to my spot. My whole family in Yemen, Gabrielle. I gotta aunt in Delaware, but I don't fuck wit' her like that. Like, it took for me to see this c/o chick, who I know from my hood, just to get my hands on this cell phone."

"So, why you just can't call somebody, and—"

"'Cause, I ain't got nobody else in Philly that I can trust."

"I got four hundred and thirty dollars."

Impressed, Hakeem grabbed his cell phone from his chest and sat up on his bunk. Gabrielle was truly winning him over, and she wasn't even slightly aware of it.

"You can have it, if you want it."

"Wanna hear somethin' crazy?"

"What?"

"I got the number for that party-line outta this old news-paper, somebody left in my cell," Hakeem revealed, rising to his feet. He suddenly felt like all of the sleepless nights he had spent, talking on the party-line, was finally bringing him the positive results he had been hoping for. "On the streets, I ain't never heard of that shit. Yo, people be callin' that shit from all the fuck over. One night, I met this white lady from New Hampshire, right. She told me she can have orgasms just from smelling mayonnaise."

Back at his cell door, Hakeem turned off his cell phone's speaker, and pressed his cell phone back against his right ear. It was aching him to ask Gabrielle for the help he so badly needed. The last female he had met on the party-line had burned him out of seventy-five hundred dollars, and one of his cars.

"Hakeem, why ya bail so high?"

"I got locked up for a shootin'."

"Oh."

"My old chick brother got me robbed for three hundred thousand."

"Dollars? Are you serious?"

"Yeah. He had me thinkin' these Mexican niggaz had all this work, and that they was cool to deal wit', but I had to fuckin' find out the hard way, that they was tryna line me up for my bread, and rock me."

"Oh, my god."

"They ain't know I had my ratchet on me, though."

"So, you shot at them?"

"I had to. It's crazy, 'cause, I wasn't on point, thinkin' no nut ass shit like that was gon' go down, or nothin' like that. Especially, wit' my man bein' wit' me. Like, I ain't even peep game, 'til my man pulled out on me, and the nigga tried to shoot me in my face, and missed. Then, his dumb ass gun jammed on him on the second shot."

"And here it is, I thought my fuckin' life was crazy."

"Gabrielle, I'm about money. I ain't into guns 'n all that other shit, but if I ever to touch them fuckin' streets again, you can best believe I'm all over them niggaz."

"Can I help?"

"No question."

"Will you help me with my foster father?"

"Gabrielle, listen to me," Hakeem replied, smiling as he plopped back down on his bunk. The sincerity he could hear in Gabrielle's voice felt like a fresh battery had just been put into his back. "That's the least I can do for you and ya daughter. This the thing of it, though. It ain't gon' be that sweet to get me out, Gabrielle. I'ma need you to come up here to see me, so I can give you game on everything that I need you to do."

"Okay."

"Now, look, I'm in the hole. So, like, when you come up, they gon' put us up in this small ass room, that's gon' have a glass between us."

"So."

Silence.

"Hakeem, I gotta black eye."

"So."

"I can wear some sunglasses."

"Gabrielle, two weeks ago, I met this chick on the party-line, and I told her the same shit I'm tellin' you, and where I had some money at, and she—"

"Hakeem, I won't be your second mistake, if that's what you gettin' at. I'm not her. All I ask, is that you keep your promise, once you come home, that's all."

"I'm sending you to all the money I got left in my stash, Gabrielle."

"I can be trusted Hakeem."

Hakeem let out a heavy sigh.

"Hakeem, sometimes, strangers treat'chu better than ya own family."

Hakeem knew this statement was true. Actually, it was this belief that had influenced him to call the party-line in the first place. He thought that after he had fully explained his predicament to someone, the promise of five thousand dollars would encourage a female to willingly come to his aid. That gamble had cost him seventy-five hundred dollars, which to him, was really nothing but pennies, but now, it was forcing him to have to turn to the money he had in his safe, at his condo. If trusting Gabrielle proved to be yet another vital mistake of his, then, he would have no other choice, but to make the unwanted phone call to his father overseas.

"Why didn't you ask the c/o that gave you that cell phone to help you?"

"I did."

"And what happened?"

"Somebody killed her at my condo."

Silence.

"Gabrielle?"

"Who killed her?"

"Taz."

"Who Taz?"

"The nigga that crossed me, I was tellin' you about earlier. My old chick brother."

"And how you know he did it?"

"She was on the phone wit' me when she got outta her car. I heard the shots, Gabrielle. After he rocked her, Taz picked up the phone.

"And said what?"

Silence.

"Hakeem, what he say?"

"That he ten steps ahead of me."

"So, he watchin' where you live, then?"

"Yeah, but that's why I want'chu to come see me first, before—"

"I don't know, Hakeem."

"Gabrielle, listen to me," Hakeem pleaded, closing his eyes tightly. He could feel his hopes slipping away from him. "That only happened to her, 'cause Taz knew who she was. She from our hood. Her mom used to live on Taz mom block. Before she knew I was here, and she saw me, Taz had asked her about me, thinkin' me and her had saw each other already. The first night I saw her, she came to my cell, and told me how she ran into Taz down South Street, and she wanted to know why I ain't make bail, and what I was locked up for. Taz ain't tell her what went down. Gabrielle, I ran everything down to her. Everything. I was tryna walk her through that shit, while we was on the phone, but Taz—That nigga must've put two and two together as soon as he saw her. He never saw you a day in his life, Gabrielle. All kinds of people be coming in and out of my condo. Gabrielle, all I need'ju to do,

17

is get a letter to the doorman at my condo. That's it. You get this letter to him and he'll let'chu right into my condo, Gabrielle. Me and you'll be on the phone the whole time. Alright?"

"I'm scared, Hakeem."

"Can you just come see me tomorrow, so I can explain everything to you? Like, then, like, you can do whatever you wanna do after that. That's all I'm askin' . . . just come see me."

Silence.

"Gabrielle, I'm comin' home the next time I go to court, no matter what. I already had my preliminary hearing, and them niggaz ain't show up. My shit gon' get put must-be-tried, the next time I go down, Gabrielle. All I got is a gun possession, and a reckless endangerment charge. Taz and them Mexicans ain't comin' to court on me. How can they? Them niggaz somewhere spendin' my fuckin' money."

"Okay, I'll come see you."

"Seriously?"

"Yeah, I'll come in the morning."

"What about dude, though?"

"Fuck him. He gon' be mad, 'cause he gon' expect me to be here when he bring my daughter back in the mornin', but that's what he get for takin' her. He got a key. After what he did to my front door, maybe when he get here, his dumb ass-s'll feel bad enough to get it fixed."

"Gabrielle, if you help me get out, what just happened to you tonight will never happen to you again."

"You sound so convincing."

"When you got faith in ya heart, it come out with the way you speak."

Chapter Two

Separated.

Together.

"I ain't think you was gon' come."

"All I got is my word and my pocketbook."

Hakeem smiled.

Chemistry.

"I would've been here sooner, but—"

"You here now, and that's all that—"

"You look tired."

"I know. My future wife had me on the phone all night, until I fell asleep on her."

Gabrielle blushed.

Hakeem felt his heart dissolve in his chest.

The two strangers both sat down and stared through the thick, plexi-glass divider at each other. Pain instantly recognized pain. The glass barrier between Hakeem and Gabrielle could have been the Great Wall of China, and this still wouldn't have stopped their connection from being made. Gabrielle studied the details of Hakeem's face as a paint collector would carefully scrutinize an exquisite piece of artwork. By far, it was Hakeem's eyes , and his thick beard, that had Gabrielle captivated the most. Hakeem's need for a haircut had him looking ruggedly handsome.

"Our eyes are the same color."

"Our complexion is, too."

Hakeem cracked a grin.

"What?"

"Yo, you pretty as shit, Gabrielle."

Gabrielle was no longer able to hold Hakeem's stare through the plexi-glass. His compliment had taken her by surprise, and had caught her totally off-guard. Gabrielle could have been dressed in the best clothes money could buy, and she still would have felt unattractive in front of Hakeem. The damage that had been done to her over the years was more internal, than external. Her insecurity issues were just the tip of the iceberg. There was a lot of unresolved sadness and pain that reached back to her years as a child, long before she had been adopted and brought to Philadelphia. Gabrielle didn't know what happiness was. Safety was a myth to her. Depression was deeply rooted in her heart, and the leaves of its branches were mirroring her profound unhappiness in her hazel eyes.

"What'chu want me to do, Hakeem?"

Hakeem stood up and sighed. He had handcuffs on his wrists, and shackles around his ankles, causing him to have to take deliberate steps to keep himself from falling. The frustration he was feeling could be seen on his face

"What did you do to get put in the hole, Hakeem?"

"When I first got here, I tried to make prayer in this holdin' cell they had me in. This fuckin' white dude started pissin' on my back, while I was prostratin'."

"For real?"

"I fucked his nut ass up, but the holdin' cell was so crowded, I really couldn't do him dirty like I really wanted to."

"I thought muslims wasn't supposed to curse?"

"We not."

"Why you do, then?"

Hakeem looked Gabrielle in her eyes, but said nothing.

He had no honest answer for her. He knew the consequences of being loose with his tongue extremely well. It just amazed Hakeem, but also shamed him, that he had just been reminded of one of his religious prohibitions, by someone that didn't even share his spiritual beliefs.

"Gabrielle, I been muslim all my life," Hakeem expressed, while sitting back down on the small, metal stool. Through the glass divider he could see all of the unanswered questions waiting in Gabrielle's eyes. "I always felt like I was the black sheep at my school. I got made fun of. I was the one who could never participate in none of the holiday stuff. No Christmas, no easter . . . no birthdays. Then, like, I was little, so I ain't know no better. I ain't even like my own name, Gabrielle. I used to be tickling my older brothers, while my dad used to be up front, leadin' us in prayer. I used to be making fart sounds 'n all that, Gabrielle. Goofy. I was young, though, Gabrielle. My whole family overseas. Like, my dumb ass so in love wit' Philly, and these streets, look what this shit got me. Feel what I'm sayin'? I could've been left the United States, if I really wanted to. Imagine if Taz gun ain't jam on him. What then? What if I ain't have my ratchet wit' me? Then, like, I'm so outta pocket, wit' all the paper I got, I was supposed to been had a lawyer on standby, just for crazy situations like this. Gabrielle, I really be feelin' like a nut in this joint. I'm in this mu'fucker, callin' the party-line, just so I can try—"

Hurt and disappointment took the rest of Hakeem's words from him. His eyes suddenly blurred with tears.

"Gabrielle, Taz muslim."

When Hakeem lowered his face down to his forearms and began to cry silently, Gabrielle knew then that Hakeem's issues with his friend were more religious, than they were personal. It also told her a lot more about Hakeem as a person.

"Gabrielle, if I rock him, Allah gon' send me to the Hell-fire."

"Even though he tried to kill you first?"

Hakeem looked up at Gabrielle and nodded his head. The confusion Hakeem saw in Gabrielle's eyes made him lower his face back down to his forearms.

It was December 24th, 2011, and it was freezing in Philadelphia. No snow had fallen yet, but the temperature was down to the mid-thirties, and the winds were cold and violent. Despite the unseasonable conditions, plenty of people still arrived at the county jail to visit their loved ones. The visiting room was crowded, and packed to its capacity. All of the inmates were wearing the standard-issued, orange jumpsuits. Some of them were smiling, and some of the inmates weren't. The happiest of the inmates were those that had already been successful at swallowing their balloons of contraband. Even with several corrections officers, walking up and down the long aisles of the humongous, visiting room, on some visits, money and drugs, were still being exchanged, and there were some inmates, who were even getting hand-jobs.

The non-contact visiting room that Gabrielle and Hakeem were in was the size of a small bathroom. The walls and ceiling were a soft, tan color, and the floor was pink, laminate tiles. A thick, glass divider, was in the center of the room, separating it into two small spaces. Both sides had one aluminum stool, and there was a desk that was the base of the glass barrier.

"I'll kill him for you, Hakeem," Gabrielle offered, leaning forward, so her whisper could float through the tiny holes in the plexi-glass, and reach Hakeem's ears. His aura, and the courage that she could see reflecting in his eyes had her feeling brave. "I can do it. I'm not muslim. I only been to church one time in my whole life. Hakeem, look at my face. Look at my eye. Hakeem, I got dog bites all over my arms and legs. If

it's a Hellfire, it can't be no worse than what I'm goin'
through already. I'm just sayin', we both need help, and, um,
and, like, I just want Mr. Dave outta me and my daughter's
lives. Hakeem, I'm serious. Why you lookin' at me like that?
You don't believe me, do you?"

"Bye, Gabrielle."

"What?"

"Knock on the door and tell the guard you ready to
leave."

"Why?"

Hakeem ignored Gabrielle as he rose to his feet. He purposely avoided making eye contact with her.

"Hakeem, what did I do? What did I say wrong?"

"It's cool. Just go 'head, Gabrielle."

"I'm not leavin'."

"Our visit about to end anyway."

"Why?"

"'Cause, our hour almost up."

"But—Well, tell me what you need me to do, so I can get
you outta here."

"Gabrielle, forget it. Forget we talked. Look, just forget
me, and just—Yo, just forget we ever met, and stop tryna kill
ya daughter, too."

Gabrielle's eyes widened, then became slits, as she stared
at Hakeem through the plexi-glass. His words had sliced and
diced her, instantly changing her previous opinion of him in
just a matter of seconds.

"Bye, Hakeem."

"Bye."

Chapter Three

Gabrielle swallowed nervously as she pushed the door open to her foster mother's hospital room. Lies to explain her black eye were on the tip of her tongue, but to both her relief, and disappointment, her foster mother was asleep. There were things that Gabrielle desperately wanted to get off of her chest. Her timing was never right, or, at least it appeared that way to her, at the moment. Before her foster mother made her departure from the world, Gabrielle wanted the truth to be known, whether what she had to say would be accepted as truth, or not.

With the same silence that she had came with, Gabrielle left, but not before placing a loving kiss on her foster mother's forehead. If there was anyone that had ever made a positive impact on Gabrielle's life, it was her foster mother.

From the hospital, Gabrielle went straight home. She arrived, only to find her daughter, Mr. Dave, and a shockingly, handsome, Japanese man, all seated at her kitchen table, eating pizza. Her arrival earned her no attention, which left Gabrielle astonished, as she walked quietly into her bedroom, and removed her black, H&M, wool coat.

"Mommy, Aunt Tracy on the phone."

Gabrielle regarded her daughter with a sad smile as she accepted Mr. Dave's cell phone from her tiny hand. Thinking of the final words that Hakeem had given her, she pecked

her daughter on the cheek with a soft kiss, then, ignoring the countless dog bites on her arms, she wrapped her daughter in a loving embrace and held her close for a few seconds. Teardrops flooded her eyes when she felt her daughter's small hands patting her back affectionately. "Mommy love you, Macy."

"Love you too, Mommy."

"Mommy want'chu to come right back in here, after you done eatin', okay?"

"'Kay, Mommy."

At the doorway of Gabrielle's bedroom, her daughter turned around and ran back for another hug. This time, she was the one who provided a kiss on the cheek. The thirst for her mother's love was dancing in her hazel eyes, and it appeared to be unquenchable.

The healing of emotional scars will always resuscitate a dying soul.

Loved ones can rescue lost ones.

Always.

"Tracy?"

"Why ya phone been off all day?"

"It need a new battery."

"Gabby , what's this my dad talkin' 'bout, you got beat up, and robbed last night, tryna buy some damn weed off of one of them corners around there?"

Gabrielle sighed and closed her eyes. When she opened them, Mr. Dave was standing in her bedroom doorway. He was holding a gun in his right hand.

"Gabby?"

"Tracy, can you watch Macy for a couple days, until—"

"Oh, I'm on my way there to get her anyway. My dad told me all about how he had came by there this mornin', and found Macy in the fuckin' house all by her fuckin' self. You—"

"Here ya dad go."

"Yeah, give him . . . "

Gabrielle tossed Mr. Dave his cell phone. After he caught it, he flashed her a smile and walked back out into her living room.

"Sick fuckin' bastard," Gabrielle thought, while kicking off her black Uggz. Her entire body ached as she climbed onto her bed and stretched out. "Now, I got robbed and beat up tryna buy some weed, huh? Asshole. It would've blew his mind, if I would've just started tellin' Tracy what really the fuck happened up in this mu'fucker last night. He lucky Ms. Tammy was sleep when I got to the hos—"

"Hey, you ready to get this party started, or what?"

Gabrielle's eyes grew large and wide, as she flipped over on her bed to her back. Down at the foot of her bed, smiling like it was his birthday, stood the attractive, Japanese man.

"Did Dave tell you what I wanted to do?"

"Get outta my fuckin' room."

"I'm willin' to pay you."

"Mr. Dave?!"

"Him and your daughter left. Hey, it's okay. I'm—"

"Get out!!"

Still smiling, the Japanese man stepped forward. Gabrielle retreated.

"I'll call the fuckin' cops on you right now, if you don't—"

"Wait a minute, wait a minute. Look, just name your price. Dave don't have to know anything."

"Five thousand."

"As soon as we're done, I'll give it to—"

"I wanna see it now. If I can't see it now, I'm callin' the cops."

"Okay, well, I have to go out to my car to get my suitcase. Will you let me back in when I come back?"

Gabrielle eyed the pretty man suspiciously. He was a lot shorter than her and reminded her of the famous, Asian actor, Chow Yun Fat. He was wearing a dark suit that looked like it had been tailored to fit only him, and him alone. His

left hand was displaying a wedding band. He had facial features that could easily allow him to pass for being twenty-something, but his eyes said that he was at least in his early forties.

"And what'chu expect on doin', if I was to decide on lettin' you back in?"

"Dave didn't tell you?"

Gabrielle held her breath as she shook her head.

"I want you to put on this strap-on dildo that I have out in my car, and I want you to go to town on my ass, like it's nobody's business."

"So, let me get this straight. You sayin' you don't wanna fuck me at all? And you don't even want me to suck ya dick, or nothin'?"

"Exactly. Why? Is doin' what I want too much for you to handle?"

"No."

"So, does that mean we have an agreement, then?"

Gabrielle nodded her head.

At 4:20 p.m., on the other side of Philadelphia, Hakeem was shedding tears, while solemnly making prayer in his jail cell. As he stood, bowed, prostrated, and sat, he was hoping to earn God's help and mercy.

"Oh, Allah, please separate me from my bad sins as you have made the distance between the east and the west, "Hakeem supplicated, after completing his fourth daily prayer of the day. His heart was heavy with trepidation. "Please reward me for my good deeds. Allah, I pushed that girl, Gabrielle away when she was willing to do whatever I wanted her to do. She might not know it, but you knew my intentions earlier. I wasn't tryna get her caught up in this drama I'm in. Allah, I chose to be patient. I'll stop hustlin'. Just get me outta here. I'm askin' you for somethin' that's easy for you to do. Allah, you control the Heavens and the earth, and all that is in between them. Nothin' happens, without your

will. Help me, please. You can do anything. You are the majestic . . . Ameen."

When a piece of mail slid beneath Hakeem's cell door, Hakeem eyed it for a moment before rising to his feet to pick it up off of the floor. In the month and a half that he had been locked up, the only mail he had received had come from the public defender that was fighting his case.

At 6:15 p.m., Hakeem made his fifth and final prayer. This particular time, no teardrops were washing his face.

Done prayer, and yawning from his exhaustion, Hakeem got back on his thin bed and dozed off. Talking to Gabrielle on his cell phone, up until the guards had changed shifts that morning had him beat. Their all-night conversation had changed his view of young, single mothers. He thought of them all in high regards now.

Eight hours later, Hakeem's jail cell door was unlocked. It was 2:24 a.m., and it was Christmas.

"Mr. Smith, your bail has been paid. Pack your shit. Let's go."

"Huh? What?"

"Your discharged. Pack all of your belongings. I'll be at the console with your pass."

"Who paid my bail?"

"Santa Clause."

Hakeem stared stupefied at the male corrections officer's back as he walked away. His cell door was left wide open, causing some light from out in the dayroom to enter his dark jail cell. For several seconds, Hakeem laid on his bed and thought of what could possibly be happening. He was forced to believe that he was about to lose his life, and that he was going to be ambushed out in the parking lot of the county prison, so as he got out of bed and began to gather his things, he asked God to place his mightiest of angels in his company.

Done.

An hour and thirty-nine minutes later, freedom was something that Hakeem once again possessed. As tense as he felt, finally being dressed in his own clothes, and inhaling the cold, winter air, made him feel almost euphoric. He couldn't wait to step off of the county prison's property. With every step that he took, his hazel eyes remained alert.

"Hakeem?!"

With the call of Hakeem's name, the vehicle the voice came from flashed its headlights twice. Next, the passenger door of the vehicle swung open.

Across the roofs of dozens of parked cars, Gabrielle and Hakeem looked at each other. It was love at second sight. Hakeem was speechless. He couldn't believe what his eyes were showing him, or what his mind was telling him. Slowly, as him and Gabrielle began to navigate their way to each other, fate was redesigning itself.

Meant.

To.

Be.

"You got me out?"

Biting her lower lip to stop herself from smiling, Gabrielle nodded her head. Inside of her, there was a little girl crying to be loved the appropriate way. Even a simple hug would suffice.

"What'chu do?"

"Gimme a hug first, then I'll tell you."

Hakeem dropped his bags and wrapped his arms around Gabrielle. They both stood the same height. Hakeem's eyes rose up to the night sky in wonderment, while Gabrielle's own eyes cried. For the first time in her life, she felt truly appreciated. Her heart was jumping for joy inside of her chest. Here, in her arms, was a man that had her feeling safe. She didn't want to let him go.

"Who that in that car, Gabrielle?"

"Somebody that think you my brother."

"Ya brother?"

"Yup, so play along when we get in the car."

Hakeem picked up his bags and followed Gabrielle.

"You might wanna stick ya head outta the window, too."

"Why?"

"'Cause, he gon' be fartin' a lot. I'll explain why, after he drop us off."

"Alright."

At Gabrielle's apartment, Hakeem saw a lot of himself in the way that Gabrielle lived. Like him, she was a neat-freak. This impressed Hakeem a lot. In the past, he had encountered plenty of women who had nice cars, expensive pocketbooks, and the like, only to later discover that the women lived like slobs, behind closed doors.

"Gabrielle, where can I pray at?"

"Anywhere you want."

"Over there cool?"

Gabrielle nodded her head as she peeled out of her coat and walked into her bedroom. When she returned to her living room, she sat down at the far-end of her black, leather sectional, and watched Hakeem as he prayed in silence. He was much different than any man that she had ever met. He had manners. His devotion to God had her wondering about the facets of her own life, not only as a person, but also as a mother. The hug that she and her daughter had shared earlier in the day had overwhelmed her completely. She wanted a new lease on her role as a mother. Her hopes were that Hakeem would be the one to help her in that transition, and be there for her, even if it was to only subtract Mr. Dave from her and her daughter's lives.

"You hungry?"

Smiling, Hakeem rose to his feet. He was hungry, happy, and he was out of jail.

"I can make you somethin' to—"

"Come on, we out, Gabrielle."

"Where we goin'?"

"To my spot."

"But what about that guy, Taz?"

"He gone."

"How you know that?"

"He sent me some pictures today. His nut ass down Miami."

"Okay, well, what if he got somebody else waitin' there?"

"Yeah, well, if he do, I feel sorry for they ass."

"Hakeem, why can't'chu just stay here for a few days?"

"Stay here?" Hakeem asked, giving Gabrielle an incredulous look. He couldn't believe that she was actually asking him such an absurd question. "Gabrielle, I'll be back in jail for murder, if I stay here. Yo, you shouldn't even wanna stay here, to keep it real. Gabrielle, ya foster father could be on his way here, right now, for all we know. What I'm supposed to act like I'm ya brother wit' him, too? You know that nigga ain't goin' for that. Gabrielle, listen, I know you scared and everything like that, but, look, it's me and you now. You said ya foster sister got ya daughter, right?"

Gabrielle nodded her head. She feared the unknown, not only for herself, but for Hakeem's sake as well. She knew what Mr. Dave was capable of.

"I'm not gon' let nothin' happen to you, Gabrielle. I promise."

"I know, but that's still not stoppin' me from bein' scared."

Hakeem walked over to Gabrielle and joined her on her couch. He placed both of her hands inside of his, and looked deeply into her eyes.

"You can go, if you want, Hakeem."

"I'm not goin' nowhere, wit' out'chu. Gabrielle, do you know why I ended our visit earlier?"

"No."

"Why you think I did?"

Gabrielle shrugged her shoulders.

His question had been something that she had been pondering over all day long, even while she had been waiting for him to come walking out of the county prison.

"Did you think I was just bein' mean to you?"

"Yeah . . . I cried at the bus stop."

"I cried when I got back to my cell. Do you wanna know why I told you to forget me, and leave, though?"

"Why?"

"'Cause, I didn't want'chu to get the sin of killin' nobody."

"Why couldn't 'chu just tell me that?"

"I should've, but—"

"Was you at least goin' to call me?"

In Hakeem's eyes, Gabrielle saw the answer to her question. He was still holding her hands in his. Had it been possible, she would have dug into her chest and handed over her heart to him, all because she felt like her heart would be safe in his hands.

"I want'chu to come wit' me, Gabrielle."

"What about my daughter?"

"We can come back and get her tomorrow."

"Mr. Dave gon' be mad, Hakeem."

"Fuck Mr. Dave. Let me worry about him."

"He crazy for real, though, Hakeem."

Hakeem snickered.

"Gabrielle, I know muslims in this city that'll have a field day wit' dude."

"Can you go up to the hospital with me tomorrow to see my foster mom, so I can tell her everything that's been goin' on?"

"No question."

Chapter Four

December 25th, 2011
9:11 a.m.

"Ay, Gabrielle, ya cell phone ringin'."

"Can you hand it to me?"

When her chiming cell phone was handed to her, Gabrielle thumbed its screen and placed it to her ear. She was too tired to open her eyes, and the warmth of Hakeem's body felt so comforting that she honestly thought that flipping her eyes open would bring her sweet dream to an abrupt end.

"Hello?"

"Gabby, get up."

"Tracy? Tracy, I'm—Why? Is somethin' wrong with Macy?"

"Gabby, my mom died this mornin'."

"What?"

Gloom.

In an instant, Gabrielle wished so badly that she had the powers to disown the sudden feelings of guilt and regret, that were stabbing at her insides. Teardrops started springing from her eyes as if a levee had been torn apart in her system. There were secrets that she had wanted her foster mother to know. With every rushed step that she took to make it to Ha-

keem's master bathroom, she sobbed, as her foster sister's own crying echoed from her cell phone, into her left ear.

From his bed, Hakeem gazed sadly at his bathroom door, wondering if he should go into his bathroom to console Gabrielle, or if he should just give her a moment to be alone, and have some privacy. He knew exactly what she was feeling. God had taken a significant number of family members from him, and had even removed his mother and grandmother from his life on the same day, while he had sat in the backseat of his mother's car. It was a memory that made Hakeem's father abhor the streets of Philadelphia, and migrate overseas to Yemen.

Hakeem loved and hated his city in an equal fashion. He was fair in his opinion of it. Up until his arrest, Hakeem had thought that he had Philly, and the circle of people he did business with, pretty much figured out. Furthermore, in hindsight, he now saw the old way that he had been doing things as simply being a disrespectful, and idiotic mindset, to have for a guy of his caliber. No more was he going to throw caution to the wind. It had almost cost him his life. The life of the female corrections officer, who had given him the cell phone in jail, had become expendable, all because of him, and this was burning his heart. Her blood was on his hands. He had to make Taz pay for that.

Mr. Dave had to pay too.

And those Mexicans.

"Gabrielle, you okay?"

"Can I be alone for a little while?"

"You hungry?"

"No."

"Alright."

Hakeem took two steps away from his bathroom door, then, with a sigh, he returned back to it. He fought the urge to open it, and won.

"Ay, Gabrielle?"

"Huh?"

"From here on out, we in this together, alright?"

"Okay."

"Alright, I'ma give you some space, now, alright?"

Separated.

"Thank you, Hakeem."

Together.

"You welcome."

Few people would have understood how Gabrielle was able to remain inside of Hakeem's bathroom for such a long period of time, without coming down with one symptom of claustrophobia. On her second hour, she made her exit with her cell phone clutched in her right hand. Her hazel eyes were a lot more mature now. Loss had brought wisdom.

"Hakeem?"

Somberly, Gabrielle searched Hakeem's entire condo, only to realize that she was there all alone. Hakeem had given her more space than she had actually desired. In his absence, she took the time to give herself a personal tour of what would now be her new home.

Hakeem's condo was on the ninth floor of a eighteen-story highrise. Its interior had the masculinity of a man, but had the finesse and style of a woman with taste. There were three bedrooms, a master bath, that was connected to the master bedroom, and a half bathroom, that stood across from an enormous living room, that had carpet the color of beach sand. On this carpet, was a vintage, cocktail table, which stood beneath a beautiful chandelier. The sofas in the living room were chocolate in color, but were decoratively spotted with white, square-shaped pillows, creating a stylish contrast. An end table beside the sofa nearest the half-bath was the home of a large, glass vase, that displayed some of the prettiest marbles the naked eye has ever seen. The walls in the living room were the same shade as the sandy carpet, and three huge windows, if their chocolate, leather curtains,

were drawn, exposed a magnificent view of City Line Avenue. A television was the only thing missing from this comfortable space. Hakeem's bedroom, and the living room, were the only two places furnished inside of the condo. Like the hallway closet, and the half-bath, the other two bedrooms were empty, as were their closets.

The kitchen was pristine. The cabinets were cherry wood, and the gigantic refrigerator, dish washer, oven, and the microwave, all had stainless steel bodies. A granite island stood center, surrounded by six, cherry wood stools. A small, flat-screen TV, and the base of a black, cordless telephone, were the only things on the surface of the granite island.

Back in Hakeem's bedroom, Gabrielle stripped naked and faced her reflection in one of Hakeem's tall, wall mirrors. Gabrielle began to study her body, asking herself what was it about her that would keep Hakeem committed to the journey him and her were about to embark on. They hadn't even kissed yet. Mr. Dave was the only man that Gabrielle had ever been with physically. What she had experienced with his boss the day before, wasn't worth counting. To her, sex, or to make love, meant to get ravished. At nineteen, with her titties still full and perky, and her stomach being stretch mark-free, and flat, and possessing curves like Kelly Rowland, Gabrielle still didn't view herself as being worthy of anyone's love; much less, Hakeem's. She deemed it unimaginable. Looking at her image, all she saw was her black eye, the bite marks on her arms, from Mr. Dave's dog, and the string from her tampon, peeking between the lips of her vagina.

"Can he accept me for who I am?" Gabrielle wondered, pulling her booty shorts back up her shapely legs. She stared into the eyes of her reflection, after she pulled her pink, Baby Phat wife beater, over her head. "What if Macy don't like him? What if he don't like her? What if he try to make me become muslim, like he is? Gabby, he can kick you out whenever he feel like it, then where you gon' go? What'chu gon' do then?"

Mad at herself, Gabrielle walked over to Hakeem's bed and picked up her ringing cell phone. She knew who the caller was, by her cell phone's ringtone.

"What?"

"Where the fuck are you?"

"I'm home."

"Bitch, see, this why I be whippin' ya—"

"I'm recordin' this conversation, Mr. Dave."

Silence.

"So, you can threaten me, and try to scare me all you want, but all that crazy shit ain't—"

"Bitch, you ain't seen crazy, yet."

"I'm tellin' Tracy everything, Mr. Dave."

Silence.

"I'm tellin' her how you—How—Mrs. Tammy died, and you—I wish it was you that died! I hate'chu!!"

"The next time I see you, it's gonna be a fuckin' murder—suicide, you funky, cock whore."

"Fuck you!!"

"Gabby, I'm gon' fuck Macy in the butt."

"Shut the fuck up, you sick pervert!"

"And if you tell Tracy any goddamn thing, I'll make sure Child Services get this sex tape of you hammerin' my boss. You'll never see Macy again, Gabby."

Silence.

"I'll always be one step ahead of you, Gabby. I know about that five grand, too."

"So."

"And when you stop by the house later to get Macy, bring that brother of yours, so everybody can meet him."

"I will. Mr. Dave, he not scared of you."

"Where's all this new heart comin' from, Gabby?"

"You'll see."

"You promise? Gabby you won't win. Oh, by the way, somebody just set ya apartment on fire."

"No, Mr. Dave!"

"Bitch, yes! Yes! I declare war!!"

To live . . . is to suffer.

Several hours later, Hakeem and Gabrielle, were both sitting dismally inside of Hakeem's silver, Porsche SUV. They were parked on the southwest corner of 6th and Girard, facing east. Their eyes were recording a scene that had both of them in utter disbelief. Hakeem's right hand was holding Gabrielle's left hand.

"Everything I owned was in that apartment, Hakeem."

Hakeem stared through his windshield up at Gabrielle's charcoaled apartment. Even with the setting of the sun, he was still able to see gray smoke rising up to the sky. Firemen were done with putting out the blaze, but a handful of them could be seen battling with some burning embers up on the roof of the apartment. From a tall ladder, one fireman was hosing down its walls, and aiming the water at the buildings adjacent to it, to keep them safe from any fire damage. Amazingly, the check cashing place beneath Gabrielle's apartment was left untouched from the two-alarm fire. Had there not been a Fire Department, located a block away, on the corner of 4th and Girard, a lot more destruction would have taken place.

"This'll be a Christmas, I'll never forget."

"So, how you wanna do this?"

Gabrielle sighed and looked sadly out at the public library, her and Hakeem were parked in front of. Her thoughts were a thousand miles away.

"You said he be actin' totally different around ya'll family, right?"

"Yeah."

"Look at me, Gabrielle."

Teardrops rolled down Gabrielle's face as she slowly turned to face Hakeem. Life as she knew it had always been unkind.

"Stop cryin'," Hakeem pleaded, using his left hand to

wipe Gabrielle's face. "We gotta go and get'cha daughter. Gabrielle, that gotta be our focus right now. As soon as the stores open back up, I'll give you some money to go and buy new clothes, for you and ya daughter, all right? Everything you lost in that fire can be replaced. That's how you gotta think, Gabrielle. I know it ain't easy, and that we only got three days in together, but just gimme a little bit more trust, and I'll show you that I know what I'm talkin' about. Just a little bit , Gabrielle. Remember who ya enemy is, and all you gotta do is, be patient, and outthink that nigga. Gabrielle, we 'bout to set the nigga whole life on fire, and he don't even see it comin'."

The seriousness in how Hakeem spoke to Gabrielle won him her trust. This changed the dynamic of their relationship in a major way.

"Where you say his house was again?"

"Lawrence and Diamond."

"What's the quickest way to get there."

"Make a right down 6th Street."

"Feel like drivin'?"

"This?"

"Yeah, why not?"

"Hakeem, this a Porsche."

"And you a dime."

At a red light on 5th and Berks, Gabrielle leaned over and planted a kiss on Hakeem's thick, bearded face. His compliment had her still feeling validated.

"What was that for?"

"For makin' me feel special, before we pulled off."

"Ay, when we get close, park somewhere around the corner, so he won't see what we in."

"Okay."

"And let me carry ya cell phone, too."

"What'chu do with the one you had in jail."

39

"Left it in the cell, for the next nigga they put in there. He might need it more than I did."

"What if they don't find it?"

Hakeem shrugged his shoulders.

"That was still nice of you, though."

At 5th and Diamond, Gabrielle pulled over and parked. Hakeem got out first. Gabrielle didn't budge.

"He been rapin' me, since I was fifteen, Mrs. Tammy," Gabrielle whispered, reciting secrets to a woman no longer alive. Her hands dropped from the steering wheel, down to her lap, and became fists. "I didn't get pregnant at a house party. I been knowin' all along who Macy's father is, Mrs. Tammy. I wanted to tell you. I swear I did. I'm sorry that I lied. Mrs. Tammy, I was comin' to tell you everything today.

Hakeem pressed his back against the passenger door of his Porsche truck and looked up and down 5th Street. Most of the houses had their windows adorned with Christmas decorations. On the driver's side of the street, up closer to Susquehanna Avenue, an elderly, black man, was sitting on his steps, smoking a cigarette, and drinking a can of beer, appearing oblivious to the bitter, night air.

"I'm sorry."

Straightening up, Hakeem walked to the rear of his SUV, to meet Gabrielle, as she stepped sideways through the tiny space, separating his truck and the dark sedan parked behind it. At the curb, Gabrielle handed over her cell phone.

"Alright, which way?"

"It's around the corner."

"Alright, come on, then."

Hand in hand, Gabrielle and Hakeem walked east down Diamond Street. When they reached Lawrence Street, they both made a right, with Gabrielle leading the way.

"That black car with the tinted windows his."

"Help me let the air outta the back tires."

"What if he catch us?"

40

Hakeem pulled up the front of his tan, Louis Vuitton sweater, exposing the two, black, Kimber 45s, that were tucked on his waistline. When he crouched beside the rear passenger tire, on Mr. Dave's Mercury Marauder, Gabrielle nervously bit down on her lip, and went to work on the opposite side.

"Alright, that's cool."

"My ears so cold, they feel like they about to snap off."

"Gabrielle, we gettin' ya daughter and we out."

"Hakeem, I'm scared."

"Introduce me as ya boyfriend to everybody, and just stay by me the whole time we in there."

"Okay."

It was fear, and not the cold winds, that caused Gabrielle's body to tremble, as she rung the doorbell to her childhood home. Her mind was telling her to run for her life, as fast as she possibly could.

"Somebody just peeked through the blinds at us."

"That was my foster sister."

"Stay close to—"

Mr. Dave opened his front door grinning from ear to ear. His eyes were telling a much different story. The awkwardness of the moment was spellbounding.

Together, Gabrielle and Hakeem entered the Devil's Lair.

"I didn't get your name."

"It's Taz," Hakeem lied, extending his left hand. Deep within, he smiled, because his left hand is what he used whenever he used the bathroom. "I'm sorry for ya loss, sir. It's Mr. Dave, right?"

"Certainly is soldier."

"Ay, I heard you gotta pit bull."

"That I do."

"Can I see it?"

"Of course . . . follow me."

Hakeem winked his eye at Gabrielle, before following Mr.

Dave's lead. As he passed by people, young and old, Hakeem politely spoke, while pulling Gabrielle's cell phone out of the front pocket of his Crooks & Castle jeans. As young as the age of eleven, secrets and strategies, of warfare, had been taught to Hakeem, by his father. At twenty-two, if Hakeem was given a well-disciplined army, he could make Homeland Security look like kindergarten cops. He was a masterful outthinker.

"Yeah, I need a cab at twenty-twenty-two, north Lawrence Street."

Making sure that Mr. Dave was listening, Hakeem purposely raised his voice, as he spoke into Gabrielle's cell phone.

"I'm goin' to 6th and Porter. Yeah . . . South Philly. Five to ten minutes? Alright . . . yeah, they can call this number when they outside. Alright, thank you."

In his kitchen, Mr. Dave stopped abruptly and spun around. War was his way of life. It was his religion. He had a storage unit with enough guns to arm every "occupy' protester in New York City. The gun in his right hand, which he was aiming at Hakeem's face, was his favorite of them all. It was a Desert Grizzly. It went with Mr. Dave everywhere.

Even to the bathroom in the middle of the night.

He slept with it.

"Mr. Dave, you ever heard of the famous, muslim general, Khalid Bin Walid?"

"Soldier, you stumbled across the most diabolical enemy you'll ever meet in your fuckin' life."

"All of the historical generals studied his tactics," Hakeem continued, unperturbed by the gun inches away from his face. His adversary's eyes were telling him that he was being underestimated, because of his age. "Napolean, Hannibal, The Ming Dynasty. Mr. Dave, Khalid Bin Walid never lost a battle. He won everytime he fought anybody. You wanna hear somethin' crazy? They say it got to a point, where people started askin' him, if it was true that his sword was sent down to him

by Allah. That's heavy, right? Guess what he told people, though? He told them that his strategy to defeatin' his enemies was patience. Patience, Mr. Dave. I'ma wait'chu out. You can let my age fool you, if you want. My name mean wise, ol'head. Even Prophet Noah let two snakes on the Ark."

Patience.

"Get the fuck outta my house."

In stature, Hakeem was taller than Mr. Dave, and he outweighed him by thirty-five pounds. Without guns, a fight between the two of them would be unpredictable. Hakeem knew mixed-martial arts. Mr. Dave knew crazy.

Simultaneously, as Hakeem raised Gabrielle's cell phone up to his right ear, Mr. Dave was lowering his gun. Their stare never wavered.

"Hello? Yeah, okay. Alright, we'll be right out. Give us a minute. Thanks."

After Hakeem ended his short conversation with the cab driver, Hakeem turned his back to Mr. Dave and walked out of Mr. Dave's kitchen. Again, as he passed back through Mr. Dave's dining room, and crowded living room, with the same politeness as before, he warmly extended condolences to each and everyone that acknowledged him with their eyes. Gabrielle and her daughter were standing at the opening of the vestibule, waiting for him. The look of concern in Gabrielle's eyes intensified his determination to show her what he was truly made of.

"Here go your car keys."

Hakeem glanced over his shoulder at Mr. Dave, then looked at his car keys in Gabrielle's hand, and shook his head.

"Our cab here."

Gabrielle gave Hakeem a puzzled look, as he began ushering her and her daughter through the vestibule and out of the front door. Out on the steps, Gabrielle scooped her

daughter up into her arms and carried her the rest of the way down the steps.

"Gabrielle, get in the cab."

"But—"

"Just get in the cab . . . trust me."

Like Hakeem had expected, once him, Gabrielle, and her daughter, were all sitting in the backseat of the cab, and being driven away, Mr. Dave had wasted no time at climbing into his car, and starting it up. Out of the cab's rear window, Hakeem and Gabrielle, both watched as Mr. Dave's car pulled out of its parking space and sped up to catch up to their cab. It appeared that sabotaging the tires on Mr. Dave's car had been a waste of time.

Patience.

"Hakeem, what we gon' do now?"

"Mommy, who him?"

"His name, Hakeem, Macy."

"Oh."

Hakeem looked down at Gabrielle's daughter and gave her the brightest smile he could get his face to display.

"Mommy, him got eyes the same color as us, right?"

"Yes, Macy."

"Oh."

At Lawrence and Berks, Mr. Dave, wearing an angry face, got out of his car and looked at the rear, driver's side tire on his car. When he looked at the cab's rear window, he saw two smiling faces, and four middle fingers, before the cab made a right turn onto Berks Street and sped off.

"Mommy, we goin' back to Mom—Mom house?"

Hakeem and Gabrielle shared a smile as they both looked down at Gabrielle's daughter. In return, Gabrielle's daughter flashed them both one of her own. Minutes later, as the three of them stood beside Hakeem's Porsche SUV, with the wind whistling every which way around them, their smiles to each

other made being out in the cold seem non-existent. In that moment, genuine love was very much alive.

"Macy, you wanna go to ya new house?"

"Can my mommy come?"

"It's ya mommy new house, too."

"Oh."

Chapter Five

Three weeks into January, the sexual tension between Gabrielle and Hakeem was put on the chopping block, as they both prepared dinner in the kitchen.

"Wanna wake Macy up now, or you wanna wait, 'til the food ready?"

"Hakeem, don't try changin' the subject."

Gabrielle pushed the refrigerator door shut when Hakeem tried to avoid her stare by opening it.

"I'm ready, Hakeem" Gabrielle announced softly, again shutting the refrigerator door, after Hakeem made another attempt to open it. With both of her hands, she grabbed his right hand and held onto it. "I wanna experience makin' love for once. Hakeem, please? I'm tired of just kissin'. And I can see it in ya eyes that'chu wanna do more, too. Hakeem, feel how wet I am. Look."

Hakeem sighed and backed away from Gabrielle.

"See, it's stuff like that, that make me feel like you not really attracted to me, like you say you is."

"It ain't that I'm not attracted to you, Gabrielle."

"Well, Hakeem, what's wrong, then?"

"We not married."

"I don't wanna be muslim, Hakeem."

"And as crazy as it may sound to you, I'm cool on us not havin' sex."

"You wasn't practicin' abstinence, before you got locked up, but now, all of a sudden, you—"

"It sound like Macy cryin'."

Gabrielle rolled her eyes at the ceiling and stormed off.

"This ain't gon' work," Hakeem realized, as he checked on the seasoned, baked chicken, in the stove. From the stove, he turned around to the island in his kitchen, and finished slicing up a cucumber for the fresh salad he was preparing. "Oh, Allah, can you please guide her to your straight path? Change what's in her heart. You see her daughter already be copyin' everything I do, when she be seein' me make salat. I don't know how long I'm gon' be able to do this. I can't put 'em out. Reward me for my good deeds, and help me with my affairs . . . please."

"Hakeem, you cookin' food?"

"Yup."

"Oh."

Hakeem and Macy flashed each other bright smiles. They had a bond. Because of Hakeem, Macy knew several verses of the Holy Qur'an in Arabic. Because of Macy, Hakeem was playing games like, hide and seek, and falling in love with the concept of fatherhood.

"You ready for ya first day at daycare tomorrow?"

"Can we wait to, um, Wednesday?"

"Tomorrow is Wednesday."

"Oh."

"Mommy, startin' school tomorrow, too, Macy."

Gabrielle rolled her eyes at Hakeem's statement as she pulled three plates out of the dishwasher and sat them on the island. She was mad at Hakeem, but not upset enough, or ungrateful, where she wished that she could return back to her old life. In just a matter of weeks, Hakeem had steered her and her daughter's lives in a completely different direction. Not only did she have keys to his condo, and to his Porsche truck, but she also had the keys to her very own

white, 2012 Infiniti M35. Hakeem wasn't stingy with her about anything, and when it came to her daughter, he was absolutely adorable.

"Hakeem, when we prayin' to Allah again?"

"After we done eatin'."

"Oh."

"Hakeem, can you finish settin' the table, while I use the bathroom.?"

Hakeem looked at Gabrielle.

"Mommy, I can set the table."

Gabrielle and Hakeem looked at Macy as she scurried over to the utensil drawer, where the forks, spoons, and butterknives, were all kept. Her pretty little face was lit with ambition. On her toes, she reached into the drawer and pulled out a handful of forks, and a can-opener. With her other hand, she withdrew three spoons, another can-opener, and one butterknife.

Over dinner, Hakeem taught Macy the first six letters of the Arabic alphabet. In silence, Gabrielle memorized them as well.

"Mommy, I'm finished my food."

"I still see vegetables on ya plate."

"Hakeem still got vegetables on his plate, too, Mommy."

"Macy, if I eat mine, you gotta finish yours, okay?"

"They nasty, Hakeem."

"Don't'chu wanna grow up to be big, and tall, and pretty?"

"I'm pretty now."

"But'chu not tall, though."

"Oh."

"Can you finish half of them for me?"

"No . . . both of ya'll gon' finish all of ya'll vegetables."

"Macy, so Mommy can leave us alone, whoever finish they vegetables first, can get the biggest bowl of ice cream."

Macy smiled from ear to ear at Hakeem's challenge.

"Alright, ready . . . set . . . go!"

Later that night, after Macy was put to sleep in her room, Hakeem and Gabrielle returned to their earlier conversation, as they both laid in bed and watched television.

"Gabrielle, what don't you like about my religion?"

"All of the rules, for one thing."

"So, it's not just one thing in particular, then?"

"No."

"Out of everything, what's the one thing you don't like most?"

Gabrielle snuggled closer to Hakeem, while thoughtfully considering his questions. There were several things about the Islamic religion that she didn't agree with.

"Is it anything about my religion that'chu do like?"

"Yeah."

"What?"

Before Gabrielle could give an answer, Hakeem's cell phone began to ring on his nightstand.

"Now, watch he answer it," Gabrielle figured, eyeing Hakeem as he grabbed his cell phone and looked at its glowing screen. To annoy him, she grabbed the remote control to the TV, and changed the channel from the basketball game he had been watching, to a reality show. "Little does he know, I believe that it's only one God, and don't have no problem—"

"Yo, turn back."

"You talkin' on the phone."

"So, what. Ay, Alfie, hold on."

With remote in hand, Gabrielle jumped out of bed and ran out of the bedroom. Hakeem didn't chase after her, although, he really deep down inside wanted to. It was the valuable news that he was receiving on his cell phone that kept him laying right where he was.

"Alf."

"Yo?"

"My fault . . . so, what'chu was sayin' about that nigga?"

"He tryna spend two hundred and fifty stacks wit' my man."

"And you sure it's Taz?"

"The nigga gotta nut ass tattoo on the side of his face, right?"

"Yeah, that's him."

"Alright, so, you tryna get'cha paper back, or what?"

"Hold on for a second, Alf."

Hakeem lowered his cell phone from his ear and took a deep breath. He wanted to let out a victory roar at the top of his lungs. After another deep breath, he smiled and placed his cell phone back to his ear.

"Alf?"

"What's up?"

"Meet me at 12th and Susquehanna, at twelve o' clock."

"Tonight, or tomorrow?"

"Tomorrow afternoon. Bring ya man wit'chu, too."

"We there."

"Alright, As Salaamu Alaykum."

"Wa Laykum As Salaam Wa Rahmatullah."

Chapter Six

"Yo, why you not in school?"

"'Cause, I was worried about 'chu."

"Gabrielle, everything gon' be cool. I told you that. You ain't got nothin' to worry about."

"Hakeem?"

"Yeah?"

"I love you."

"I love you, too, Gabrielle. I love you and Macy."

Gabrielle switched her cell phone to her other ear, and turned her back to the relentless wind that was having its way with Chestnut Street. Center City felt like Chicago and Alaska, all in one. Philadelphia was dealing with record low temperatures.

"I don't want nothin' to happen to you, Hakeem."

"See, now, you got me feelin' like, I shouldn't've told you what I told you."

The disappointment in Hakeem's voice caused Gabrielle's hazel eyes to fill up with tears.

"Call me on ya lunch break, alright?"

"Be careful, Hakeem."

"I am. Now, go back in there and show The Art Institute how you get down."

"Okay."

"Ay, did Macy cry when you dropped her off at daycare?"

"Not one teardrop."

"I promised her a rabbit, if she didn't cry."

"She told me."

"Alright, Superstar. Get back in class."

"Bye."

No matter what Hakeem said, Gabrielle couldn't stop herself from being worried about him. However, him telling her that he loved both, her and Macy, had helped her to focus, as she sat through two hours of introductions and orientation, in school. Being around so many talented individuals, and being exposed to all of the diverse, career opportunities, made her feel like she was being involved with the positive flow of the world. It was something that her heart had been needing. At one moment, while listening to another art student speak on her personal ambitions, Gabrielle's left eye had produced a single teardrop, as her own ideas and new goals ran races in her head. She was about to be somebody.

At lunch, Gabrielle went into The Library Place to eat. It was crowded with all sorts of people, and as she moved amongst them all, Gabrielle felt like she belonged. To her, it was a defining moment in her life.

Up North Philadelphia, on the corner of 12th and Susquehanna, Hakeem was sitting in the backseat of his friend's 2012 Land Rover Evoque. Hakeem was giving his full attention to the friend of his friend, Alfie, who was sitting in the front passenger seat. His name was Keyz.

"The nigga grabbed two bricks off me before, so—"

"Did he have his cousin, Fresh, with him, when ya'll seen him?"

"Naw, he was wit' these two chicks."

"Was they Rican?"

"I ain't sure. They stayed in the car."

"Yeah, Hak, they was Rican."

Hakeem met Alfie's eyes in his rearview mirror.

"Why? What's up?"

"Alf, them the bitches who them Mexican cartels be sendin' to the United States, when niggaz be fuckin' up they paper."

"Yeah, well, they make caskets for bitches, too. They can get pink jawns, if they want."

"Alright, look, Keyz, this what I need you to do for me."

For the next twelve minutes, Alfie, and his friend, Keyz, listened as Hakeem put together a beautiful, double-cross for Taz. Hakeem's cell phone never stopped ringing throughout his entire conversation.

A little while later, Hakeem was in the company of another reliable associate of his. His name was Bill-Bill, and he was from 12th and Susquehanna. He was someone that Hakeem trusted with his life. He was the man that taught Hakeem that, with some people, loyalty was for sale. As Hakeem and Bill-Bill sat at the kitchen table, inside of Bill-Bill's two-story, rowhouse, the two of them kept it real with each other, as they always did.

"Hakeem, smart men know when to pick they battles."

"So, what I'm supposed to just bow outta this shit?"

"It's cats in jail doin' forever, and niggaz in they graves, who, no mu'fuckin' doubt, wish they could rewind back to when, bowin' out was an option, Hakeem."

"Like my dad, huh?"

"Hakeem, you gotta learn how to let some shit go sometimes."

Hakeem clenched his jaws and stared angrily at Bill-Bill's white, refrigerator door. Letting go what had happened to his mother and grandmother was impossible for him.

"You thirsty?"

"Naw, I'm good."

"It was an unfortunate accident, Hakeem."

Teardrops filled Hakeem's eyes, as the biggest mental and emotional scar, unpeeled itself inside of his mind. Ha-

keem lowered his face down to Bill-Bill's kitchen table and unleashed what was inevitable.

"We muslim, Hakeem. Let that shit out. When we cry, it soften our heart."

"Bill-Bill, man, I can cry for the rest of my life, and I think my heart gon' still stay hard."

"When your next court date?"

"Next month."

"What day?"

"The eighth."

"Tell me about this lawyer you hired."

"She cool."

"What's her name?"

"Tobi Russeck."

"I want'chu to let this thing wit' Taz go, Hakeem."

Hakeem frowned and stared across Bill-Bill's kitchen table into his eyes.

"Go overseas wit' the rest of ya family. Get married, Hakeem. This doonya got more wins, than losses."

Sighing, Hakeem lowered his eyes down to his folded hands. He knew he could easily ignore, or let go, his situation with Taz. However, moving overseas to Yemen, with his father, and three older brothers, meant that he first would have to find it within himself to forgive them for not avenging the deaths of his mother and grandmother.

"Why didn't you gimme a call, while you was locked up?"

"I ain't wanna be no burden."

"Ay, I might be outta the game, but I still gotta few nickels layin' around."

"I know."

"You spoke to ya dad lately?"

"Nope."

"How about ya brothers?"

"Nope."

"You know what Allah says about cuttin' the ties of kinship, right?"

"I know."

"Tighten up, then."

"I am."

"Insha Allah."

"Na'am, Insha Allah."

The.

Big.

Payback.

Hakeem stretched his legs and shifted uncomfortably. He was inside the trunk of a parked, blue, Pontiac Bonneville, and he was sweating profusely. In his hands, Hakeem was choking the rubber grips of two, Israeli hand-Uzis. His face was covered with a Barack Obama, Halloween mask, which was given to him by Alfie, and he was wearing a one-piece, black, Dickie overall. The car he was in was parked on Jefferson Street, between 7th Street, and Marshall Street. This area was known as Homicide Hell. It was here, where Hakeem chose to ambush Taz. His only hopes were that the two Mexican women weren't tagging along with him.

It was a few minutes after midnight. Homicide Hell was eerily quiet. The Grim Reaper was twiddling his skeletal thumbs with boredom.

The sound of car doors being slammed reached Hakeem's ears. His anxiety was running rampant within him. He didn't want to kill Taz. He just wanted his money back. He only wanted what belonged to him.

"If them bitches wit' this nigga, I'ma have to air—"

Click.

From the grassy lot across the street, Alfie thumbed the key-less remote in his hand, popping the trunk on the Bonneville, where Taz was under the impression that eight kilos of cocaine were waiting for him. With Alfie, also hiding in

the tall grass, were some young murderers, who thrived on making Homicide Hell exactly what it was.

"Pussy, drop that fuckin' bag!"

Surprise.

The Grim Reaper stopped twiddling his boney fingers and smiled.

"Drop that shit!!"

Taz earned his nickname for having a wild and unpredictable personality. In the Grays Ferry section of South Philadelphia, where him and Hakeem both grew up, Taz was feared by many, and loved by none. Taz was actually short for Tazmanian Devil. He always carried a gun and wore a bulletproof vest. He was short, skinny, and his beard was so big that it covered the entire front of his neck, and upper chest. His face had six blotches on it, from where he had gotten shot with a Tec-22 as a teenager.

Taz hadn't come alone, as Hakeem quickly learned. To Taz's right, and to his left, were two, Mexican women. The hand-Uzis that Hakeem had leveled at their pretty faces didn't even make the two women bat their eyelashes.

"Hak, that's you?!"

After Taz's question, Alfie and his assembly of shooters, all blitzed out of the tall grass with their guns raised. Upon seeing this, the two, Mexican women pushed Taz forcefully into Hakeem, and drew hand-Uzis of their own, from beneath their waist length, white, fur coats. At that moment, Hakeem's only disadvantage was that he only stood a foot away from the still-open trunk of Alfie's Bonneville, and that his back was to it. Catastrophically, when Taz was shoved into him, Hakeem had tried to side step him, while also attempting to spray off some gunshots, but, with unhumanlike speed, Taz had rushed Hakeem, sending them both toppling into the open trunk of the Bonneville.

Death match.

While Hakeem was in a small, dark space, fighting to

save his life, at his condo, Gabrielle was in her walk-in closet,
trying to decide what she was going to wear to school the
next day. She was sitting in the center of the floor with her
knees pulled up to her chest. Beside her, she had her new
iPhone that Hakeem had bought for her. He was on her mind
heavy, and she didn't want to miss his call. With a sigh,
Gabrielle did another once-over of her closet. She was surrounded by racks and racks of dresses, furs, jeans, shearling
coats, designer pocketbooks, and expensive shoes and sneakers. She now owned items that she once used to stare into
stores and admire as a window shopper.

"Mommy?"

"Macy, what'chu doin' woke?"

"I miss Pop-Pop, Mommy."

Gabrielle wrapped her arms around her daughter and sat
her on her lap. She prolonged the warm squeeze she was giving her daughter, because she was at a loss for words. Her
daughter's revelation had struck her soul like a lightening
bolt.

"Mommy, can Pop-Pop pick me up from school tomorrow?"

"No, Macy."

"Why?"

Tears slid down Gabrielle's face.

"Mommy, why you cryin'?"

"'Cause, Mommy sad."

"Oh."

With her little hands, Macy reached up and helped
Gabrielle wipe the tears from her face. Macy was wearing
some Missoni pajamas that Hakeem had ordered from their
website.

"Can I get my bunny rabbit tomorrow, Mommy?"

"Only if you go get back in bed, and—"

Gabrielle's cell phone started ringing on the floor.

"That's Hakeem, Mommy?"

"Yup."

"Can I—"

"Hakeem?"

"Gabri—Gabrielle?"

In that one second of Gabrielle hearing how difficult it was for Hakeem to say her name, she knew then and there, that something was terribly wrong.

"I . . . need—Gabri—"

"Hakeem, what's wrong?"

"I got—I—Gabrielle, I got shot, and I keep passin' out."

"Oh, my God. Hakeem, where you at?! What happened?"

Hakeem told Gabrielle where he was, and briefly explained to her what had happened to him. Hakeem also gave her a number to call, along with some specific instructions that he wanted conveyed to the person that he had her call. Gabrielle had remembered every detail word for word.

"Gabrielle, call him right now."

"Okay."

"Tell Macy I—"

The other end of Gabrielle's cell phone went silent.

"Hakeem?!"

"Mommy, what's wrong with—"

"Macy, go wait for me in the living room," Gabrielle ordered, tearing off Hakeem's Yves Saint Laurent bathrobe. Frantically, she dialed the number Hakeem had asked her to call, as she stepped into a pair of sneakers. "I told him not to —Hello? Is this Bill-Bill?"

"Yes?"

"Hakeem got shot, and he locked inside the trunk of a car. He keep—"

"Wait a minute, wait a minute. Slow down."

"He want'chu to call ya friend with a tow truck."

Chapter Seven

Two weeks later . . .

"Tracy, can you come to the door for a minute?"

"Gabby?"

"Yeah."

"Girl, oh my—Where you at?"

"Out front."

"Why ya number came up blocked?"

"I'll explain that when you come outside."

"Okay, I'll be right out."

Gabrielle kept her eyes in her rearview mirror as she sat her cell phone down in her lap. The reflection of cars driving east on Diamond Street behind her, had her feeling nervous and jittery, while she sat in her car. She was gambling with her life, and she knew it. Going against Hakeem's strict orders to stay away from North Philadelphia, after leaving school, Gabrielle had daringly traveled up North Philadelphia anyway, to visit her foster sister. There were issues that Gabrielle desperately needed to get off of her chest. It was time that her foster sister knew the truth about everything.

It was a sunny, February afternoon. School was letting out. In her rearview mirror, Gabrielle was watching as kids dispersed from the elementary school behind her at the intersection of Lawrence and Diamond. The sight brought back

memories of when she was once a student at the very same school.

When Gabrielle's foster sister came out of her house dressed in all-black, muslim overgarments, Gabrielle stared at her in open-mouthed fascination. Likewise, when Gabrielle's foster sister saw Gabrielle sitting behind the steering wheel of the sleek, four-door, Infiniti, she too, gawked in open-mouthed fascination.

"Gabby, where you get this car from?"

Gabrielle wasn't trying to press her luck. As soon as her foster sister pulled her passenger door shut, Gabrielle stomped her mid-calf, buckle boot, down on her gas pedal. She knew that Mr. Dave was most likely at work, but she wasn't taking any chances. She flew down Lawrence Street at a break-neck speed, and didn't slow down, until she was making a left turn onto Berks Street.

"Gabby, slow down. Why you drivin' so damn fast?!"

"When I pull over, I'll tell you."

On 4th Street, a few houses before Oxford Street, Gabrielle pulled over and parked. She kept her car running, and her eyes were playing all of her mirrors, until her nerves gradually settled down. When she turned and faced her foster sister, Gabrielle quickly noticed that she was being inspected from her Whiting+Davis boots, up to her Dominican-styled, Chinese wrap. Her foster sister had judgment in her eyes.

"So, you muslim now?"

"Before we even think about gettin' to me, and what I am, you gon'—"

"Tracy, ya father been rapin' me, since I was fifteen. Well, actually, since I was fourteen."

"What?"

"Macy is ya dad's, Tracy."

With these words, Gabrielle placed her back to her driver's side door. Her Bruno Mars CD was whispering lightly

out of her car speakers. The small speaker that her back was pressed against was sending rhythmic trembles up and down her spine.

"Just think back to two thousand and six, Tracy," Gabrielle recommended, watching as her foster sister's eyes brimmed with tears. Her own eyes did the same. "Remember how bad I started doin' in school? Tracy, he would pick me up at the bus stop, then he would make me suck his dick in his car all the way home from school. He used to tell me he'd kill all of us, if I ever said anything to you, or ya mom. Then, when you went away to school, he just got worse. When ya mom used to be at work, he used to make me put on her lingerie and do it to me in they bed, Tracy."

For an hour, Gabrielle and her foster sister cried, hugged, and talked. During this sixty minutes, day became night.

"Gabby, can you take me to that masjid right there, so I can make prayer?"

Sadly nodding her head, Gabrielle looked through her windshield at the large masjid down the street. Its property stretched from Germantown and Jefferson, and went as far over as Orianna and Oxford.

"I'm getting married on Friday, Gabby."

"Married?"

"My dad put me out, because I took my shahadah. When you called, I was in there packin' all my stuff."

At 4th and Jefferson, Gabrielle turned left. At the corner of Germantown and Jefferson, she made another left, and parked behind a taxi cab.

"He keep pullin' my kimars off my head, too."

"Tracy, he the one that gave me that black eye. He the one that set my apartment on fire, too."

"Gabby, I'm sorry you had to—"

"It's not your fault, Tracy."

For five straight minutes, Gabrielle and her foster sister hugged and cried some more.

"I have a letter for you from Mommy."

"How?"

"One of the nurses had found it under her pillow when they was cleanin' her hospital room. I meant to give it to you the night you came to the house with that guy to pick up Macy, but when I came back downstairs, you was gone. You left without even sayin' anything."

"I had to."

"Then I tried callin' you, to let you know we was cre-matin' Mommy, but'cha cell phone was off.

After giving her foster sister another apologetic glance, Gabrielle accepted the envelope that she had pulled out of her pocketbook. Her name was written on it, and the envelope was still sealed.

"You the only person she wrote, Gabby."

Gabrielle looked up from the envelope. Her foster sister was crying again. Teardrops were sliding down the front of her pretty face, and falling down to her black overgarment. It was visible in her watery eyes that she wished that a letter had been written for her too.

"I never opened it, or anything. You can read it, while I go pray."

"Tracy, what made you wanna become muslim?"

"A lot, really."

Gabrielle's cell phone started ringing.

"You should come inside and take ya shahadah, Gabby."

"No, I shouldn't, either."

"You would, if you knew what was best for you."

"And who's to say, takin' my shahadah is what's best for me?"

"Billions of muslims all over the world. The one who cre-ated all of us, whether we acknowledge him, or not . . . that's who."

"I acknowledge that there's a God, Tracy."

"On your terms, or his?"

Gabrielle's cell phone stopped ringing.

"Do you like wearin' all that stuff?"

"I do now. Everybody got so much to say about how muslim women dress, but don't nuns dress just like us? Gabby, I get more respect from people out in public, than I ever did."

Gabrielle's cell phone started ringing again.

"Answer your cell phone. I'll be right back."

After Gabrielle's foster sister got out of her car, Gabrielle picked up her cell phone and answered it.

"Yes?"

"Mommy, Hakeem said him gonna beat'chu butt."

"Oh, really?"

"Yes."

"Give Hakeem the phone, Macy."

"Mommy, where you at?"

"In my skin."

"Oh."

As Gabrielle waited for Hakeem to get his phone, she opened her foster mother's letter, and began to read it.

"What's up, Superstar?"

"Hakeem, I'm on my way to pick you and Macy's prescriptions up right now."

"She threw up again."

"Did she eat anything?"

"That's what made her throw up. She ate some pop tarts."

"Pop tarts?"

"That's what she wanted."

Macy had a stomach virus. She caught it from someone at daycare. Since Hakeem was recovering from his gun shot wounds at home, he was caring for Macy during the day, while Gabrielle attended school. When Gabrielle got home, she acted as Mommy and nurse.

"Alright, we'll see you when you get here, then."

"Okay."

Off of her cell phone, and more able to fully concentrate,

Gabrielle decided to reread her foster mother's letter over, starting from the beginning. It was a one-page letter, written on both sides. The handwriting was in cursive. The message was a dying confession. As Gabrielle finished the last line at the bottom of the front-side of the letter, her face became a mask of several emotions, all of which were dreadful. She started to hyperventilate. Unable to stop reading, Gabrielle flipped the letter over, and with crying eyes, she continued to read. When her foster sister returned from the masjid, and got back into her car, Gabrielle's eyes were just completing the last sentence of the letter.

"Gabby, what's wrong?"

Like an avalanche that occurred all of a sudden, Gabrielle released a scream that came from her soul, and started to sob uncontrollably, as she placed her face on her steering wheel.

"What Mommy say, Gabby? What she say?"

The weeks with Hakeem had transformed Gabrielle in a lot of positive ways; both inwardly, and outwardly. Not smoking weed had caused her to add on a few pounds, giving her body a thickness that made her curves much more appealing. Inwardly, her most drastic transformation was what she thought of herself. It wasn't just good for her personality, or that her newly-discovered, self-worth, was just enlightening for her as an individual, but what Hakeem had pointed out to her, was how her own daughter was beginning to adapt to the inspirational vibes as well. Now, with learning that she had only been adopted by her foster mother, for the pleasure of satisfying her foster father's perverted appetite, Gabrielle was feeling like a meaningless human being all over again. Near the end of the letter, her foster mother had expressed her deepest regrets, and apologies, but for Gabrielle's sake, this was simply like applying a small band-aid to a wound that needed a hundred stitches.

To live . . .

is to suffer.

Gabrielle's foster sister removed the wrinkled letter from Gabrielle's clenched fist, and took her turn at reading the damning confession for herself. When she was done, she got out of Gabrielle's car, and went across the street, back into the masjid. A short moment later, she came back out with an older, muslim woman, who followed her closely over to Gabrielle's car.

Far across the city, Hakeem's eyes were wet with tears. He was laying in his bed, flipping through the pages of an old photo album of his. Macy was beside him, sleeping quietly.

A loud knock at Hakeem's front door sent his nerves into an immediate frenzy. Macy's safety was his first concern. At first instance, Hakeem's protective nature was to wrap one of his bulletproof vests around Macy's tiny body, then hide her some place safe. When the knocking at his door became more incessant, Hakeem snatched his gun from beneath his pillow, and went to face whatever danger was waiting for him on the other side of his front door. The gunshot wound to his stomach made him slouch as he walked. While crossing his living room floor, Hakeem's mind speculated about who his uninvited guest, or guests, could be. He knew it wasn't Taz for sure, and he didn't think that it could be the two, Mexican women, because after their arrest, the night that all of the drama had went down, the two of them had both gotten deported back to Mexico, or at least, that's what the word on the streets was.

With his gun aimed at his front door, Hakeem placed his left eye up to his peephole. The door vibrated against his face as the person on the opposite side started knocking again. What Hakeem saw made his mouth go dry, and both of his eyes widen. On the other side of his front door stood a muslim couple, and two, federal agents.

"Hakeem, that's Mommy?"

Slowly backing away from his front door, Hakeem shook his head.

"Who—"

"Go back in the room, Macy."

Macy didn't budge. She simply rubbed both of her eyes sleepily, and watched Hakeem as he hid his gun under the center cushion of his couch.

"Macy, go get my cell phone off the bed."

"'Kay."

"Hurry up."

Hakeem walked back over to his front door, unlocked it, then pulled it open. He gave all four of his unannounced visitors annoyed stares.

"Sir, we'd like to speak to Gabrielle Epps."

"About what?"

"These are her parents, and they would very much like to see her."

"Gabrielle mom and dad dead."

"Sir, who—"

"Here go your cell phone, Hakeem."

Everyone's eyes lowered down to Macy as she squirmished her way by Hakeem. The muslim couple gasped when they were able to get a good look at her.

"Hakeem, there go Mommy!"

"Macy, that's not—"

Hakeem's voice was lost by a vision that was both stunning him, while at the same time, amazing him. He swore to himself that his eyes were playing some kind of cruel joke on him, or that his pain medication had to be causing him to experience some type of delusional side-effect. For clarity, he blinked his eyes, and like everyone else, he continued to stare as the young, muslim woman, who had just stepped off of the elevator, began to walk towards them.

"See, that's Mommy, Hakeem."

Seconds after Gabrielle had exited the elevator, two other

people had also stepped off of the elevator behind her. One was a black, muslim female, with a very, light complexion, who was wearing all-black overgarments, and a black, fur vest. Beside her was a tall man, that was clean-shaven, who had on some expensive sunglasses, and an outfit that looked like it had cost him a pretty penny. Hakeem and these two individuals knew each other very well. They were all raised on 27th and Wharton, in South Philadelphia. The muslim woman was Taz's older sister, and Hakeem's ex-girlfriend. Her name was Alicia, but she went by her muslim attribute, which was Bayyinah. The guy with her was her cousin. His name was Fresh, and him and Taz shared a loft apartment on 11th and Vine.

Hakeem could smell trouble.

Gabrielle could too.

So did the two federal agents that were standing beside Gabrielle's clueless parents.

Chapter Eight

That same night . . .

Hakeem had Gabrielle by the hand, and Gabrielle had Macy by hers. With Hakeem in the lead, all three of them filed into the bathroom and closed the door behind them, leaving Gabrielle's parents, the two federal agents, and Taz's sister, and his cousin, out in the living room by themselves.

Organized.

Confusion.

"Hakeem, what's goin'—"

Placing his index finger up to his lips, Hakeem silenced Gabrielle, then turned on the faucet on the bathroom sink.

"Mommy, Hakeem gotta gun."

"Yo, you ain't recognize them people?"

"The ones that was on the elevator with me?"

"Not them . . . the ones wit' them two fuckin' feds?"

"Mommy, Hakeem said a bad word."

"Hakeem , who are they?"

"Gabri—Ay, yo, they talkin' 'bout they ya mom and dad."

"My mom and—"

With a disbelieving frown on her face, Gabrielle reached over Macy's head to open the bathroom door, but Hakeem quickly caught her right hand, and held onto it. Bored, Macy flushed the toilet.

"That's Taz sister, and his cousin, Fresh, I was tellin' you about."

Some nights, Hakeem and Gabrielle would lay in bed, and talk, until the sun came back up. Their topics had no limits, or barriers. They were both opinionated, and sometimes, their late night talks ranged from how well their first, black president, was doing, to Macy, their dream vacations, life in general, and even how an orgasm felt, because Gabrielle had never had one. For the both of them, the act of not having sex was an uphill battle, but its highlights were that it allowed both of them to fall in love fairly, without any physical biases clouding their judgements. At twenty-two, and nineteen, Hakeem and Gabrielle were ahead of the game.

"Hakeem, what they doin' here?"

"Look, I'm on they top as soon as we walk out, but, yo, while I'm hollerin' at them, you need to be seein' who the fuck them—"

"Hakeem, said, another bad word, Mommy."

"I took my shahadah."

"You look real pretty, covered up, too. Let's get this drama outta the way, then we'll—"

"Ya'll medicine in my pocketbook."

"Yo, my gun under the middle couch cushion."

"Want me to get it, Hakeem?"

"No," Hakeem and Gabrielle both said together, looking down at Macy, as she put her tiny foot on the weight scale, which occupied the small space, between the toilet and the sink.

"Alright, come on."

Macy flushed the toilet again.

Gabrielle opened the bathroom door.

Hakeem turned off the sink's faucet.

All eyes were on Hakeem, Gabrielle, and Macy, when the three of them came marching out of the bathroom. Hakeem's eyes flicked from the two federal agents to Taz's family mem-

bers. Gabrielle's eyes flicked from Taz's family members, to the muslim couple, that were obviously impostering as her parents.

"Ay, Fresh, and, Bay? Let me holla at ya'll back here."

As Gabrielle and Taz's sister crossed paths, they both glared at each other with open resentment. The two of them were sisters in Islam, but new enemies for no reason.

"Bitch," Gabrielle thought, rolling her eyes in response to Taz's sister's sneer. Going into the living room, she picked Macy up and stared daggers at the couple, pretending to be her mother and father, giving no acknowledgement to the authorities, standing closely beside them. "What they think I'm slow, or somethin'? Look how pointy her nose is. Look at his—His—No. Oh, my—Fuck no. This can't be . . . "

Gabrielle fainted.

"What happened?" Gabrielle wondered, blinking her eyes open, three minutes later. Someone had laid her across the couch, but she didn't know who had done it, or how she had gotten there, as she groggily propped heself up on her elbows. "Did I pass out? Who—"

"You made me fall and hit my head, Mommy."

"Sorry, Macy."

"Are you okay, Gabrielle?"

"Khaleemah, give her a moment to get her head together."

"Is askin' her is she okay a crime, Basil?"

As Gabrielle sat up slowly, Macy climbed on the couch and worked her way onto her lap.

"I know this is going to sound unbeliev—"

"Who are ya'll?"

"I'm your father, Gabri—"

"And I'm your mother."

"Gabrielle, we were never dead. We've—Me and your mother been in the Witness Protection Program."

"But—"

"I know there's a lot to explain."

Gabrielle stared at her father as he sat down beside her and took her right hand, and enclosed it inside of his. Minus the thick, salt and pepper beard, and the aging wrinkles around his eyes, he looked exactly like the tall man in the only photo she had of her parents. His eyes matched hers. The scar beneath his bottom lip was there, and his hair was straight, and satiny, just like hers. Turning to face her mother, Gabrielle not only felt overwhelmed, but she felt like the floor had gotten snatched from under her feet. Nothing was what it was anymore. Her history as she had always believed it to be was now baseless. She had experienced enough heartache for the day. First, it was her foster mother's letter. Now, here were two ghosts from her past, trying to tell her that their deaths were a hoax, and that they had been living in the witness protection program for the past fourteen years.

"How did ya'll find me?"

"They did."

Gabrielle looked from her mother, to the two federal agents, standing silently beside the opening to the kitchen. They both seemed to be more concerned with what was being discussed down the hall, in Hakeem's bedroom, than they were with the two people they were obviously there protecting. This made Gabrielle even angrier. She sat Macy on her little feet, and rose to her own. As she became madder, her thoughts grew clearer.

"Get out."

These words of Gabrielle's got the federal agents' full attention. Both of them watched Gabrielle as she stormed over to her pocketbook, and pulled out an envelope.

"Read this on the way to wherever ya'll goin' from here," Gabrielle snapped, shoving her foster mother's letter into her mother's hands. With a face of contempt, she snatched open the front door and stepped to the side. "Ya'll was better off

lettin' me think ya'll was dead. At least, then, I couldn't've blamed the two of ya'll for all the horrible shit I had to fuckin' go through. Witness Protection Program, my ass! I was ya'll fuckin' daughter! I was damn near the age, my daughter is now. Guess who her dad is?!!"

Gabrielle's parents held onto each other as they followed their black-suited protectors out of the front door. Their heads were hung low. Gabrielle's mother was crying.

"Daddy, my foster father is my daugther's dad! He started rapin' me when I was only fifteen, Daddy! While you was bein' fuckin' protected, your damn daughter wasn't!"

Out in the hallway, Gabrielle's mother dropped the letter that Gabrielle had forced her to take.

"Yeah, read it, Mommy! Read how my fuckin' foster mother knew what was goin' on the entire fuckin' time!"

Hakeem had never witnessed Gabrielle so upset before; much less, raise her voice. It alarmed him to see her so out of character. As he walked down his hallway towards her, with Taz's sister, and cousin, in front of him, his thoughts at that moment was that he should run up to her and try to hug all of her pain away. It was still difficult for his mind to grasp onto the fact that she was wearing overgarments, and that she had taken her shahadah, and had become muslim.

After Taz's sister, and cousin, stepped foot out of the condo, Gabrielle slammed the door at their backs, and ran to the bedroom. Macy started to cry, because her mother was.

"Want some ice cream, Macy?"

"I want Pop-Pop."

Hakeem looked at Macy dumbfounded. The love that he felt for the pretty, little girl, was superior. To comfort her hurt, was calling for him to return her to the very same man that he had rescued her and her mother from. Looking into Macy's crying eyes, Hakeem wished that she had've asked

him for anything else in the entire world, when suddenly, a bright idea popped into his head.

"Macy, you still want that rabbit?"

Macy's eyes grew large and hopeful. She was still crying, but in her hazel eyes, the glow of the sun could be seen, appearing behind the clouds.

"Alright, let's go check on Mommy, Macy."

"'Cause—'Cause, Mommy sad?"

"Yup . . . now, we gotta think of somethin' to make her happy all over again."

"Oh."

"Oh," Hakeem repeated, teasing Macy, as they walked hand in hand down the hallway to his bedroom. Macy's bright smile was pulling on his heart strings. "Macy-Macy . . . Fo-Facy. Anna-Anna . . . Fo-Fanna."

Gabrielle wasn't crying anymore when Hakeem and Macy came walking into the bedroom. She was laying across the bed hugging a pillow close to her chest, and staring blankly at the mirrored-door, that led to Hakeem's walk-in closet. The black kimar she had on her head was pulled back a little, exposing the edges of her hairline. Her Whiting+Davis boots were down on the floor, beside her pocketbook, and one of her portfolio sketch-books, from school, was sticking out from beneath the bed, where her cell phone was laying.

"Mommy, we here to, um, make you happy, um, all over and over again."

"And I'm goin' first, so may I have your attention, please?"

"I'm not in the mood, Hakeem."

"You will be after this performance I'm about to put down, ain't she, Macy-Fo-facy?"

Grinning from ear to ear, Macy nodded her head with much enthusiasm, as she climbed up on the huge bed with her mother. She loved Hakeem with all of her little heart.

When it came to making her laugh, Hakeem never disappointed, so as he picked up the remote control to his entertainment system, and then disappeared into his walk-in closet, she jumped up and down, clapping her hands excitedly.

Non-stop, for an hour and a half, Hakeem entertained Gabrielle and Macy by throwing a mini-concert for them, in the middle of his bedroom floor. With every song, he went into his closet, and had changed into an outfit to imitate that particular artist, or group, then performed their songs as best as he knew how. The staples in his stomach had prevented him from doing his best Chris Brown moves, but when Michael Jackson's 'Thriller' album came on, he put some socks on his feet, and moonwalked from one wall to the other. Macy had fallen asleep during his Jay-Z concert, but with a smile on her face, Gabrielle had sung along with Hakeem to each and every song.

A point came in the night, where the seriousness of all that was going on made its entrance again. This happened when Gabrielle returned from putting Macy to sleep in her own bed.

"So, what should we talk about first?"

"That was my real mom and dad."

"Yeah, I kinda figured that from the way you was snappin'."

"Like, how was I supposed to react, Hakeem? What they expected from me? Was it supposed to be all smiles, and hugs?"

"Ay, man, anybody who been through all the stuff you went through, then had the picture remixed on 'em like that, would've reacted the same way. I know I probably would've."

"So, I wasn't wrong?"

"Do you feel wrong?"

"No."

"What they in The Witness Protection Program, or some-thin'?"

"That's what my dad said."

"That's crazy."

Hakeem and Gabrielle walked into the bathroom to-gether. Both of them grabbed their toothbrushes, put tooth-paste on them, then began to brush their teeth, as they watched each other's reflections in the mirror.

"So, where you take ya shahadah at?"

"At the masjid."

"Which one?"

"Don't get mad at me, okay?"

Hakeem gave Gabrielle a confused glance as he returned his toothbrush to its holder.

"After school, I went and picked up my foster sister, and—"

"So, you went up North Philly?"

"Hakeem, Mr. Dave was at work."

Letting out a long sigh of frustration, Hakeem stepped around Gabrielle and walked out of the bathroom. He un-derstood what she obviously didn't. Mr. Dave was in no type of way to be taken lightly, or to be played with. Hakeem was certain that Mr. Dave was anxiously waiting for their paths to cross again, and that the crazy man was going to try some-thing over the top, so he continuously made emphasis of this to Gabrielle, and had warned her how it was always impor-tant for her to be aware of her surroundings, and to stay away from North Philadelphia.

"I told Tracy the truth about everything, Hakeem."

"Yeah, well, clearin' ya conscience could've got'chu rocked."

Gabrielle removed her kimar, her overgarments, and outfit that she had on beneath it. After putting all of this stuff away neatly, Gabrielle climbed back into bed with a heavy heart. Her day had been long and exhausting.

"Hakeem, ya medicine in my pocketbook."

"I'm cool."

Gabrielle sighed and watched Hakeem as he used the re-mote control to dim the lights, and cut on the huge, flat-screen, TV, that was slowly lowering down from the ceiling, on the other side of the bedroom.

"What did Taz sister and cousin want?"

"Some bullshit."

"Feel like talkin' about it?"

"Not really . . . but it wasn't what I thought it was gon' be about, though."

"They know about Taz?"

"His cousin think he scrambled to Mexico wit' them chicks, but I think his sister . . . "

"You think she know you killed him?"

"Naw, but from the way she was actin', I think she know that nigga ain't in no fuckin' Mexico."

For a few seconds, Hakeem and Gabrielle stared quietly at the TV, as Hakeem searched for something for both of them to watch.

"You got court tomorrow, don't'chu?"

"Yup."

"Want me to stay home and watch Macy?"

"Yo, you ain't missin' no school days on my watch."

"But—"

"It's a daycare center on 4th and Market."

"Hakeem, but she not enrolled there, though."

"Money talk, Gabrielle."

"Can I make salat with you in the mornin'?"

"Absolutely."

"Can we get married tomorrow, too?"

"Can we what?"

"All I want for my dowry, is some books, and more over-garments."

"And what if I told you that Taz sister pregnant?"

Gabrielle took the remote control from Hakeem's hand and muted the flat-screen. The silence became loud instantly. Hazel eyes stared into hazel eyes.

"You told me you stopped messin' wit' her five months ago."

"That's how many months she said she is."

"So, you actually not only believe that, but'chu also believe it might be yours, too?"

"She showed me her stomach, Gabrielle."

"Hakeem, you a drug dealer. Well, you was. Look, you might know the difference between real drugs, from fake drugs, but can you honestly say you know what a girl stomach should feel like, or, Hakeem, for that matter, even look like at five months?"

"Let me tell you somethin' about me, Gabrielle," Hakeem responded, wincing in pain, as he sat up in bed. He hated that Gabrielle was questioning his intelligence. "I ain't get to where I'm at, by not payin' attention. And I ain't sayin' that on no cocky shit, either. Gabrielle, she could've walked in here with a baby that looked just like me, and I still would've got on some shit, like, I want a paternity test. I'm far from slow, Gabrielle. My dad had me and my brothers playin' chess when we was pups. You feel what I'm sayin'? Like, I hate to compare myself to a fuckin' animal, but I'ma beast when it come to most of this street shit, Gabrielle. I ain't sayin' I know it all, but I definitely know a little about a lot. Now, not to change lanes, but Macy brought up Mr. Dave when you ran in here cryin' earlier."

"What she say?"

"Just that she wanted him, that's all."

Gabrielle pulled the pillow from under her head and smothered her face with it. A second later, she let out a muffled scream, as Hakeem looked down on her.

"Don't go up North no more, Gabrielle."

"I'm not."

"So, how you end up at the masjid, while you was up there, though?"

After taking the pillow off of her face, Gabrielle told Hakeem all about her trip to see her foster sister, and how she had ended up inside of the masjid. As she spoke, Hakeem soothed her by playing with her hair and massaging her scalp.

"So that's the letter you was tellin' ya mom to read earlier?"

Gabrielle nodded her head.

"I heard you tellin' her to pick up a letter, but I ain't know what'chu was talkin' about."

"Today was a long day."

"Yo, I ain't know what to think when I saw them agents through the peep-hole."

"That's how I was feelin' when I got off the elevator."

"Did they say how they found you?"

"Them agents, I guess."

"Plus, it's in the system, from when you renewed ya driver's license, and changed ya address to here."

"Doin' that got me so wet."

Hakeem frowned in confusion. A second later, he stopped massaging the nape of Gabrielle's neck and pulled his hand away.

"Hakeem, why you stop?"

"'Cause, this ain't one of them nights, where I got it in me to turn you down."

"You ain't gotta say it like I be tryna take advantage of you."

"I'm just sayin'."

"Wanna feel how wet I am?"

"Gabrie—"

"Just gimme ya hand, dag."

"Yo, you outta pocket."

Gabrielle hissed in satisfaction as she guided Hakeem's

right hand down into the front of her black, laced, La Perla panties. The heat of his touch, made her inhale quickly. Her clit shot off fireworks when three of Hakeem's fingers trailed across it. Spreading her legs open wider, Gabrielle arched her back and chewed on her bottom lip, as Hakeem's middle and forefinger slowly began to curl, parting her pussy lips.

"Alright, I felt it."

Gabrielle shrieked when Hakeem snatched his hand out of her panties.

"Gabrielle, we already outta pocket for doin' all this."

"So, why can't we just get married tomorrow, then?"

"I mean, we can, but . . . "

"But what?"

"Naw, I'm just sayin, we could've used ya dad as ya Walee, and—"

"Hakeem, they can be pretendin' to be muslim for they cover, for all we know."

"True."

"Can't we just go to the masjid?"

"Yeah."

"Hakeem?"

"Yo?"

"Why you never let me see ya dick? Is it little, like a pinky finger, or somethin'?"

"What? Man, you trippin'. This jawn so long, you can tie it in two knots."

"Let me see, then."

"Chill, man."

"So, we gon' get married tomorrow?"

"Insha Allah."

"That mean, God willin', right?"

"Yup."

"Hakeem?"

79

"Gabrielle, you know we gotta get up to pray in a few hours, right?"

"Oh, I forgot all about that."

"See."

"Hakeem, when you gon' tell me what happened to ya mom, and why you don't speak to ya dad and brothers?"

"Gabrielle, I be wantin' to, but, then, I just be like—I don't know, man."

"It don't have nothing' to do with you not trustin' me, do it?"

"Not at all."

"Oh."

"Yo, that's where Macy get that from."

"What?"

In the best Macy voice he could muster up, Hakeem said, 'Oh.' This earned him a series of giggles from Gabrielle.

"Yo, that's how she be soundin', though, don't she?"

Gabrielle nodded her head against Hakeem's shoulder, still laughing.

"Gabrielle, after we get married, I wanna adopt—Oh, shit. Yo, ain't that ya foster sister?"

Gabrielle sat up in bed as Hakeem unmuted the TV, and proceeded to turning up the volume. On the flat-screen, behind the white, male, news reporter, stood Gabrielle's foster sister, Tracy. She was crying hysterically as she stood in front of her house. A number of cops, and plain-clothes, detectives, were standing around her. The camera man then panned right, out to Lawrence Street, bringing into view, a black, BMW, that was riddled with bullets. As the camera man panned back left, once again, putting the camera back on Gabrielle's foster sister, a small picture of Mr. Dave was then posted up in the top-right corner of the flat-screen.

"Oh, shit."

"Hakeem, they was gon' get married tomorrow."

"Damn, that's crazy."

"Hakeem, that guy just came back to the United States to marry Tracy, then they was leavin' next week, to go back overseas."

For some unknown reason, Hakeem suddenly started to have a sick feeling in the pit of his stomach. Slowly, a question began to crawl up his chest, and marched its way to the tip of his tongue.

"Oh, my God. I gotta call Tracy."

"Gabrielle, where dude was from overseas?"

"Tracy said, he live in Yemen, but that he was originally from down South Philly, somewhere."

To live . . .

is to suffer.

"What she say his name was?"

"Um, I think it was Shampsideen, or somethin' like that."

Hakeem covered his face with his hands and let out a gut-wrenching sob, that slowly became a painful sounding howl. Hakeem was feeling a thousand regrets as the face of his older brother flashed in his mind. Remorse started swimming laps through every vein in his body. Lowering himself back to his pile of pillows, still covering his face, Hakeem let his crying have a voice and let his anguish fly free.

"Hakeem?! Hakeem, what's wrong?"

Time brings change.

Change brings time.

"That was my brother, Gabrielle. That was my fuckin' brother. That was Shamps. That pussy killed my fuckin' brother."

Chapter Nine

Outside, on the sidewalk of the Criminal Justice Center, Hakeem powered his cell phone back on and looked around for a moment. He had a lot of things that he wanted to get done, and only a small window of time to do it in. It was 12:15 p.m., and the weather was freezing. Everyone on foot in Center City was bundled up, and moving like the cold air was their worst enemy.

Hakeem raised his hand to hail a passing cab, but then decided against it. His Porsche jeep was only two blocks away, parked inside of a parking garage, on 12th and Sansom. However, that wasn't his first destination; neither was the daycare center, on 4th and Market, where Macy was. He had something more important he wanted to get done. As he began to stroll east on Filbert Street, he raised his cell phone to his ear and called back the person that he had received the most missed calls from.

"What happened?"

"The judge threw it out."

"So, that's good, right?"

"Yeah."

Hakeem stopped at the corner for 13th and Filbert. The traffic light on the opposite side of 13th Street was red. It wasn't the red light that Hakeem was respecting. He was

simply waiting for the traffic that was speeding north up 13th Street to slow down before he crossed the intersection.

"So, where you at now?"

"Just leavin' outta CJC."

"Oh."

Hakeem switched his cell phone to his other ear, and jammed his left hand into the pocket of his A Bathing Ape Jacket. He was cold, but he welcomed the discomfort. He was grieving tremendously.

"You okay?"

"Naw."

"Hakeem, we can wait to get married, if you want."

"Naw, we still gon' do it, Insha Allah."

"Well, I gotta get back in class, okay?"

"Alright."

"I love you, Hakeem."

"I love you, too."

"As Salaamu Alaykum."

"Wa Laykum As Salaam Wa Rahmatullah."

"What was the extra stuff you just said?"

"I'll teach you later on."

"Insha Allah."

At 12th and Filbert, Hakeem turned right, and then proceeded to walk down 12th Street, until he reached the double-glass doors of the Gallery Mall. Inside the Gallery, he paid attention to nothing and no one. He was numb. Mr. Dave was on his mind. He came out of the Gallery Mall at 8th and Market, and walked south all the way down 8th Street, until he was standing outside of the well known jewelry store on 8th and Walnut. It was here, where Hakeem's senses slowly began to return. It was here, where Hakeem wanted to purchase a wedding ring for Gabrielle. This was the place that had his mother and grandmother so excited, and where the three of them had been headed, on that fateful afternoon, that had tore his family into shreds.

"Good afternoon, sir. How can I help you today?"

"I wanna, um, buy a real nice wedding ring that gotta decent-sized karat on top of it, and like, a bunch of smaller karats goin' around the band."

"Sounds nice. If you don't mind me being forward, what's your spending expectations?"

"I got thirty thousand on me right now."

"Cash?"

"Cash."

With that magic word, Hakeem dug down into the front, right pocket of his Naked and Famous jeans, and withdrew a roll of money, that was secured by a thick, blue rubber-band. From his front, left pocket, he pulled out another one, only this roll of money was wrapped tightly by a red rubber-band. From the inside pocket of his jacket, Hakeem pulled out a third roll of hundred dollar bills, and then lined it beside the other two, on top of the spotless, glass jewelry case.

"I'll have to count it, and then verify that each bill is authentic, sir."

"Be my guest. Matter fact, I'll be back for my ring in two hours."

"Are you sure?"

Hakeem forced a smile on his face and extended his hand over the glass showcase. The white jeweler shook his hand firmly, and deftly removed Hakeem's three rolls of money from between them.

"I'll be back in two hours."

"What's your name, sir?"

"Hakeem."

"Akeem?"

"Hakeem."

"Oh, Hakeem . . . with an 'H'?"

"Yeah."

"Okay, I'll see you in two hours, Hakeem."

Thirty thousand dollars lighter, Hakeem stepped back

outside to the frigid temperature. His exhales could be seen drifting away from his face, as he looked up and down 8th Street. It was freezing. Still, Hakeem, welcomed it. To get a move on with his list of things he wanted to get done, he stepped off of the sidewalk and hailed down an unoccupied cab that was coming his way, up Walnut Street.

Minutes later, in the back seat of the cab, Hakeem pulled out his ringing cell phone and answered it.

"Hello?"

"Guess who just had the audacity to come into my school?"

"Who?"

"My mom and dad."

Hakeem placed his hand over the speaker of his cell phone, and told the cab driver to take him to 4th and Market.

"Did you hear me, Hakeem?"

"Yeah, I heard you."

"They right here, parked in front of my school."

"So, you gon' talk to 'em?"

"Didn't you say we needed my dad for our marriage?"

"I mean, well, first, you gotta find out if they really muslim, or not, before we do anything. If he is, though, it'll save us from havin' to go to the masjid, and gettin' somebody to step in as ya Walee."

"Okay, I'ma call you back."

"Alright."

Hakeem palmed his cell phone and stared out of the cab's rear window. At 9th and Walnut, as the cab driver was turning right, his hazel eyes lit up like small balls of fire. A short, white man, was walking down 9th Street, reading a newspaper. Mr. Dave's face was on the front page. Glaring out at the newspaper, as the white man passed, Hakeem answered his ringing cell phone and pressed it against his left ear.

"So, what they say?"

"They muslim."

"Al Hamdulillah."

"Alright, so, what we gotta do now?"

"Tell 'em to meet us at the house, at like six."

"That's it?"

"Yup."

"Okay. Oh, um, As Salaamu Alaykum."

"Wa Laykum As Salaam Wa Rahmatullah."

Hakeem had never been married before. When him and Taz's sister were dating, they had discussed it on numerous occasions, but that was as far as the two of them had ever gotten, because Taz's sister had wanted Hakeem to stop selling drugs. This ultimatum eventually brought an end to their two-year relationship. Now, Hakeem viewed his position in life much more seriously. He saw marriage as a balance for him. How he was going to earn his money was still something that Hakeem was trying to figure out, but Hakeem was at a point, where he was now open to trying a legitimate business hustle, that wouldn't land him behind bars. He had college in mind for Macy. He had a clothing line in mind for Gabrielle. For himself, however, he didn't know what his calling was going to be.

"You can pull over right here. Ay, yo, I'll give you an extra twenty dollars, if you wait for me, and take me back to the parking garage, on 12th and Sansom."

"The ticket I'll get for parking in this bus lane'll cost me more than twenty dollars, young'n."

"Man, it ain't even no buses comin', ol'head."

"Look, I ain't denyin' that, young'n. All I'm sayin' is, the people drivin' them there buses ain't the ones down here writin' the damn tickets. You dig what I'm sayin'?"

"Alright, how 'bout this, then," Hakeem reasoned, understanding the cab driver's point. He knew all too well how vindictive the cops and parking authority were in Center City. "All I'm about to do is, run in that daycare center over there, and get my peoples. Ol' head, we comin' right out. My

wheel parked up at that garage on 12th and Sansom. All you gotta do is spin around the block, and we'll be right there on that corner, waitin' for you. From there, we can be out."

"Sounds like a plan to me."

"See, that's what I'm talkin' about, ol'head."

"Alright, get a move on."

Hakeem got out of the cab and zig-zagged his way across Market Street. It took him three minutes to get Macy, help her into her gloves, hat, scarf, and coat, and another two minutes, to make it over to where he had told the cab driver he would be waiting.

"Where your car, Hakeem?"

"We about to go get it right now."

"Oh."

"You still wanna go get ya bunny rabbit?"

Macy nodded her head as she climbed into the back seat of the cab. Hakeem got in after her and pulled the door shut behind them.

"What'chu gon' name ya rabbit, Macy?"

"Um, I don't know."

"It's cool. We can wait, 'til you pick it to name it."

"'Kay."

The black, cab driver looked over his right shoulder and gave Hakeem and Macy a warm smile, before pulling out, and merging in with the westbound traffic, on Market Street.

"Here you go, ol'head."

The cab driver pulled Hakeem's fifty dollar bill through the small, square slot, cut into the plexi-glass divider, and grinned sheepishly. Hakeem had impressed him.

"I'd make the turn, if I could, young'n."

"Naw, this cool right here, ol'head."

"You be safe."

"No doubt . . . you, too."

Hand in hand, Hakeem and Macy got out of the cab and walked into the parking garage on 12th Street. Once both of

them were back inside of Hakeem's Porsche SUV, a certain sense of comfortability reflected on both of their faces. Hakeem was in deep thought, as he drove to South Philly. Macy was strapped in her car-seat, playing with a doll she had brung along from the house.

"Who my daddy, Hakeem?"

Macy had asked Hakeem this question, while the two of them were waiting for a red light at 12th and Spruce to turn green.

"Who Mommy tell you ya dad was?"

Macy shrugged her little shoulders.

Hakeem forced himself to meet Macy's innocent eyes in his rearview mirror. He saw unconditional love in Macy's eyes, but most of all, he saw that she wanted to be a daddy's girl, and simply be loved by whoever this man might possibly be. Everyone at his condo was under the assumption that she was his daughter. This was believed everywhere him and Macy went together. Even in Gabrielle's eyes, he had seen that she too wished that he was Macy's father.

"Can I be ya dad, Macy?"

This question choked Hakeem up, and caused his eyes to become blurry with tears. He used his left hand to clear his vision as he crossed Washington Avenue, and continued driving South.

"You can be my daddy, Hakeem."

"You promise?"

Macy nodded her head.

"I'ma take care of you and Mommy, alright?"

"'Cause, Mommy sad?"

"Hold on, Macy."

Hakeem picked up his ringing cell phone. He accepted the call, put the phone to his ear, then made a left onto Oregon Avenue.

"Who this?"

"It's Abi, Hakeem."

"As Salaamu Alaykum Wa Rahmatullah."

"Wa Alaykum As Salaam Wa Rahmatullahi Wa Barakatuh."

For a full minute, Hakeem and his father just listened to each other cry, on both ends of their cell phones. They had a lot of unresolved issues, and the main person that had tirelessly attempted to mend their differences was now gone.

"Bill-Bill called me this mornin', and—"

"Abi, I know who did—"

"Hakeem, I've arranged for your brother's janazah to take place over here, Insha Allah. Bill-Bill already gave me the details of the conversation you and him had, so it's no need for you to repeat anything to me.

"So, you just gon' let another one of our family members get murdered, and you not gon' do nothin' about it, Abi?"

"Ibn, the strong man is not the one that can throw another man down, the strong man is . . . "

Hakeem lowered his driver's side window and tossed out his cell phone. Clenching his jaws, trying his hardest not to snap in Macy's presence, he raised his window back up, then calmly pulled into the small, strip plaza, where the pet shop that sold rabbits was. The pet shop was located on Front and Oregon.

"You cryin', 'cause you sad, Hakeem?"

"Yup."

"Why?"

"'Cause, my heart hurtin' real bad."

"Oh."

"Ready to get'cha rabbit from this store?"

"Yes."

"Alright, Macy-fo-facy, come on."

At six o'clock, Hakeem pushed open the door to his condo and let out a long sigh of exasperation. He was tired, stressed out, grieving over his brother, and carrying a gray rabbit, in its cage, who Macy had endearingly named, Fo-

facy. To top it off, the gunshot wound to his stomach felt like he had hot hands plucking at his internal organs. The death match with Taz had been the most vicious battle that Hakeem had ever experienced. Some of his scars were unseen, and some were visible. He had two bite marks on his face, that were healing, from where Taz had bitten him savagely, during their intense fight for survival. That night, Hakeem had learned a lot about himself. He had realized that he feared standing before God, and being judged, more than he was afraid of death itself. He had also discovered that he had owned a strong tolerance for not only emotional pain, but for physical pain as well, and that by bringing the faces of his mother and grandmother to mind, this instantly had provided him with an untapped amount of anger that numbed his physical senses completely. How laying with his childhood friend's lifeless body on top of him for nearly two and a half hours had affected him was another story within itself.

After shutting his front door, Hakeem gazed around his living room at everyone. There was Gabrielle, who was rushing towards him with a timid smile on her face. Gabrielle's parents, her foster sister, and two, older muslim men, were all regarding him and Macy with pleased smiles, from his living room.

"Hakeem, where ya'll been? What happened to—"

"I ain't late."

"I know, but I was just worried, 'cause I kept tryna—"

"Look at my bunny rabbit, Mommy."

Hakeem sat Macy's rabbit carrier down, then slowly, with Gabrielle's help, took his jacket off. His face frowned in agony.

"Why you leave ya medicine in my pocketbook?"

"I forgot it."

"So, you mean to tell me, you went all day without—"

When Macy unlatched the door to her new pet's carrier, the small rabbit darted out like a gray ball of lightening. With

Macy shrieking excitedly, right on its fluffy tail, the fast, fur ball zig-zagged in the kitchen, out of the kitchen, around the living room twice, and then down the hallway into the bedrooms.

"Ay, I need to lay down for a second."

"Okay."

"This ya dowry."

Gabrielle took the two bags from Hakeem's left hand. One bag contained several black overgarments, with matching kimars, and in the other bag, there were Islamic books for a new convert, and a pocket-sized, Noble Qur'an.

"Thank you."

"We can get'chu some more stuff over the weekend."

"Those men from a masjid in West Philly. They the ones that was gon', um, marry ya brother and Tracy today."

Hakeem cut his eyes over Gabrielle's shoulder to look at her foster sister. Her face was the essence of sadness. She looked devastated and fragile. Knowing her pain, it made Hakeem want to comfort her. He had questions for her, and at the moment, he almost wanted to talk to her, more than he wanted to get married. After all, she was the daughter of his brother's killer.

"Tell 'em to give me a minute, Insha Allah."

"Okay."

Hakeem headed down the hallway to his bedroom. At his bedroom door, he just barely got out of Macy's way, as she giggle and chased after her rabbit, heading back out to the living room. After using the bathroom, Hakeem sat on the side of his bed and exhaled a heavy sigh, then lowered his face down into his hands. He wanted to holler. He wanted his father to hear the pain in his voice on the other side of the Atlantic Ocean.

"Here go your medicine, and somethin' to drink."

"So, you really ready to be my wife?" Hakeem asked, raising his head with a sigh. From Gabrielle's left hand, he took

the tall glass of orange juice, and from her right palm, he removed the two percocets. "Gabrielle, you see what my life like? When they take these staples outta my stomach, I'm on Mr. Dave fuckin' top, Gabrielle. For all the shit he did to you, and you definitely know I'm all over that mu'fucker for what the fuck he did to my brother yesterday. So, if we walk out there and get married, Gabrielle, I want'chu to know that shit might get bad, way before it get better.

"Hakeem, I already know what bad feel like."

Holding Gabrielle's stare, Hakeem took his pain medication and drunk some of his orange juice.

"I want'chu to marry Tracy, too, Hakeem."

"What?"

"You allowed to have more than one wife, right?"

"Yeah, but she—"

"Not tonight, but I'ma talk to her and see what—"

"Gabrielle, hold up. Pump ya brakes . . . just stop talkin' for a—"

"Is what I'm askin' you to do, a good deed, or a bad one?"

"I ain't sayin' it ain't permissible, or haram, but—"

"Alright, well, just come and marry me first, "Gabrielle ordered, taking Hakeem's empty glass out of his hand. She looked over her shoulder at him as she walked towards the bedroom door. "I know all about co-wives beefin', Hakeem. I'm just simply thinkin' ahead, that's all. At least me and Tracy are already close. And she can teach me stuff about the religion, from a female perspective, which you can't. Plus, we both know how she feel about Mr. Dave, now, right? Hakeem, this'll be good for all of us. Maybe, this what Allah wanted. And if that is ya baby by Taz's sister, you marryin' her, too. What? Am I comin' at'chu too strong? The cat got'cha tongue, huh? Yeah, I'm wifey number one, and I'm callin' the shots, Hakeem Smith. Now, come on."

Chapter Ten

The next morning, Gabrielle woke up first. The smile on her face was luminous. As she laid beside Hakeem's sleeping body, she raised her hand up to the ceiling and admired her sparkling wedding ring. She loved it, and she loved the man laying next to her, who had given it to her. Opening her eyes a married woman was an undescribable feeling for Gabrielle. She had never felt so happy in her entire life. Her only gripe about her wedding night was that, before her and Hakeem got the chance to officially consummate their marriage, the percocets Hakeem had taken had kicked in, sending him right to sleep, while she had been out in the living room, saying her goodbyes to her parents, and her foster sister.

Seeing Tracy leave had brought Macy to tears, so Gabrielle had suggested that Tracy and Macy go stay at a nearby hotel on City Line Avenue, and to just return the next day, whenever they chose to.

"Yo, why you ain't wake me up to pray?"

"Don't even try it, Hakeem," Gabrielle countered, as she turned over on her side, to face the man that had her heart in his hands. Between her legs, was shouting for his attention. "I woke you up twice. No, three times, matter fact. The last time, you told me to give you five minutes. Talkin' 'bout how you was gon' make wudoo, and we was gon' pray, but when

I tried to get'chu up five minutes later, you wouldn't even budge. I just went out and got one of them books you bought me yesterday, and I just said, and did, everything it said to do. It wasn't as easy as I'm probably makin' it sound, 'cause I kept mispronouncing a lot of the arabic words I had to say, but I tried my best, though."

Hakeem caressed Gabrielle's right cheek tenderly with his left hand. He was thoroughly impressed with her.

"I'm responsible for my own salats, right?"

"Yeah . . . we wait for prayer, prayer don't wait for us. And don't let nobody, not even me, 'cause you to neglect any of them."

"I'm not."

Hakeem smiled at Gabrielle.

Gabrielle returned Hakeem's smile with a soft kiss on the lips. Her libido had her skin hot, sensitive to the touch, and her clit was thumping like a tiny marching band.

"Let me go make up the prayer I missed, and I'll be right back, alright?"

"Okay."

"You like ya ring?"

"I love it."

"I wanted to get'chu one the size of a suitcase."

"Hakeem, you make me feel loved."

"Ay, why Macy ain't come in here yet?"

"She at a hotel up the street with Tracy."

"Oh, we about to have some butt-naked fun, and show off up in this joint, huh?"

Gabrielle's arousal influenced her to kiss Hakeem, again. His tongue danced with hers, then he moved his mouth under her chin, and slowly licked down her throat. With her eyes closed, Gabrielle reached between Hakeem's legs. He didn't stop her. When she had what she was searching for, in the grip of her left hand, Gabrielle opened her eyes.

"It's hard for me, Hakeem?"

It was a telling question that was innocently asked. Soft and sweet, and followed by a throaty moan.

"Let me go pray."

"I'ma be waitin' right here."

"Naw, go put them stilletos on that I picked out for you, when we was at the mall."

"The Louboutins?"

"Them the red-bottom ones, right?"

"Umm hmm."

"Yeah, them."

Finally.

Time to have sex.

"I want'chu to fuck me with ya fingers first, Hakeem. Then, ya tongue. Then, ya dick."

Hakeem hooked both of his thumbs inside the waistband of his Hanano, surfboard shorts, then pulled them down, along with his boxers. He was standing down at the foot of his bed, with his eyes studying Gabrielle's birthday suit. He was anxious to touch her.

"Fingers, tongue, dick."

"I can't remix the order?"

Gabrielle shook her head and seductively caught her bottom lip between her teeth, as she unshamefully admired Hakeem's hard dick. From where she was positioned on the bed, it appeared like it was curving to her left. Slowly, Gabrielle brought her eyes up to Hakeem's handsome face. The lust glowing in his hazel eyes made her insides warm all over.

"You sure you don't want the dick first?"

"I—I wanna—" Gabrielle lost her answer, and held her breath, as Hakeem grabbed her left Christian Louboutin, and kissed her inner thigh. To accommodate him, she opened her quivering legs wider and let out a ragged string of exhales. "I want the best for—For last, Hakeem. Only—Hakeem, only fingers. Mmmmmmm."

Hakeem was cheating. He was using his fingers and his

95

tongue at the same time. He wanted Gabrielle to remember their first episode for the rest of her life

"Hold ya pussy lips open for me."

Gabrielle never had oral sex performed on her before.

"I'ma show you how special ya clit . . . is."

Extreme pleasure engulfed Gabrielle's mind, body, and spirit, when Hakeem put his warm mouth on her clit, and began to do slow circles around it with his tongue. Gabrielle felt nerves and tingling sensations coming to life in places of her body that made her feel like she was inside of someone else's skin. Watching Hakeem lick, slurp, and suck, on her joy button, had her fascinated. They were now intimately connected, and as she laid there on her back, holding the opening to her love tunnel open, Gabrielle swore to herself, that no other man, but Hakeem, would ever be allowed to touch her in such a way. What Hakeem was doing to her had her ready to bite her lip. His right, middle finger was jabbing in and out of her wet pussy, in a screwing motion, and saliva from his mouth was mixing with her own juices, allowing his steady finger-jabs to touch her back pussy wall.

Two rainbows were arched over the back of Gabrielle's pussy. Her clit was producing falling stars.

"Hakeem, what's that?!"

Finally.

"Hakeeeeeeeeem?!!"

Gabrielle had no idea what an orgasm actually felt like. At first, she became frightened, but then, as the storm of tingles, rushed up her legs, high and higher, euphoria intoxicated her senses, and she erupted—literally. Gabrielle's cum juices squirted Hakeem in his face, causing him to first think that he was being peed on. The suddenness of it made him frown with disgust, spit, move away, and swipe at the thin-stream, that eventually became a trickle, then seconds later, became nothing. Blown away, and breathing super-heavily, Gabrielle looked from Hakeem, down to her pussy, then back

at Hakeem. She was mystified, but sexually elated, and wanting to repeat what had just happened to her.

"Yo, why you ain't tell me you had to pee, man?"

Stupified, Gabrielle stared at Hakeem as he used the bedsheet to wipe his face and beard, while he climbed off of the other side of the bed.

"Pee?" Gabrielle thought, following Hakeem with her eyes. She didn't understand what had went wrong. "What he think I—was I peeing on myself? That wasn't pee. I—That was an orgasm, wasn't it?"

"Yo, we gotta change them sheets, man."

"Okay, but I—"

"You should've told me to stop, so you could've went—"

"Hakeem, I didn't pee on you."

"Man, you did so."

Gabrielle grabbed a handful of the wet bedsheet beneath her legs, and leaned forward to sniff it.

"I can't believe you peed in my mouth, man."

"Hakeem, this not pee."

"Yeah, alright."

"Come smell it."

"Naw, I'm good."

"Well, smell the sheet in ya hand, then."

Reluctantly, Hakeem smelled the satin, bedsheet in his left hand. The expression on his angry face became quizzical. Looking at Gabrielle, he raised the bedsheet up to his nose and gave it another whiff.

"Satisfied, now?"

"Damn, so you squirt when you cum?"

"I guess."

"I ain't know what that shit was."

"No other girls you ever been with did that before?"

"Naw, but I seen a couple porno chicks do it on DVDs before, though."

"Boy, you had me scared, thinkin' I was gon' have to

make a doctor's appointment, to see my OB/gyn, on Monday."

"We good. I just gotta cop up some scuba goggles, that's all."

Hakeem and Gabrielle laughed together, then continued where they had left off. This time, they skipped the foreplay.

Round two.

"Gabrielle, look how that shit look, goin' in and out."

"I see it, Hakeem. I . . . see it."

The gift of Hakeem's gunshot wound to his stomach was that him and Gabrielle had to be very meticulous with how they were having sex. Their movements had to be slow and careful. There could be no rushing. There was a pace. Slow . . . slower. The two of them were sitting on an ottoman, facing their naked reflections, in the wall mirror, out in the hallway. Both of their bodies were glistening with beads of sweat, as they moved together methodically. Slowly, Gabrielle was riding Hakeem in a reverse-cowgirl position. Her hips were winding in a hoola-hoop motion, while she was slowly sliding up and down on Hakeem's dick. Gabrielle's hands were cupping her titties, sometimes teasing her nipples. Hakeem's hands were cupping her ass cheeks, to balance her weight, as they both watched Gabrielle's wet pussy, cause Hakeem's dick to appear, then vanish, right before their watching eyes.

"When can I suck it, Hakeem?"

"Gabrielle, go slower at the top."

Gabrielle had no idea of what Hakeem wanted. By them making love so slowly, she was able to feel Hakeem's dick throbbing against the walls of her pussy, whenever she rose to the point, where only the fat head of his dick was left inside of her.

"Right—Damn . . . yeah, right th—"

Pleasure and pain collided in Hakeem's system. Muscles in his stomach were contracting. The zipper of staples up the center of his stomach felt like they were being removed, one

by one. His reflection in the mirror was displaying only the pleasure he was feeling, as Gabrielle reached down, grabbed his dick, then did slow, deliberate circles, on just the helmet of his sex weapon.

"Like that . . . that's what'chu want?"

"Yeah."

Gabrielle ran the tip of Hakeem's dick across her pussy lips for herself, then put it back at the entrance of her pussy for Hakeem. She wanted him to have what he wanted. Watching herself in the mirror had her pleasured beyond describable words.

"I wanna suck it, Hakeem."

Everytime Hakeem's dick pulsed, Gabrielle responded by tightening her pussy muscles, and allowed more of Hakeem's dick to slowly re-enter her. She never let her hoola-hoop fall.

"Hakeem, ya dick so big and thick."

"I'm about to cum, Gabrielle."

"I want'chu to cum down my throat."

Hakeem gripped ten dimples into Gabrielle's ass cheeks. Her dirty talking was intensifying the momentum of his climax. Pleasure was overcoming pain. Gabrielle's pussy was so wet, and felt so tight, he wanted to live in it. He squeezed her ass cheeks tighter.

"I'm—Arrrgghhh . . . what'chu doin'?"

Gabrielle pulled Hakeem's dick out of her pussy, and turned around and faced him, just as his first spurts of cum started to fly. Quickly dropping to her knees, Gabrielle put Hakeem's cum-spitting dick inside of her mouth, with a look of lust, and dedication on her face. Sucking and swallowing, she stroked the length of Hakeem's dick with her hand, until Hakeem's sex weapon stopped shooting at the back of her throat. When she was done, she kissed the head of Hakeem's dick, and released it with a toothy smile.

"Damn girl."

"You not the only one who seen pornos before."

Chapter Eleven

"He did what?"

"He snuck around there, and blew our house up, and they said he sicked Sammy Davis on Mrs. Santiago, and her gran'son."

"And who told you this?"

"Shakarra."

"From across the street?"

"Yeah . . . she sent me a text, a little while ago. She saw the whole thing."

"So, knowin' the cops lookin' for him, and that they been showin' his face all over the news, he still gon' go around there, like that shit don't matter."

"This him callin' me again, Gabrielle."

"Tracy, hold on."

"And he keep leavin' me all these crazy messages, talkin' 'bout, how I'm Benedict Arnold, and how he gon' butt-rape me, and kill me, for tellin' the cops what happened."

"Hakeem wanna say somethin' to—"

"Gabrielle, I'm scared."

"Don't be, I'm about to come and pick you up right now, Tracy."

"Okay."

"Talk to Hakeem, while I throw somethin' on."

Gabrielle handed her cell phone to Hakeem and climbed

out of bed. The two of them had been cuddled up in bed when Gabrielle's cell phone had started to ring. It was Sunday, and a few minutes before midnight. Macy was in her room asleep, or at least, that was the impression that Hakeem and Gabrielle were under. Macy was actually holding a conversation with her rabbit about her favorite movie, which was 'Happy Feet.'

"Tracy?"

"Yes?"

"So, what he do?"

"He blew up our house, and he keep leavin' me all these crazy messages. Hakeem, he won't stop callin' me. I'm—I'm scared."

"Where you at?"

"Still at the hotel?"

"The one you and Macy was at the other night?"

"I had got a room for the weekend, and I was just gon' give them more money tomorrow, to stay for another night, until I figured out what I—"

"Tracy, you ain't gotta stay at—Hold on, here go Gabrielle."

Hakeem gave Gabrielle her cell phone back, but he also handed her the gun from beneath her pillow. The twin to the new Glock 40 he was handing her was under the pillow his head was on.

"You remember how to use it, right?"

Nodding her head, Gabrielle put her cell phone to her ear. She had her black overgarments on, and she was wearing her face veil, for the very first time. On her feet, she had on her black, Ugg boots. As she walked out of the bedroom, talking to Tracy on her cell phone, she put on her black, mink vest. Her heart was pumping bravery into her veins. She couldn't wait for her and Mr. Dave to cross paths again. It was slowly becoming the thing that she wanted most.

Hakeem yawned and got out of bed. When he made his

first step out into the hallway, Gabrielle was shutting the front door behind her. For a moment, Hakeem just stood in the darkness of his hallway, allowing his mind to wander. It was right then and there, that the understanding came to him as to why his father had chosen to move overseas, and not go down the unpredictable path of seeking revenge. Just as Hakeem was thinking about Macy's future now, and wanting to give her a fair shot at becoming someone in life, his father had been trying to do the same exact thing for him, and his older brothers, over a decade ago.

The ringing of the house phone pulled Hakeem out of his deep thought, and put him back in motion. His first assumptions were that Gabrielle was calling to tell him that she had gotten pulled over by the cops, and that they were disregarding the fact that she had a driver's license, and insurance, which ultimately meant that they wanted to search her car. In the kitchen, Hakeem flipped up the light switch, and snatched up his cordless phone from its base. When he saw the name that was showing on the caller ID, it instantly brought him a wave of stress.

"As Salaamu Alaykum."

"Wa Laykum As Salaam . . . Hakeem, is what I heard about Shamps true?"

"Yeah."

"What was he doin' back over here?"

"He had met this sister on-line, and he came over here, so they could get married. They was gon' go back over to Yemen, but the sister dad shot him up, while he was outside in the car, waitin' for the sister to come out."

"So, why ain't you call me?"

Hakeem walked out of his kitchen, and went into his living room. He could hear the genuine concern in Taz's sister's voice, but this didn't stop him from being suspicious of her intentions for calling, at such a late hour of the night.

"And why ya cell phone been goin' to voicemail all week-end?"

"I lost it."

"So, where was Shamp's janazah at?"

"My dad sent for his body."

"So, you talked to ya dad."

"Briefly."

Hakeem sat down on his couch with a sigh.

"Insha Allah, you and ya father need to stop swingin' the hatchet, and bury it. Hakeem, you know it's definitely what Shamps would've wanted ya'll to do."

"I know."

"Who was that girl at'cha condo?"

"My wife."

"She know about me."

"Ask her yourself."

Hakeem rose to his feet when he heard his front door being unlocked. He felt relief in knowing that Gabrielle had returned home safely. She had been on his mind the entire time she was gone.

"Who that?" Gabrielle asked, reading Hakeem's lips, as she accepted the cordless phone from him, and raised it up to her ear. After flipping up her face veil, she stepped around Tracy and locked the front door, all the while, wondering why Hakeem wanted her to talk to his old girlfriend. "Hello? Wa Laykum As Salaam Wa Rahmatullah . . . Gabrielle. What's yours?"

As Gabrielle disappeared down the hallway, Hakeem cut on the lights in the living room, to make Tracy feel a little more comfortable.

"As Salaamu Alaykum."

"Wa Laykum As Salaam."

"On the way here, Gabrielle talked to me about becoming her co-wife."

"That was her idea, not mine," Hakeem clarified, as he

103

walked into his kitchen, and took a seat on one of the wooden stools, outlining his kitchen's center island. He turned around and faced Tracy, and watched her as she removed her leather jacket and sat down on the couch, out in his living room. "Tracy, this all new to me. Like, I been muslim all my life, but this my first time bein' married. Then, like, it's a lot goin' on right now. A lot. Not only that, but'chu and my brother was—"

"I only knew your brother for two weeks, Hakeem. My reasons to get married was for the sake of Allah only. I just wanted to marry a brother that was on his Deen, that's all."

"Al Hamdulillah, but I'm just not—"

"Hakeem, I don't want nothin' crazy for my dowry. Teach me a surah. My mom left me eighty-five thousand dollars. I have money. All I want is a husband that fears Allah, and that can teach me."

"I don't know if I can be fair to two wives, though, Tracy."

"Just juggle us, like all these guys be doin', that's out here cheatin' on their wives, and their girlfriends. In this case, everything is out in the open. I can find another apartment, or house, and just give us our rights, Insha Allah."

Bowing his head, Hakeem shut his eyes and exhaled a long sigh. When he raised his head, he saw Gabrielle coming down the hallway, out of the corner of his left eye. She had a smirk on her face.

"That was real cute, how you gon' give me the phone, so she can see that'chu not hidin' nothin' from me, Hakeem. I like that."

At Gabrielle's return, Tracy joined her and Hakeem in the kitchen. She chose a stool opposite Hakeem, beside the one that Gabrielle was positioning herself to sit on.

"Hakeem, that sister Bayyinah nice."

"Yo, let's forget about ya opinion of Bayyinah, and focus on what the three of us gon' do, 'cause I'm startin' to feel like

decisions bein' made for me, and that the two of ya'll think ya'll got everything figured out."

Gabrielle and Tracy shot glances at each other, but neither dared to look across the granite-topped island, into Hakeem's serious eyes. The comment that he had made had been chilly, and all of his words had dripped with sarcasm.

"Don't everybody speak at once."

"I think all of us should just move overseas somewhere, and never come back."

"Just like that, Tracy?"

"What's here, Hakeem?"

"Gabrielle, how you feel about what Tracy just suggested."

"I don't wanna go nowhere, 'til Mr. Dave dead."

Hakeem fixed his eyes on Tracy's face, to see how she reacted to Gabrielle's statement. Her facial expression was unreadable.

"Tracy, can you see ya self killin' ya dad? I'm sayin', like, if he was to kick the door in right now, and he said, he'd spare you, despite all the shit he been sayin', but that he was definitely rockin' me, and Gabrielle, what would you do?"

Teardrops filled Tracy's eyes, and started to fall.

"Gabrielle, what's gon' happen to Mr. Dave when you see him?"

"You already know."

"Tracy, you see how easily Gabrielle answered that?" Hakeem asked, staring over into Tracy's brown eyes, as Gabrielle comforted her, by holding her hand. He thought that Tracy was beautiful, and was reminded of the actress, Reagan Gomez, whenever he looked at her for too long. "I wanna share somethin' with both of ya'll. My mom was my dad's second wife. All of my older brothers is by his first wife. I'm the youngest. So, it was me, my mom, and my gran'mom ... my mom's mom. My dad had gave my mom some money, to get this gold chain she had wanted. My, um, my gran'mom

was drivin'. We was comin' down Dickinson Street. I heard the shots, but, like, for some reason, I just thought somebody was lightin' firecrackers somewhere. I was little, and ain't know no better. Some niggaz was shootin' at each other on 15th Street, though. Three bullets hit my mom in the face, while she was smiling at me, and fixin' a button on my shirt. My gran'mom got hit in the head, once, and crashed into a mailbox. When the car flipped over, I landed on my mom lap."

The unbearable ache in Hakeem's chest forced him to lay his face on his crossed forearms. His thick beard was wet with tears, and his crying was sounding like the first stages of a tea kettle, with its whistle call. Gabrielle and Tracy sat across from Hakeem with their own crying faces buried in their hands.

"I wanted my dad to kill every fuckin' thing movin'," Hakeem continued, wiping his hands down his face, as he raised it. He took a moment to regain his composure, by swallowing, and taking a few deep breaths, before he went on with telling his painful tale. "Instead, though, he took a second job, and started tellin' me and my brothers, and they mom, that we was gon' be movin' overseas, once he had enough money saved up. That crushed me. It made me see my dad as a coward. Like, I just didn't understand, that he was doin' what he thought was best for his whole family. Doin' what I wanted him to would've got him the death penalty, or he could've got rocked. Then, it ain't no tellin' how me and my brothers would've ended up. Plus, my gran'pop ain't help. He was a kafir. He was my mom's dad, and for him to lose his wife, and his daughter . . . on the same day? That shit had him on my side all the way. That's who I stayed wit', when my dad and them left. My gran'pop died when I was seventeen. He left me some money, and I just started hustlin' from there."

"How old was you when—"

"Ten."

"Did the cops ever find the guys that was havin' the shootout?"

"Bill-Bill did."

"The guy from that night with Taz?"

"Yeah . . . that's my dad bestfriend. He put the work in, without my dad knowin', though."

"But he told you?"

"Yeah, when I got older."

"I know who can help us get my dad."

Hakeem and Gabrielle turned their attention to Tracy.

"I never met him before, but from some of the stories my mom told me, he supposedly hate my dad with a passion."

"Who, Tracy?"

"Remember when we was little, and my mom took us to that retirement center, and that old man we visited, shitted in his hand, and threw it at us?"

"The one who started chasin' us all around?"

"Gabby, that was my dad gran'father."

"Seriously?"

"That was my first, and only time, that I saw him. My mom called him one day when I visited her at the hospital, so me and him could talk."

"What he say?"

"He told me to kill myself, and hung up on me."

"Why don't he like ya dad?"

Tracy answered Hakeem's question by shrugging her shoulders.

Gabrielle let out a yawn.

"Gabrielle, what day ya dad, and ya mom leavin'?"

"I think Thursday."

"Alright, I gotta plan for us, Insha Allah. Tracy, you know what retirement center they got ya great-gran' father at?"

"I can make some calls in the mornin', and find out. Him and my dad got the same name."

"You ain't erase the messages ya dad left you, did you?"

"No."

Gabrielle yawned again, then reached across the island for Hakeem's hands. Together, they used both of their left hands, and made a hand-bridge.

"Tracy, we gon' get Gabrielle dad to be ya wali, so we can get married, Insha Allah. I'm gon' let him known about our whole situation wit'cha dad, and since I think he owe Gabrielle big time, I'm gon' call him on it."

"Hakeem, you might get mad, but while you and Tracy was out here talkin', I was in the room tellin' Bayyinah, you'll marry her this week."

"Wait a minute, wait a minute . . . who is Bayyinah, ya'll?"

"This muslim sister that's pregnant by Hakeem. She Taz's sister."

"And who is Taz, "

"Hold up . . . back up. Oh, so, now, you think the baby mines, huh?"

"Can one of ya'll tell me what's goin' on?"

"Tracy, I'ma let Gabrielle fill in the blanks, since she—"

"Hakeem, where you goin'?"

Hakeem stood up and walked out of the kitchen.

"Hakeem?"

"I'm goin' to sleep. Salat come in, in like three hours. And don't forget you gotta drop Macy off, before you go to school. You know how ya'll be on Mondays."

Hakeem took his attitude with him down the hallway, and into his bedroom.

"Gabby, who is Bayyinah and Taz?"

"Well, first, I gotta rewind things a little bit, and explain how me and Hakeem really met."

Tracy yawned.

"So, you and Hakeem didn't meet at a thrift store, like you originally told me."

"Tracy, somebody could write a urban novel about how Allah put me and Hakeem together."

"Well, I'm all ears."

"Alright, so, this how we really met."

Chapter Twelve

Two days later . . .

Good deeds.
Erase.
Bad ones.
"Hakeem, you wanna be with Gabby, don't'chu?"
"Why you ask me that?"
"'Cause it's our first night together, and my period came on."
"So, because we can't get it in, you thinkin' I don't wanna be here wit'chu?"
"Kinda."
Hakeem turned over onto his side and faced Tracy. He noticed immediately that her eyes were wet with tears.
"We only been married like six hours, Tracy, "Hakeem reminded Tracy, while using his left thumb to stop a teardrop, that was trailing down her left cheek. The sadness in Tracy's eyes forced him to feel guilty, although he knew he had no reason to feel that way. "We not gon' be used to bein' around each other that fast, Tracy. Stuff take time. I can control my desires. So what'cha period on. I'm here 'cause it's ya night, and 'cause I wanna be here. I ain't no pussy monster, Tracy. You my wife. Like, my bad for just layin' here, and bein' all quiet, but I was just doin' a lot of

thinkin', but that's all. My fault. I ain't pressed, 'cause we can't get it in, if that's what'chu was thinkin', though. My bad for bein' inconsiderate, alright."

"Do you always get so quiet when you gotta lot on ya mind?"

"Most of the time."

Hakeem and Tracy were in the bedroom of their new apartment. It was a spacious apartment, located in West Mt. Airy. The apartment overlooked Lincoln Drive, and had off-street parking, which turned out to be a determining factor for Hakeem, when he and Tracy had viewed the handsome place, two days earlier.

"I really was just layin' here wonderin' how ya great-gran'father gon' act when me and Gabrielle dad show up tomorrow."

"You really think lettin' him hear all them crazy messages my dad left on my phone, gon' get him to listen to what you have to say?"

"I hope so."

"Hakeem, can I ask you somethin'? It don't have nothin' to do with what we was just talkin' about, though."

"What?"

"Suppose, you go ahead and marry that sister Bayyinah, then she find out what really happened to her brother? How you plan on dealin' with her, then?"

"I know . . . that crossed my mind a couple of times."

"Even worse, what if she already know what really happened, but she just pretendin' like she don't, just so she can get somethin' done to you?"

"Damn."

"What?"

"I like the way you think, Tracy."

"Hakeem, ain't no way she ain't hear about what he did to you, before you got locked up. You know how the streets is. Now, you home, and he just got up and vanished? Let's

not even talk about his cousin. Who knew he robbed you for all that money."

"Once Fresh hear from them Mexican chicks, everything gon' definitely come out in the open. That's all Fresh do is run his mouth."

Tracy sat up in bed Indian style. It was in the middle of the night. Like Hakeem, Tracy often did a lot of reflecting herself. However, instead of becoming withdrawn, she had a habit of vocalizing her thoughts. Since learning about Hakeem's twisted predicament, from Gabrielle, Tracy's mind had become the storage pace for many deep worries.

At just twenty-five, Tracy had settling down, and raising a family on her mind. Losing her mother had been a life-altering experience for her. She no longer craved being at the popular Philly nightclubs, or wanted to know about the latest gossip going on in the streets. Becoming muslim had been her own choice. A personal relationship with God was what she wanted, and now that she actually had this, along with all of the madness, that seemed to be popping up, every which way she turned, she felt that her struggling would only better her chances at being a pious, muslim woman, in the near future.

"Hakeem, did you ever see that movie, 'Heat'?"

"Yeah, that's my movie. Why? What about it?"

"A couple of years ago I used to mess with some guy name, Hoose, from Abbottsford projects. Do you remember how Robert De Niro's character could've gotten away?"

"Yeah, he fucked up when he went back to rock Wayne-gro."

"That's what Hoose used to always say, Hakeem."

"Tracy, you pretty, and you smart."

"Hakeem, we can get away. You, me, Gabby, and Macy. All of us can."

"We will."

"Not if you and Gabby let my dad be ya'll Wayne-gro."

That night, Hakeem went to sleep with Tracy in his arms. She was his new treasure. His talk with her had sent him to sleep with a lot to think about. Tracy had given his intellect some nourishment, and because Hakeem had never encountered a female that was able to appropriately feed his wisdom, he was sensing that what he had with Tracy, was going to be something that he would grow to respect and appreciate.

A little before sunrise, Hakeem got up and prayed. Afterwards, he climbed back into bed with Tracy. Because of her menstrual cycle, she didn't have to perform her daily prayers with him.

"Hakeem?"

"Yo?"

"Call and check on Gabby and Macy, and see if they're okay."

"Gimme a kiss first."

Hakeem and Tracy had never shared a kiss. After their marriage ceremony, under everyone's watchful eye, the two of them had entangled in a hug, but that had only been for a quick second.

On the same pillow, Hakeem and Tracy kissed, then kissed some more. It was a meaningful moment for them both. The symptoms of the kiss was still present in Hakeem's system, as he placed his new cell phone to his ear, and called Gabrielle. The screensaver on his cell phone was a picture of Macy hugging her rabbit.

"As Salaamu Alaykum, Baby."

"Wa Laykum As Salaam."

"Hakeem, I'm over here missin' you sooooo much."

"Everything okay over there?"

"Just got done prayin'. Ready to wake Macy up in a little bit, so we can get ready for school."

Hakeem talked to Gabrielle a few minutes longer, then

he handed his cell phone over to Tracy. After showering, Hakeem got dressed, and returned back to the bedroom.

"Gabby said she'll call you on her lunch break."

Hakeem smiled as he climbed back into bed with Tracy. He accepted his cell phone back from her, and stuffed it down into the pocket of his black, Banana Republic corduroys.

"What kind of boots are those?"

"Roc climbers."

"They go nice with that sweater."

"So, what's on ya menu for the day?"

"Go get me a new cell phone. Most likely, after that, I'll just come back here and wait for them to deliver our new furniture."

"Yea, 'cause this air-mattress corny."

"Hakeem, do you think ya brother would've liked me, once he got to know me?"

"Absolutely. Tracy, Shamps would've loved you."

"Can we name out first son after him?"

Hakeem closed his eyes and saw his brother's face. When he reopened them, he saw Mr. Dave.

"Hakeem, he was only tryin' to introduce himself to my dad, and shake his hand."

"Ay, do you think ya dad boss would let ya dad use one of his cars, since he can't drive around in his?"

"Over the weekend, one of the detectives called me and told me that my dad boss, and his wife, was missin'."

"You think ya dad got somethin' to do with it?"

"The cops do."

"You don't?"

"Hakeem, at this point, I'm convinced my dad is capable of doing just about anything. What's sad is, Macy ask about him everytime she see me."

"We gon' have to tell her the truth one day, Tracy."

"I know."

"Want me to do anything, before I leave?"

"Just gimme a kiss, and promise me you'll think about what we talked about last night."

Out in his Porsche, Hakeem sat behind his steering wheel for a moment, and tried as best as he could, to put his life into perspective. He found this extremely hard to do. His eyes kept shooting up to his rearview mirror, to look at Macy's empty car-seat. It wasn't until its second ring, that Hakeem realized that Tracy's cell phone was chiming in the right pocket of the black, mink vest, that he had on, over his black, Rag & Bone sweater.

"Hello?"

"Who the fuck is this with my daughter goddamn cell phone?"

"Her husband."

"Her what? Listen, you little punk bitch . . . hand my god-damn daughter her cell phone, before—"

"Before what?"

"Before I tear off ya goddamn head, and shit down ya mother fuckin' neck!"

The threat made Hakeem smirk, as he started up his jeep and slowly pulled around Tracy's rental car.

"Young nigga, you must not know who the fuck I am."

"Yea, I do. You the nut ass ol'head, who ain't know who the famous, muslim general, Khalid bin Walid, was, right?"

Silence.

"I'ma feed ya dog dick to you, you freak."

"It's Taz, ain't it?"

Hakeem merged his Porsche with the southbound traffic, on Lincoln Drive. His emotions were burning holes in his heart. As he drove, he sunk lower in his seat, to avoid any po-tential cops from seeing that he was talking on a cell phone. The tears in his eyes were for his brother. So badly, he wanted to reveal to Mr. Dave, that he was the brother of the man he had killed in front of his house, but his instincts were

screaming for him to withhold this information. Keeping this from Mr. Dave, was hurting Hakeem more than a snake bite would hurt a child.

"How's my girls doin', Taz?"

"Better than you."

"I miss fuckin' Gabby. When I get her back, I think I'll make her mouth my toilet for a week straight."

"Why you called me from a blocked number, freak?"

"Cowards die twice, Taz."

"My name Hakeem, freak."

"Ya name's gonna be whatever I decide to call you."

"Where you wanna meet at, freak?"

"In Hell . . . meet me there, and I'll show you just how freaky I can get. Make sure you bring Macy along. You know ya'll won't get away from me so easily the next time, right, Taz?"

"The next time, I won't be tryna get away."

"Joker, my aim so goddamn good, I can shoot the nuts off a fuckin' mosquito, at nine at goddamn night. If you wanna shot at this here title, come out when the mu'fuckin' wolves howl."

After those words, Mr. Dave ended his call with Hakeem, and he never called Tracy's cell phone back. For the remainder of the drive, to pick up Gabrielle's father, Hakeem listened to all of the psychotic messages, that Mr. Dave had left on Tracy's cell phone. It was twenty-nine of them.

Blind.

Faith.

"What?"

"You heard exactly what I said . . . I'm just sayin', since you can quote the Qur'an, and the sunnah so well, then won't'chu tighten up, and obey them."

"I'm old enough to be ya father, Hakeem."

"Man, how old you is don't give nobody no free pass to be wrong," Hakeem argued, killing the engine on his jeep. He

was furious that Gabrielle's father had shaved his beard completely off. "I wouldn't care if you was old enough to be my gran'father. Okhi, we muslim. The reminder benefits the believer, right? Ya'll ol'heads be crackin' me up, like somebody younger than ya'll can't never check ya'll about nothin'. That's that pride, man. Ya'll got so much to say when we don't listen to whateva ya'll gotta say, though. None of us ain't perfect, and we all gon' make mistakes. We can't get around that, okhi. Look what Allah say in Surah Asr. He say mankind is in loss, if we don't help each other tighten up."

Hakeem exhaled an exasperated sigh when Gabrielle's father said nothing, and just continued to stare forward. The two of them were parked in the valet lane of the Center City hotel, where the Witness Protection Program, currently had Gabrielle's parents staying. The hotel was on 4th and Arch.

"Plus, that jawn was lookin' decent on you, too."

"My wife said I look like a tree jumper."

"What's that?"

"A rapist . . . you know how they be—"

"Yea, I get it. Ay, well, at least it'll grow back."

Just like that, the tension between Hakeem and Gabrielle's father had disappeared. It was a bonding moment for both men. For Hakeem, however, as he started his jeep back up, and blended in with the southbound traffic, on 4th Street, it seemed like it was also the perfect time for him to ask a pressing question, that had been lurking in the back of his mind, since the first time he had met Gabrielle's father.

"Ay, yo, what's you and ya wife situation with the—"

"I knew this was gon' come sooner, or later."

"Alright, so, to make us both feel comfortable, let's get it outta the way."

"We muslim, Hakeem."

"Yea, but, we men, too. And I'm the type that don't bang wit' rats. I mean, like, at all."

At 4th and Market, Hakeem made a right. As he drove

up Market Street, he waited impatiently for Gabrielle's father to start talking. At 5th and Market, he made another right turn, but instead of proceeding forward, with the northbound traffic up 5th Street, Hakeem pulled over and parked.

"I didn't tell on any muslims, if that's the impression you under."

"In my book, tellin' is tellin'."

"True."

"Alright, so, spill what happened."

"Also, keep in mind, that this all took place, before I converted."

It was 9:17 a.m., and it was cold and treacherous outside. Behind where Hakeem's Porsche was parked, a small line of people stood bundled up, and shivering, as they braved the nippy conditions, to give their orders of coffee and breakfast specials, to the old, Polish man, running the mobile, food truck.

"Okay, here's what went down," Gabrielle's father began as he scratched his hairless cheeks with his left hand. His hazel eyes went sad. "I got introduced to this Haitian dude named, 'City Lights', through one of his nieces. Me and this particular niece used to mess around, here and there. So, uh, at this time, I'm handlin' about half a kilo. Never could get to a whole one, 'cause I would drink that damn syrup, Hakeem. Drink it like water, too. Turned out to be my downfall."

"What happened?"

"It came to City Lights' attention, that I had gotten his niece pregnant, and because she was the only daughter of his favorite sister, he decided to offer me the position of a lifetime."

"So, this was all before ya relationship with Gabrielle mom?"

"Durin' it?"

"So, she knew about the Haitian chick?"

"She had her suspicions, but when everything sank like

the Titanic, she got the truth from the streets, then from the FBI."

"Damn."

"So, City Lights put me in charge of this crib, that he used to stash all of his kilos, and some of his guns and money. For a hot month, I was happier than a dog with two tails. You hear me?"

Hakeem was so intrigued with Gabrielle's father's story, he ignored his cell phone when it alerted him that he had received a text-message.

"But'chu know Allah don't be blessin' nothin' that's evil," Gabrielle's father confirmed, giving Hakeem a sideways glance. His tone of voice became sorrowful. "One night, I'm syruped up. You hear me? Dead to the world. So, I wakes up, to all this hollerin'. Now, mind you, when I dozed off, City Lights' niece was beside me in bed, and a young cat we used to call, 'Plus', was out in the living room, with the neighbor's daughter. Now, like I said, I wakes up and hear all this screamin' and damn yellin'."

"Who was it?"

"The neighbor's daughter."

"What dude was tryna rape her?"

"Plus was down on the living room floor dead, and she was runnin' all around, asshole naked, with her throat slit from ear to ear."

"Oh, shit."

"Little brother, that's not even the worst of it."

"What—"

"City Light's niece was back in the bedroom, on the floor with her head chopped off."

"But'chu—Yo, I'm loss. How you ain't see her when you woke up?"

"The lights was out, and she was on the other side of—"

"So, who was in the spot doin'—"

"Rohan."

"Who the fuck is that?"

"One of City Lights' nephews, who had just came from Haiti, and thought that my position should've been his."

"Wasn't shorty his cousin, though?"

"That ain't matter to Rohan, Hakeem," Gabrielle's father continued, unzipping his black, leather jacket. Looking Hakeem in the eyes, he pulled up his shirt, to show Hakeem the old gunshot wounds, decorating his torso, and left side. "As soon as he seen me standin' there, in the hallway, he shot the neighbor's daughter in the face, then he came after me."

"You ran?"

"Like the damn Road Runner. Made it back to the room, got my gun, and we did it like the cowboys used to."

"What happened after that?"

"Woke up the next day in the hospital, under Federal arrest, for one hundred and fifty-five kilos, thirty guns, three murders that I didn't do, and one attempt."

"Damn . . . so, hold up, who was the attempt on?"

"Rohan."

"But he—"

"His crazy ass flipped the script. While I was in and out of surgery, he was droppin' dimes on his uncle, me, even said we had brought him from Haiti, so that he could sell drugs in Miami. Rohan was sayin' anything he could think of."

"He was on some silly shit, huh?"

"Hakeem, I never told on City Lights. I did tell the truth about what really went down with Rohan, but that's it."

Hakeem's cell phone alerted that it had received another text-message.

"Of course, they gave me a polygraph test, to see if I was being honest."

"You passed it?"

Gabrielle's father sighed and nodded his head.

"Alright, so, if the nigga, City Lights, know what really

went down that night, and he definitely know you ain't rat on him, then who they hidin' ya'll from?"

"Rohan."

"They let that nigga go?"

"A prison guard helped him escape."

"Why his uncle ain't just get him rocked, once his nut ass hit the streets, then?"

"Somebody poisoned City Lights' food in prison."

"And this nigga ain't get caught, yet, after all this time?"

"They'll find Hoffa, before they find Rohan, Hakeem."

"He mean like that, huh?"

"He meaner."

With a better understanding of Gabrielle's parent's history, Hakeem put his Porsche SUV into drive, and pulled out into the flow of the northbound traffic. He followed 5th Street all the way up to North Philly. At Cecil B. Moore Avenue, Hakeem made a left turn. When he reached 8th Street, Hakeem turned left, and slowly pulled into the large, parking lot, of an even larger retirement center, which appeared to rise up to the skies.

"I hope this work."

"Let me do the talkin'."

Hakeem looked at Gabrielle's father and raised his eyebrows.

"Maybe me lookin' like a tree jumper might be our advantage."

"Why you think that?"

"I can show you better than I can—What's his name again?"

"David Epps. Tracy dad is his gran'son."

"Yeah, I got that part . . . okay, let's go."

Seven minutes later, Hakeem and Gabrielle's father returned back to Hakeem's jeep with solemn expressions on their faces. They didn't speak until Hakeem started up the

SUV and steered out the retirement center's parking lot, and it was a half a block behind them.

"Out of all the days he could've died, he had to check this mornin'."

"Don't get upset with the decree, little brother. Patience brings victory."

"I know, but damn," Hakeem complained, turning left on Thompson Street, behind a school bus. He felt like his only chance at getting Mr. Dave had just been spoiled. "I gotta—"

"When do the wolves howl, Hakeem?"

"At night, right?"

"There go your answer right there. That's when he said he'll be out, ain't it?"

"Yea, but I don't know what this nigga drivin', and at night, the only shit floatin' around is cops and cabs."

Gabrielle's father nodded his head thoughtfully, as Hakeem paused for a stop sign at Marshall and Thompson.

"Definitely can't afford to get pulled over by the cops, with a bunch of guns on you."

"That's what I'm sayin'. Plus, it ain't like I know where to start lookin' for him any—"

Hakeem stopped at a red light on 6th and Thompson, then dug his cell phone out of the right pocket of his mink vest. He caught Gabrielle's call on the second ring.

"As Salaamu Alaykum."

"Why you ain't been respondin' to me, or Tracy's text-messages."

"Can you greet me back first?"

Hakeem smiled when Gabrielle's father smiled. He switched his cell phone to his left ear, and pulled off when the traffic light ahead turned green.

"Wa Laykum As Salaam, Hakeem."

"You said that wit' some attitude."

"We was textin' you, 'cause one of Tracy's friends saw Mr. Dave when she was goin' to work this mornin'."

"Where?"

"You know where the Spring Garden Street, El-stop is?"

"Yeah."

"Alright, so, you know that tunnel, between there, and 2nd Street?"

"Where the train go under, and come out, right?"

"She was on the El, and she seen him goin' into the tunnel, Hakeem."

Hakeem could hear the excitement in Gabrielle's voice. He was feeling excited himself.

"She saw that mother fucker."

"How sure is she, though."

"Hakeem, she saw Sammy Davis with him, and everything. It was him."

"Don't it be a lot of bums, livin' down there in that tunnel?"

"Yup."

"You thinkin' what I'm thinkin'?"

"You already know."

"What time you get outta school?"

"I'm out already."

"Alright, well, meet me at that thrift store on 8th and Moyamensing."

"Right now?"

"Yeah, right now. I'll be right there, after I drop ya dad off."

"My mom called me and told me he shaved his beard off."

"Wanna talk to him?"

"No."

Chapter Thirteen

The following day . . .

Hello.

"Gabrielle, me and your dad was allowed to move overseas, to Cairo."

"In Egypt?"

"Our flight leaves tonight, at eight."

Goodbye.

"Hakeem, you knew and ain't tell me?"

When Hakeem shook his head, Gabrielle looked back across their restaurant table at her parents. She felt like they were abandoning her all over again. All week long, she had mentally, and emotionally, prepared herself for this moment. For the past fifteen years of her life, not a single day had ever gone by, where she didn't wish that her parents could return from the dead, to rescue her from the tortured life she was living. Now here they both were.

Never dead.

Leaving her again.

"Mommy, wanna French fry?"

"No, Macy."

"Oh."

Gabrielle's black, face veil, was hiding the teardrops that were crawling down her face, but her body language dis-

tinctly showed everyone at the restaurant table, that she was breaking down. Her entire body was shaking, like the last leaf on a tree in autumn. With all the strength she was able to muster up, Gabrielle rose to her feet, grabbed her clutch-purse, then started walking towards the restaurant's exit.

For it to only be a mid-Thursday afternoon, the popular Manayunk restaurant, where Gabrielle had come to meet Hakeem, Macy, and her parents, was packed like it was a weekend evening. More rudely than she would have wanted to behave, Gabrielle, still crying, bumped her way through the restaurant's crowded waiting area, and squeezed her way by a white, lesbian couple, to make it to the restaurant's all-glass doors. She was met by a gust of wind when she stepped outside. The black denim fabric of her overgarments flapped around her body like a boat sail.

"You knew this day was comin' all week," Gabrielle thought, eyeing the roof of her Infiniti, as she worked her way through the restaurant's small parking lot, to get to it. She sighed when her cell phone started ringing in her purse. "Cairo? They spend what . . . a week with me, and expect me to get over the fifteen years they was unaccounted for? Are they serious? How about tryna really get to know me, before leavin'. Cairo? All these places in the United fuckin' States, and they chose Egypt."

Gabrielle got into her car and drove home. Her cell phone rung the entire drive. When it wasn't ringing, it was alerting her that text-messages were being sent to it. Gabrielle never looked at her cell phone once.

Goodbye.

At home, Gabrielle got undressed, put on something comfortable, and got into bed. All of the crying she had done had given her a headache. She dozed off with a pillow hugged close to her chest, and thinking about her school project, that was due the next morning. It was 5:12 p.m. when she fell

asleep, and 12:31 a.m. when she opened her eyes and rolled over and faced Hakeem, who was sitting up watching TV.

"Hakeem, what time is it?"

"Twelve somethin'."

"My mom and dad left?"

"What'chu think?"

Gabrielle closed her eyes, regretting her earlier behavior. From Hakeem's tone of voice, it was clear that he was upset with her. A lump formed in the back of Gabrielle's throat, and when she swallowed it down, it stubbornly came right back. Teardrops tried to squeeze their way through her shut eyes,

"Me and Macy went wit' them to the airport."

"Why you let me sleep so long?"

"'Cause when somebody make it perfectly clear to me that they don't wanna be bothered, I—"

"Hakeem, it wasn't'chu I was mad at."

"That's besides the point, though. I'm ya husband, Gabrielle. You left me there, feelin' all awkward. That was corny, man."

Gabrielle sighed and opened her eyes. A teardrop snuck out of her left eye. Gabrielle could sense that an argument with Hakeem was on the horizon. It would officially be their first one.

"Macy sleep?"

"Yup."

Gabrielle rolled her eyes.

"Ay, you know, I was 'posed to be wit' Tracy tonight, right?"

"Well, why ain't'chu, then, Hakeem? Ain't nobody stoppin' you from goin' over there."

"Oh, so, what, I was 'posed to just come in here, and drop Macy off, then just leave, huh?"

"Evidently."

"Man, you was—Man, I'm out."

Propping herself up on her elbows, Gabrielle watched as Hakeem silently started to dress. She wanted him to stay, but couldn't fix her lips to ask him to get back into bed, because somewhere, deep down inside, she felt like she truly still wanted to be alone. After taking one last look at Hakeem, she laid back down on her bed, and pulled the comforter over her head, until a thought crossed her mind, that made her sit back up.

"We still goin' to look for Mr. Dave tomorrow night?"

"Gabrielle, get the fuck outta my face."

"Hakeem, you ain't gotta talk to me like that."

"Man, I wish I could have my fuckin' mom back from the dead," Hakeem vented, frowning in disgust, as he paused in his bedroom doorway. His tears blurred his vision, as he stared through the darkness at Gabrielle. "Gabrielle, yours got her life fucked over, 'cause of ya dad. Not for her own shit. I'm sayin', like, I feel you bein' upset, and I'd be outta pocket, to say you ain't gotta valid reason for feelin' how you do, but come on, man. Ya mom don't deserve the same blame ya dad do, Gabrielle. She don't, man. Even wit' all the shit Mr. Dave and Tracy mom took you through, do you honestly think they would've gave you up, if they both knew you was gon' have to deal with all that bullshit? Be mad, but like—Yo, if you would've seen how fuckin' hard ya mom started cryin' when you left, you would've knew her love for you was deep as shit, Gabrielle. You would've knew. At least in Cairo, they ain't gotta worry about that Haitian nigga. Macy cried at the airport."

With his last words, Hakeem sighed and walked off. The echo of him closing the front door was heard moments later.

For Gabrielle, school was a helpful and positive distraction from all of the drama, that was going on in her private life. In her class, Gabrielle wasn't the most talented student, but what she lacked in talent, she made up for with her raw skill, and ambition, which always left her fashion instructor

genuinely impressed. Wiping away her tears, Gabrielle dragged herself out of bed, with all that Hakeem had said to her, and her homework, on her mind. Before getting started on her art, and fashion project, which she assumed was going to take her all night to finish, Gabrielle went into Macy's bedroom, to check on her. In there, she started crying again.

The next morning, only having gotten two hours of sleep, Gabrielle took Macy to daycare, then drove herself to school. The voice messages her parents had left on her cell phone had her feeling terrible. The day crawled by like a snail for Gabrielle, and it didn't help that Hakeem was ignoring her phone calls, and all her text-messages.

"As Salaamu Alaykum, Tracy."

"Wa Layum As Salaam."

"You talk to Hakeem?"

With her question, Gabrielle braked her Infiniti at the pavement of The Liberty Place's parking lot, allowing the northbound traffic, going up 16th Street, to maintain its pace.

"Not since last night. Why? What's wrong?"

"He not answerin' none of my calls, or none of my text-messages, Tracy."

"Mines, either."

"What'chu mean?" Gabrielle asked, pulling off of the sidewalk, and fitting her car into the 16th Street traffic. When the light drizzle, falling from the gray afternoon skies, became heavier, she switched her cell phone to her other ear and turned on her windshield wipers. "Tracy, wasn't he with you last night?"

"No."

"No?"

"Gabrielle, the last time me and Hakeem spoke, he was tellin' me about what happened at the restaurant, with you, and your mom and dad. So, since I knew you was feelin'

messed up, I gave up my night, and I told him he can stay with you."

Confused, but listening, Gabrielle made a right onto Market Street. A knot of anxiety was beginning to form in the pit of her stomach.

"Is somethin' goin' on that I don't know about, Gabby?"

"Tracy, Hakeem didn't stay with me."

"Okay, so, he wasn't with me."

"Well, where was he, then?"

"You know him better than I do, Gabby."

"I'm startin' to have a bad feelin', Tracy."

"And now I am, 'cause you are."

"Somethin' wrong, Tracy."

Chapter Fourteen

Gabrielle, Tracy, Macy, and a friend of Tracy's, who was the one that had spotted Mr. Dave on her way to work, all looked at Hakeem with surprised expressions, when Hakeem pushed open his front door and came walking nonchalantly into his condo, as if he hadn't been missing for the past day and a half. For Gabrielle, Tracy, and Macy, Hakeem spared a charitable grin. For Tracy's friend, he displayed a vengeful stare.

"Gabrielle, lemme holla at'chu in the bedroom for a second. You, too, Tracy."

With a hundred and one questions on the tips of their tongues, Gabrielle and Tracy followed Hakeem down the hallway, and into the bedroom. Skipping, with a handful of pretzel sticks, Macy brought up the rear.

"Hakeem, Where you been?"

"Gabrielle, chill. Ay, Tracy, cover Macy ears real quick."

"Chill? What'chu mean, chill?"

Tracy squatted and placed her hands over Macy's ears.

"What the fuck is that bitch out there doin' in my spot?" Hakeem questioned, looking from Tracy, to Gabrielle, who was standing closest to him. There were some crazy voice messages on his cell phone from Gabrielle, and he couldn't wait for an opportune moment, to confront her about every last one of them. "Man, that's the bitch I told you about, that

burnt me outta that seventy-five hundred, and my fuckin'
Acura wagon. Now, either, ya'll gon' go out there, and tell her
to pass off the keys to my shit, and put her funny lookin' lazy-
eye ass, outta my spot, or I'ma go . . . "

Gabrielle took a swing at the left side of Hakeem's face,
like she was swinging at a handball. The sound of her right
palm, making contact with Hakeem's right cheek, sounded
like the gunclap of a .22 handgun.

"Man, what the fuck you hit me for?!"

"What'chu think I'm blind, Hakeem?!"

With her question, Gabrielle took another swing at Hakeem, but this one didn't find home, because Hakeem had
caught a hold of her wrist mid-swing.

"You got the nerve to come up in here . . . "

Gabrielle swung at Hakeem with her free hand, but this
one was also intercepted by Hakem's other hand.

". . . with a fuckin' passion—"

"Ay, yo, you better stop—Man, Macy right there!!"

"Get off me, Hakeem!"

While Gabrielle struggled to free her wrists from Hakeem's grips, not wanting Macy to stand witness to any further domestic violence, Tracy scooped Macy up into her arms
and scrambled frantically out of the bedroom. Out in the living room, Tracy's friend stood, paralyzed, holding Hakeem's
car keys, and the title, and registration, to his cinnamon-col-
ored, 2011 Acura TSX sport wagon, but when Gabrielle came
flying down the hallway past Tracy, and Macy, Tracy's friend
broke into a panicked flight, into Hakeem's kitchen.

"Don't run now, bitch!"

Gabrielle was similar to a lake that owned a calm surface,
but had a dangerous current beneath it. Tracy was well aware
of this, which explained why she ran over to help her friend
when Gabrielle cornered her in the kitchen, and removed a
meat cleaver from the kitchen sink.

"Oh, you up in here, pickin' mu'fuckin' sides, Tracy?!"

"That's not what I'm doin', Gabri—"

With the meat cleaver in her hand raised high, Gabrielle charged Tracy, and Tracy's friend. All three women clashed head-on, and with fists swinging, and a meat cleaver being wrestled for, their fight quickly went down to the kitchen floor. Macy's crying joined in with their screaming and shouting, as Hakeem crawled over to where Macy was in the living room. Forgetting about the staples in Hakeem's stomach, Gabrielle had brought a swift knee up to Hakeem's groin, and had punched him in the stomach, which immediately had melted Hakeem down to the bedroom floor. Fortunately, for everyone in the condo, Hakeem had made it out to his living room when he did, because although, he would never know it, and neither would anyone else, but Macy was just two steps away from reaching her little hand under the middle cushion of the couch, where she had seen Hakeem hide one of his guns, weeks earlier.

"Gabby, let her hair go!"

"Tell her to let go of my kimar!"

"Stop punchin' her, Gabby!"

"Bitch, be happy I ain't the fuck punchin' you for tryna help her!"

"Tracy, she still tryna get that meat cleaver!"

"Gabby, stop!"

Hakeem was in too much pain, and felt too weak to do anything, but listen, and hold Macy against his chest. He had his eyes closed. Not only did he feel slightly disoriented, as he thought about the blood that was trickling across his ribcage, but he felt stupid for not handling things a lot differently when he first walked into his condo.

"Gabby, listen to me. It's a blessin' what Nita did. Had she did what she was supposed to do, you and Hakeem would've never met, because he wouldn't've had no reason to call the party-line back."

"Where his car keys at, Nita?"

"Over there."

"Over where, bitch?"

"Over—by, the, um, by the couch."

Hakeem opened his eyes. He saw his Acura keys, and paperwork for it, over near his couch, on the floor.

"Gabrielle, can you please let my hair go?"

"Gabrielle, I gave Hakeem that passion mark two days ago. You smacked him for nothin'."

"Wallahi, Tracy?"

"Wallahi."

It took everyone in Hakeem's condo almost three hours to relax and settle down. It wasn't until after Tracy's friend had left, that Hakeem, Gabrielle, Tracy, and Macy, were all able to simmer down, in their own personal ways. As midnight approached, and Saturday became Sunday, Gabrielle and Tracy talked out in the living room, while Hakeem rested in bed, and Macy slept in hers.

"And so, he never reported the car stolen, because he thought Nita would probably snitch him out to the cops, and tell them all about the stuff that he was into?"

"Well, that's what he told me."

"Gabby, you say that like you don't believe him."

"Tracy, he ain't report it stolen, 'cause it's in Bayyinah's name."

"How you know?"

"'Cause she told me."

Tracy gave Gabrielle a strange look.

"The only reason he ain't report it stolen, is because he ain't wanna have to deal with Bayyinah, so all that about him bein' worried about Nita tellin' on him, is just a bunch of bullshit, Tracy."

"Okay, and? What's so wrong about—"

"I'm done, Tracy."

"Done with what?"

"All of this shit. Bein' muslim. Bein' married. Every-thing."

"Gabby, but—"

"Let's kill him, Tracy."

"Kill who?"

"Who else?"

"Hakeem?"

"Yeah."

"What? Gabby, you—"

"Tracy, I told Bayyinah what he did to her brother, and she—"

"You did what? Gabby, Hakeem is our husband."

"Tracy, you can die with him, or you can stay alive, and split all of his money in that safe with me and Bayyinah. The choice is yours, Tracy."

Hakeem didn't stand in the darkness of his hallway long enough to hear Tracy's response. He had overheard far more than enough, and he was convinced that he was definitely sleeping with the enemy; two of them, actually. With quiet steps, Hakeem walked backwards to his bedroom. Before getting back into bed, and pretending to be asleep, Hakeem put on two of his bulletproof vests, and he put a hand grenade in the pocket of his bathrobe.

Two birds.

One stone.

Chapter Fifteen

On Sunday night, a few minutes after ten o'clock, Hakeem walked into the apartment that he shared with Tracy. After shutting and locking the door, Hakeem stood completely still and listened to his surroundings. The Mac-11 he held in his right hand was pointing down at the hardwood floors, beneath his brown and cream, hi-top, Hennessy sneakers. With alert eyes, Hakeem began to follow the low sound of Tracy's voice, until he found her in their bedroom making prayer. The smell of Egyptian musk from an oil-burner over on the windowsill, greeted Hakeem's nostrils at the doorway. Unaware of Hakeem's presence, because her back was to him, Tracy's sobbing voice rose, and lowered, as she recited a short surah from the Noble Qur'an, that Hakeem had recently taught her.

No matter how hard Hakeem tried, he couldn't stop his own teardrops from falling from his eyes. He was suffering from two heartbreaks at the same time. No where in his memory was he able to hunt down any past moments that would provide him with an explanation why Gabrielle and Tracy would suddenly want to betray him. Hakeem had spent his entire morning, and afternoon, at a Germantown masjid, praying, crying, and drowning in heartache, and disappointment.

Done praying, Tracy slowly rose to her feet. When she

turned around and saw Hakeem in their bedroom doorway, she jumped and raised her hands up to her chest.

"What's up, Tracy?"

"As Salaamu Alaykum, Hakeem."

Tracy's voice was barely a whisper. Because she was still crying, her greeting had left her lips, carrying with it all of the emotions that she was feeling on the inside.

"Wa Laykum As Salaam."

Peace.

"Why you cryin' like that?"

"Hakeem, Shaytan . . . messin' . . . everything up."

At first, Hakeem stood stiff, and unresponsive, when Tracy wrapped her arms around him, and buried her face in his chest. He wanted to push her away, and set her chest on fire with his Mac-11, but the harder Tracy cried against him, the more Hakeem became convinced that Tracy's loyalty with him was still alive. He could sense it in the protective way in how she was pressing her body against his. Tracy was hugging him as if she was shielding his body from an enemy that only she could see.

"Come over here and sit down on the bed, Tracy."

Wiping her tears and sniffing, Tracy followed Hakeem over to the side of their bed, and sat down.

"Tracy, I heard what'chu and Gabrielle was talkin' about last night," Hakeem revealed, kneeling down in front of Tracy. A balance of anger, confusion, and sadness, had his heart and mind in dark places. "If Macy wasn't there with us, I would've rocked both of ya'll."

"Hakeem, it's Gabby and that girl, Bayyinah, that's—"

"You want me and my brother blood on ya hands, huh, Tracy?"

"Hakeem, no."

"Well, tell me what the fuck is goin' on, then."

"It's Gabby, Hakeem. It's her . . . not me."

136

"So, why you ain't come in the room, and tell me what was goin' on, before you left last night?"

"When I was about to, she reached under the couch, and pulled a gun out on me. Hakeem she took my cell phone and made me leave. Wallahi."

"It's a thousand pay phones between there and here, Tracy."

"I—I know, but I just—Hakeem, I'm sorry."

Hakeem's cell phone started ringing in the pocket of his brown, leather, Gucci jacket. Leaving his gun on the floor, he stood up straight. To secure Tracy's silence, Hakeem pressed his index finger against his lips, before answering his cell phone.

"What's up?"

"Dag, I get a, 'What's up', now?"

"Gabrielle, what's—"

"Why was ya cell phone off all day?"

"I was in the masjid."

"All day?"

"That's what I just said, ain't it?"

"Hakeem, this the second time you pulled a disappearin' act, and claimed to be at the masjid. I don't understand why you can't just put'cha phone on mute, so you still can at least text."

"Yea, well, it's a lot that'chu wouldn't understand."

"Look who's talkin'."

Hakeem sat down on the bed next to Tracy. He had a look in his hazel eyes that was cold and deadly. The way that Gabrielle was pushing his buttons had him ready to go bezerk.

"That's the least you can do for the person that bailed you outta jail."

"You right."

"Especially since you not keepin' ya end of the bargain."

"Which was?"

137

"Well, obviously, ya word don't mean nothin' to you, if you can't even remember what'chu told me."

Rising back to his feet, Hakeem clenched his jaws. He had to move, because he was getting too upset to stay seated. After picking his Mac-11 up off of the floor, Hakeem walked out of the bedroom. Tracy followed him.

"So, where you at?"

"Over here wit' Tracy."

"Oh, really?"

"Stop questionin' me, Gabrielle."

"Can I talk to her?"

"For what?"

"It's—Hakeem, can you just—She left her cell phone over here yesterday."

"Why you ain't say that, then?"

"Why did I have to?"

"Yo, man, the fuckin' way you talkin' to me is real crazy right now."

"Hakeem, just give Tracy the phone, and calm down."

"You know what, Gabrielle? You a wolf in sheep's clothin'."

"Mr. Dave called me worse."

"'Here go Tracy."

"'Bout time, dag."

"Yo, this bitch really think it's sweet, or somethin'," Hakeem figured, as he handed Tracy his cell phone. His heart was pumping lava through every vein in his body. "Little do her dumb ass know, I'm up on game. Then, of all people, she gon' let Bayyinah be the one that pull her fuckin' strings? Bayyinah? She the fuckin' smartest dummy in the world. Gabrielle listenin' to her, though? Alright. Then, instead of rockin' me to sleep, she talkin' greasy to me. That alone would've woke me up. Slapped me yesterday. Like, how she don't think that I'd peep how she different she actin'? Even Macy actin' funny towards her."

"Hakeem?"

In the middle of the living room, Hakeem stopped pacing, to take his cell phone back from Tracy.

"She want me to pick Macy up from daycare tomorrow."

Hakeem took off his jacket and tossed it on the arm of the couch, then he started pacing again. He was thinking. His lips moved as he mumbled something incoherent under his breath.

"Hakeem, did you hear everything she was sayin' last night?"

"I heard enough."

"She messin' with that guy, Fresh, Hakeem."

At hearing this, Hakeem took a deep breath and shook his head. His eyes flooded with tears as he exhaled and continud to pace. It was hard for him to come to grips with Gabrielle's deceit, as it was, but to be told that she was dealing with Taz's cousin, only broke his heart that much more. His hate for Gabrielle transcended past his love for her, in those few seconds.

Dishonor.

Before.

Death.

"She just threatened to kill Macy in her sleep, if I told you anything."

"Tracy, she bluffin'."

"What if she not, though?"

Hakeem joined Tracy on the couch. They both sat in silence for several seconds.

"It's like our lives became one of them crazy TV shows, or one of them scary movies, or somethin'."

"Tracy, I need to know everything you know, so we can both be on the same page wit' this shit. I need to know everything."

"Okay, um, well, she mad at'chu, 'cause ya'll ain't go lookin' for my dad the other night."

"How long her and Bayyinah been talkin'?"

"Since that night when you gave her the phone, so they could talk. They be goin' to lunch together, and everything."

"And she fuckin' wit' Fresh?"

"That's what she told me last night."

"Alright, so, what else she say?"

"That she not muslim no more."

"And all this, 'cause—"

"Hakeem, they supposed to be goin' to look for my dad tomorrow."

"Who?"

"Her, Bayyinah, and Fresh. That's why she want me to . . . "

"Pick Macy up?"

Tracy sighed and nodded her head sadly.

"She probably don't even be goin' to school no more."

"She still be goin'. Her and Bayyinah supposed to be movin' to New York, to start they own clothing line."

"With my fuckin' money, huh?"

"She said, after Fresh help them kill you, her and Bayyinah gon' kill him."

"Both of them bitches crazy."

"Hakeem, they girlfriends."

"What? As in they fuckin' each other?"

"And Bayyinah not pregnant, either."

Hakeem left his gun on the couch and stood up. His face was a portrait of bewilderment, as he looked down at Tracy.

"Hakeem, she was wearin' somethin' she bought from some costume store."

"Did she say how they gon' try to rock me?"

"They tryna figure out how to get the combination to your safe first. Once Gabby got the combination, she gon' replace all of your money with all this counterfeit money that Bayyinah got."

"And that's they master plan? Some dumb ass shit like that?"

"Hakeem, then, Gabby gon' put all this, um, stuff in ya food, so you'll fall asleep."

"So, Fresh can come into the condo and rock me?"

"Yup."

"And what about Macy?"

"Gabby wanna leave her with me."

"That's like the brightest part of her plan right there."

"She goin' to CJC tomorrow, on her lunch break, to get her bail money back she used to bail you out."

"And what she supposed to be doin' wit' it?"

"She ain't say."

"You was right, Tracy."

"About what?"

"How this shit like one of them crazy movies."

"What we gon' do, Hakeem?"

After pacing back and forth a few more times, Hakeem sat back down beside Tracy and grabbed her hands. With sad eyes, Hakeem looked at Tracy and kissed her softly on the lips. He was grateful for her devotion to their marriage.

"I'm on ya side, Hakeem. I never even considered doin' anything to hurt you."

"Yeah, but, I'ma need you to keep actin' like you not on my side, though, alright?"

"Okay."

"Just for a few days, Tracy. That's all."

"I can't believe this happenin'."

"All we gotta do is outthink three people, Tracy. That's far from hard."

"Why can't we just go to the cops?"

"'Cause, I gotta spine."

"But I don't wanna kill Gabby, Hakeem."

"Do you want her to kill me?"

"Hakeem, of course not."

141

"And are you gonna let her kill you?"

"No."

"Look, I'm not tryna have us locked up for three bodies, but if they—"

"Hakeem, why we just can't figure out a way to outthink them, like you—Like you just said, and—"

"What if my hand get forced? My hand already gettin' forced, Tracy."

"Well, use ya other hand, then. Hakeem, don't let them force you to become impulsive, like they is. We muslim, right? Let's be different, and meticulous, Insha Allah."

The next morning, which was a Monday, Hakeem woke up to pray. It was still dark outside. Together, him and Tracy both sleepily went into their bathroom, and made ablution. Done doing that, Tracy put on her kimar and her overgarments, then stood a few feet behind Hakeem. It took them only six minutes to complete their prayer. Afterwards, Hakeem climbed back into bed, and Tracy quickly joined him, after taking off her overgarment and kimar.

"Ay, did that chick, Nita, call you, yet?"

"I gotta text from her yesterday."

"Ay, yo, it's a small world, ain't it?"

"She had me thinkin' her babyfather bought that car for her, all this dag on time."

"She wish."

"But what's so crazy is, before you walked in the door, she was just askin' me and Gabby how you looked."

"The note on that car six and some change."

"Can I keep it?"

"For a kiss."

Tracy smiled and gave Hakeem a kiss. While kissing him, as she always did, when the two of them kissed, Tracy affectionately began to run her fingers through Hakeem's thick beard.

"She broke my heart, Tracy."

"Baby, she don't—Hakeem, don't cry."

"I treated her daughter like she was mine, Tracy. I bought Gabrielle shit she never had."

"And for that, and all the other nice stuff you did for them, some of your bad deeds will get wiped from your record, Hakeem. Macy appreciate everything you do for her. Hakeem, that little girl love the mess outta you."

"Tracy, how you gon' start cryin', and expect me to stop?"

"Hakeem, how could a wife not cry, when her husband cryin' right in front of her?"

Chapter Sixteen

"Mommy, you not gon' be bad today, 'kay?"

"Macy, didn't I tell you . . . " Gabrielle raised her hand and smacked Macy to the kitchen floor. Tempted to do more, she stood over Macy, and glared down at her. "You better stop actin' the fuck grown. Do you hear me? You wanna get choked?"

Teary-eyed, Macy sniffled and shook her head. Grape jelly from the butterknife in Gabrielle's left hand, dripped down to the chest area of her pink sweater.

"I didn't think so. Now, get up, before you make both of us late for school."

"'Kay, Mommy."

"And like I said yesterday, if you tell Hakeem, Tracy, or anybody at daycare, about me fuckin' hittin' you, I'ma kill that stupid ass rabbit, and set it on—"

Gabrielle's neck whiplashed when Hakeem pushed the front door open, and came walking into the condo. Fidgety, Gabrielle returned back to the kitchen island, and went back to making Macy's two peanut butter and jelly sandwiches. Hakeem's sudden arrival was entirely unexpected, bringing an instant sense of relief to Macy, and a bunch of evil thoughts to Gabrielle.

It was 8:13 a.m., and according to every local news station, Monday was going to evolve into a bright and beautiful

day. For Hakeem and Gabrielle, it was going to be one full of surprises, and a day that both of them would never forget.

"Hakeem, can you change Macy sweater for me, while I finish gettin' her lunch together?" Gabrielle asked, using the nicest voice she was able to muster up. Out of the corner of her left eye she watched Hakeem spitefully, as he took Macy by the hand and disappeared with her down the hallway. "In her tall dresser, in the second drawer, she got another pink sweater, like the one she got on, but it gotta white trim around the collar. And you can change her sneakers, and put on her pink Ugg boots."

When it rains . . .

it pours.

In Hakeem and Macy's absence, Gabrielle's first premiere of her being pregnant, introduced itself as morning sickness. A sudden flash of nauseousness washed over her entire body, sending her scrambling over to the kitchen sink, where she flipped up her face veil, and started vomiting up the spaghetti she had eaten the night before. Standing there, distracted by all sorts of conflicted thoughts, Gabrielle lost all sense of time, until she began to dry-heave, over the kitchen sink. When Gabrielle raised her head to reach for the paper towels, Hakeem and Macy came into view. The two of them had been watching her from the opening of the kitchen.

"You cool?"

"Do I look like it?"

"What'chu pregnant?"

"Hakeem, ya guess is as good as mine."

For a moment, Gabrielle and Hakeem just stared at each other in silence. The hidden war between them had expired for the span of six seconds. It was the first time in days, that the two of them were actually sharing an intimate conversation. For Hakeem, however, knowing all that he knew, he saw the sensitivity reflecting in Gabrielle's eyes as nothing more than generic emotions. In Gabrielle's mind, the very

idea that she was pregnant, and that a child inside of her had been made by a man that loved her, completely uprooted all of the faith she had invested into Bayyinah and Fresh. How quickly her mindset had altered itself back to wanting to be faithful to Hakeem, had Gabrielle so confused with her own rationality, and logic, she started to panic as she thought about the terrible train wreck of a plan, that she had conspired, and had set into motion.

"Macy, come on."

"Ay, where Tracy cell phone at?"

"In the room, on ya nightstand."

On the elevator, Gabrielle held Macy's hand, which was something that she hadn't done in a while. Every so often, Macy would stare up at Gabrielle in confusion. Through the condo's lobby, Gabrielle squeezed Macy's little hand tighter, as a hot flash, and a dizzy spell, almost caused her to melt down to the lobby's carpeted floor.

Out in the condo's parking lot, a watchful set of eyes paid close attention to Gabrielle's every move, until Gabrielle pulled off in her Infiniti. In the same parking lot, behind tinted windows, another pair of eyes were watching the person, who had been watching Gabrielle.

After Gabrielle dropped Macy off at daycare, she nervously dialed Bayyinah's cell phone number, and placed her cell phone up to her ear. As she followed the early morning, eastbound traffic, on the I-76 expressway, Gabrielle's level of anxiety soared with each ring of Bayyinah's cell phone.

"Speakin' of the devil."

"Hey, Bayyinah."

"Girl, I was just talkin' about'chu."

"To who?"

"Them two Mexican girls that used to be with my brother. They came back."

"They got out?"

"A few days ago. One of them cartels about to help them get back across the border tonight."

"They comin' back to Philly?"

"Well, they wasn't, but after I told them all about'chu, and the plan we got for Hakeem, they wanna be the ones to kill his dumb ass. They don't like what he did to my brother, either. Look, I'm gon' call you as soon as I get off the phone with them, okay?"

"Okay."

Angry with herself, Gabrielle pulled her lower lip into her mouth, and bit down on it, until she could taste her own blood. There was no one else to blame for the perfect storm that she had created, but her own self. The guilt she felt was punishing her heart, and while she drove behind a slow-moving, school bus, down the Ben Franklin Parkway, her mind terrorized her, by flashing images of Hakeem lying in a pool of his own blood. As Gabrielle made a right off of the Ben Franklin Parkway, and turned down 17th Street, she picked up her cell phone, and called the only person that she felt could possibly provide her with the help she so desperately needed.

Back at the condo, Hakeem was moving in and out of every room, like a private investigator, while talking to Tracy on his cell phone. He had freed Macy's rabbit from its cage, and every so often, the two of them crossed paths.

"But what if she really is pregnant, Hakeem?"

Hakeem sighed into his cell phone as he walked into his bedroom. At his bed, he dropped down to one knee and looked under it. Nothing was hiding under his bed, except for a few dust balls, so Hakeem rose back to his feet.

"Want me to call her?"

"For what?"

"To see if she'll tell me."

"Tracy, I'm ready to empty this whole condo out, so when she walk back in this mu'fucker, won't nothin' be in—"

147

Hakeem removed his cell phone from his ear when it beeped twice. He looked at the screen for a quick moment, then put it back to his ear, as he sat down on the side of his bed.

"Ay, Tracy, hold on, alright?"

"Okay?"

While reaching over to pick up Tracy's cell phone, from his nightstand, Hakeem answered his second call.

"What's up, ol'head?"

"Hakeem, if you never mow the lawn, you'll never see the snakes."

"What'chu mean?"

"How long have you known me, Hakeem?"

"All my life."

"And do you consider me to be someone you can rely on?"

"Absolutely . . . where you goin' wit' this?"

"I just got off the phone with Gabrielle. Now, you of all people know that I ain't never been a morning person, and normally cuss a mu'fucker out for even wakin' me up, but the conversation I just had with ya wife was so damn bizarre, I don't know right now, if I'm fuckin' comin', or goin'."

"Bill-Bill, don't believe nothin' that bitch—"

"Hakeem, listen to me. Just listen to—"

"Alright, hold on real quick."

Hakeem sighed and switched his call back over to Tracy, who he had totally forgotten about, until he looked down at her cell phone in his left hand.

"Tracy?"

"I'm still here. Everything okay?"

"Yeah, my fault. Ay, look, my ol'head Bill-Bill just—"

The sound of someone knocking on the front door rattled Hakeem's nerves, and quickly put him on alert. He left his cell phone on the bed, and as he rose to his feet, he pulled his gun off of his waist. His mind was racing as fast as his

heartbeat. Down his hallway, he went marching, wishing he had x-ray vision, while he stared angrily at his front door, wondering who was on the other side of it.

"What the fuck is she doin' here?" Hakeem wondered, glaring through his peephole with one eye at Bayyinah. The urge to spray his Mac-11 through his front door was a powerful emotion, that wasn't easy for him to suppress by no means. "Fuck she carryin' that big, dumb ass bag for? Why the fuck would Gabrielle call Bill-Bill? What she tryna get him to cross me, too? All these mu'fuckers suspect."

Hakeem stepped back and snatched his front door open, just as Bayyinah was raising her left hand to knock on it again. Their eyes engaged in a battle over Hakeem's raised Mac-11. The nozzle of the hand-uzi was inches away from Bayyinah's face.

There.

Will.

Be.

Blood.

"What's up Bayyinah?"

"I need to talk to you."

"About what?"

"A lot of stuff. Can I come in?"

Hakeem didn't budge.

Bayyinah's brown eyes became tearful.

Showing reluctance, that was clearly visible for Bayyinah to see, Hakeem stepped aside and let Bayyinah enter his condo. Before closing the door, Hakeem looked out into the hallway to make sure that Bayyinah was alone.

"If you gotta answer ya door with a gun, maybe you should really consider doin' somethin' different with ya life."

Hakeem figured that it was best to be thought dumb, so as he locked his front door, while watching Bayyinah closely, he remained silent. Hakeem knew Bayyinah like the back of his hand. The arrogant expression on her face told him that

she was gloating in believing that she knew what he didn't. Because he did know what was going on, Hakeem gave Bayyinah's back an evil smirk, as he followed her into his living room.

"Is that the gun you used to kill my brother?"

"No, but it can be the one that kill you, since you wanna get right to it."

Shaking her head sadly, Bayyinah sat her duffel bag on Hakeem's couch. A single teardrop escaped her right eye when she placed her hand on her swollen stomach, and slowly sat down on the empty couch cushion, beside her duffel bag. Letting out a sigh, she readjusted her black kimar around her face.

"What happened to us, Hakeem?"

"What'chu mean, like, between me and you, or you talkin' 'bout wit' me and Taz?" Hakeem asked, slightly raising his voice, to be heard over his ringing house phone. He took a seat across from Bayyinah, and rested his gun on his lap. "Wit' me and you, if that's what'chu talkin' 'bout, you wanted me to stop hustlin', and I ain't want to. Then, like, I 'on't know if you called ya self tryna call my bluff, but 'chu moved out. That was that. Come on, Bayyinah, man. We been over this shit a thousand times. As far as Taz, that nig—"

"Hakeem, I know how my brother was."

"I had to do what I had to do, Bayyinah. That nigga tried to shoot me in my fuckin' face, but his gun jammed. We was cool, 'til he started fuckin' wit' them Mexican bitches. He shot Rachel down in the parkin' lot, just 'cause she was tryna get to my money, so she could bail me out, Bayyinah. That nigga was trippin'."

"Where his body at, Hakeem?"

Hakeem shrugged his shoulders. He honestly didn't know where Taz's body was. He didn't care.

"So, you did my brother like they did Bin Laden? You just let somebody do what they wanted with him?"

Both of Bayyinah's questions had cracked with emotions.

"Did the mu'fucker who told you what happened, tell you that I let somebody do what they wanted with him?"

"You should've called me, Hakeem. Why didn't you call me?"

"And said what? That I rocked Taz?"

"No . . . you should've called me from jail, and told me what was goin' on. Maybe, if you had've, shit wouldn't've gotten this far. Rachel wouldn't be dead. My mom started gettin' high again, Hakeem. All because she stressed out about where Taz might be. Can you imagine how I feel, when I know what happened, and have to be in her presence, and act like I don't? You have no idea what that's like, Hakeem. I know everything that happened, because Gabrielle told me. Hakeem, ya wives don't care about'chu. They—"

"I already know about ya'll whole plan, Bayyinah. Just like I know that'chu fraudin' 'bout bein' pregnant, too."

"So, you think—You know what, Hakeem? We can . . . settle this, right . . . fuckin' . . . here, and right . . . the . . . fuck . . . now."

Right before Hakeem's eyes, while his house phone run incessantly in the background, Bayyinah had stood up, peeled out of her leather jacket, pulled her black overgarment over her head, then had unbuttoned the peach, Via Spiga shirt, that she had on. With her hands on her hips, Bayyinah then walked over to Hakeem, and stood directly in front of him.

"And it's a girl, if you even care to know. My due date is on your mom's birthday."

Speechless, Hakeem placed his hand softly on Bayyinah's pregnant stomach. When Bayyinah covered his hand with both of hers, Hakeem looked up into her eyes. It was true. She really was pregnant.

"I wanna name her Kareemah, after ya mom. I think we made her that weekend we stayed in Atlantic City. Hakeem, we can get a paternity test as soon as I have her."

"So, all that stuff you was tellin' Gabrielle was bullshit?"

"Most of it. Why? What she tell you?"

"She ain't tell me shit."

"So how—"

"Tracy told me the other night," Hakeem explained, moving over so that Bayyinah could sit down on his couch beside him. He found it hard to take his eyes off of Bayyinah's exposed stomach, so he stopped trying, and just gazed at it. "I overheard her and Tracy talkin' a couple of nights ago. I was standin' over there in the hallway, listenin' to they whole conversation. I been knew. So, when Tracy told me everything, like, how ya'll was gon' drug my food, after ya'll got the combo to my safe, so that Fresh could rock me, I just added that shit to what I already knew. Bayyinah, I know everything. How you and Gabrielle fuckin'. How ya'll gon' rock Fresh. Ya'll clothin' line. New York. I—"

"All lies, Hakeem."

Hakeem and Bayyinah glanced over at Bayyinah's Gucci pocketbook when her cell phone started ringing inside of it. Neither of them moved to get it.

"So, first of all, ain't nothin' about my sexuality has changed, since we broke up. Hakeem, the last dick that was inside of me, belong to you. Two, gettin' Gabrielle to believe that I was a lesbian was so damn easy, it's pathetic. Hakeem, I been gettin' in her ear for the past two weeks. We go to lunch together, and to be honest with you, I just wanted to have enough proof, so I could show you that these chicks you married, ain't the ones for you."

"So, what'chu tryna say, you are?"

"You sayin' I'm not? Hakeem, think about it . . . our only issue was that I wanted you to have a halal way to make

money. That's all. Other than that, as far as I know, things between us was okay, Hakeem."

"Fresh know what happened wit' me and Taz?"

"He know. He told me how Taz was mad at'chu for breakin' up with me, and how when Taz started hangin' with them Mexican girls, you stopped hangin' with him and Taz, and Taz ain't like that."

"You told him I rocked Taz, or Gabrielle did?"

"I did."

"Taz knew I wasn't feelin' them Mexican chicks. I told him that the first time he introduced us."

"He was mad, too, 'cause I was pregnant."

"Why he ain't tell me? I ain't even know."

"I told him you ain't think it was yours and that'chu had put me out."

Hakeem sighed and lowered his face down into his hands. Taz's betrayal was making sense to him now.

"Hakeem, Fresh really think we gon' do all this stuff tonight. You remember Amir?"

"Norvick cousin?"

"Yeah."

"What about him?"

"Well, he goin' with Gabrielle and Fresh, to look for Gabrielle's foster father tonight. Hakeem, I told Amir to kill Gabrielle and Fresh when they get down there."

At approximately 12:17 p.m., on the corner of a bank, on 15th and JFK Blvd, Gabrielle received a phone call from someone that caused all of her emotions to shatter into pieces. Gabrielle stood frozen on the sidewalk, as the pedestrians walked by her in haste, to escape the low temperatures, and to handle their personal duties, before their lunch hour came to an end. For Gabrielle, time no longer mattered.

"Mom?"

"Are you in school?"

"I'm—I'm on my, um, lunch break," Gabrielle answered,

happy to hear her mother's voice. Switching her cell phone to her other ear, she adjusted the straps of her pocketbook on her shoulder, and began walking south on 15th Street, against the wind. "I just came outta the bank. I cashed the check the, um, courts, or CJC, gave me, for payin' Hakeem bail a few—"

"Who was that girl that came to see Hakeem, who was with that guy, that night, me and your father first came to see you?"

"Who? Bayyinah?"

At Market Street, Gabrielle turned west, and continued walking. She was wearing a full-length, lynx coat, that Hakeem had bought for her. On her head, she had on a black, kimar, and under her expensive coat, she had on a black overgarment, that was made of denim fabric. Beneath her overgarment, Gabrielle was wearing a red, Foly+Corrina sweatsuit, that matched her spiked, Christian Louboutin sneakers. The cold weather wasn't bothering her one bit; life was.

"Gabrielle, she was just up in ya'll condo with Hakeem for over a damn hour. And she don't have the duffel bag that she went in there with, either."

"Mom, what'chu talkin' 'bout? How you know that?"

"Mothers know they children, Gabrielle. All the way on the other side of the ocean, I had this strong feeling that mine needed me. I got here last night, not sure, if I should call, just stop by, or what. Then, this mornin', I'm sittin' in your parkin' lot, and I see that same girl from that night, watchin' you and my gran'baby with her seat leaned all the way back. I been here ever since. Now, what's—"

"What kind of car was she in?"

"A Porsche jeep like Hakeem's, but it's silver. Now, Gabrielle, I'm still sittin' here, watchin' this same girl, who didn't get outta her car, until after you left, get back into her car. She leavin' now. Smilin', too. Now, I might be wrong, but either she up to no good, or Hakeem is, or they both are. I

don't know. All I know is, I don't like what I just sat here and saw today. And I most definitely don't like this worried feelin' that I got, Gabrielle. I don't."

"Mom, it's all my fault."

"What's all your fault? Gabrielle, what's going on?"

"I messed up, Mom. I had it so good, and I messed it all up, bein' stupid."

"How?"

From 16th and Market, all the way to the fifth floor of the parking garage, where Gabrielle had her car parked in the Liberty Place's parking facility, Gabrielle spoke on her cell phone to her mother, and told her all about everything, leaving out nothing. At times, she cried, and was forced to stop talking. The gravity of what was going on had Gabrielle feeling like she had the weight of the world on her shoulders. She was also feeling ashamed of herself, cranky, and she was having a strong craving for celery sticks, that was driving her crazy.

Gabrielle was on the verge of hysteria, but when her and her mother's conversation was interrupted by another phone call, which, much to her surprise, was coming from Hakeem, Gabrielle nearly pissed on herself.

"Mom, this him, callin' me."

"Hakeem?"

"Yeah . . . what should I do? Should I answer it?"

"Talk to him, Gabrielle."

"But—"

"Baby, trust in Allah, and talk to your husband. I'm not at all supportive of these choices you been makin', but as your mother, I'm inclined to help you right your wrongs. Gabrielle, your husband is your way into Paradise. Make sure you let him know about them Mexican girls, and let him know that I'm down here in the parking lot, too."

"Okay."

Afraid of what was to come next, Gabrielle took a deep

breath and accepted her call from Hakeem. Her hand that held her cell phone was shaking nervously.

"Hello?"

"You in class?"

"No."

"Where you at?"

Silence.

"Bill-Bill called me, Gabrielle. He told me everything you told him. But'chu knew he was gon' do that anyway, though, right?"

Silence.

"Gabrielle, I been knew what was goin' on. I was standin' in the hallway, that night you was tellin' Tracy how you was done bein' muslim, and bein' married. I heard all'lat dumb ass shit you was sayin'. What's so crazy is, Bayyinah had you on some puppet shit the whole time, Gabrielle. Yo, and guess what? Gabrielle she did all'lat, just to show me that'chu and Tracy wasn't loyal to me."

"I'm sorry, Hakeem. I'm so sorry. Wallahi, I am."

"Gabrielle, I'm gon' bottom line this shit for you. This scar you gave me is too fuckin' big, and too fuckin' deep, for a sorry."

"Hakeem, what do I have to—"

"Where you at?"

"In the Liberty Place, parkin' garage," Gabrielle answered, using her free hand to flip up her face veil. She wiped her face clean of her tears, then sighed as she switched her cell phone to her right ear. "Hakeem, I know me sayin' what I'm about to say might sound desperate, but I'm—I'm, um, I'm willin' to do whatever it takes, to make—Hakeem, just gimme a chance to make it right. Gimme a chance to right my wrongs. I'm pregnant, Hakeem. I got the pregnancy test right here. It's right here in my pocketbook, Hakeem. I'll show it to you. I stopped at CVS, before I went to school this—"

"That shit probably Fresh's."

"No it's not. It's yours, Hakeem. I never kissed Fresh. Ask Bayyinah. You can ask Fresh, Hakeem. The most we ever did was send each other some nasty text messages, and that's about it. Hakeem, I swear."

"You was wit' poisonin' my food, and lettin' that nigga come in the spot to rock me. You told Bayyinah about Taz, Gabrielle. Like, yoooo . . . I can't believe you, Gabrielle. Me? How you gon' flip on me? I was for you, Gabrielle. Like, all the way for you, wit' no pauses, or nothin' man."

Silence.

"And don't think I ain't been peepin' how different Macy been actin' around you, either."

The disgust and disappointment in Hakeem's voice was tearing Gabrielle's heart into shreds. Looking back at everything, Gabrielle knew that she had made many terrible mistakes. Bayyinah had humiliated her, and had her feeling like an idiot, and a fool. With her mind games, Bayyinah had shown Hakeem that she was weak-minded, and that his life in her hands, was potentially expendable.

"Hakeem, can I come home?"

"Don't'chu still gotta schedule to follow?"

"With who?"

"Fresh and Amir?"

"But, I thought'chu said it was all a lie?"

"That was the only part of the plan that was authentic. The only remix is, after ya'll holla at Mr. Dave, Amir got instructions to down you and Fresh, too."

"Why?"

"That's how Bayyinah wanted to play it. Gabrielle, Bill-Bill gon' be down there. I just got off the phone with him. Only you and him comin' outta there alive, Gabrielle."

"But—"

"Ain't nothin' gon' happen to you."

157

Gabrielle didn't believe Hakeem. She wanted to, but something inside of her just wouldn't allow her to do so.

"I'm sayin', all this nut ass shit over Mr. Dave, right? You said, I ain't keep my word, and all'lat. How you paid my bail, and I ain't never keep my end of the bargain. That's what all this shit about, right? Well, you gon' get'cha chance to holla at Mr. Dave tonight. You gon' get what'chu wanted."

"Hakeem, can I come home first?"

"Yeah, after Mr. Dave goin' away party. Call Bill-Bill. He waitin' for you to call right now."

"Did Bayyinah tell you about them Mexican girls?"

"She told me about everything."

"She was lyin' about that, too?"

"Yup . . . guess what she wasn't lyin' about, though?"

"What?"

"Bein' pregnant. That wasn't nothin' from no costume store. She showed me her stomach. Gabrielle, look, just call Bill-Bill, man."

"Hakeem, I love you."

"Yeah, right. You don't even love Macy, so I know that's bullshit. Gabrielle, you too cynical to love anybody. You love Gabrielle, and that's about it."

"Are you bein' this mean to Tracy? She knew, too."

"Gabrielle just call Bill-Bill. Worry about that. Listen to what he tell you to do, too."

"Hakeem, what if something go wrong?"

"Insha Allah, it won't."

Chapter Seventeen

"And when Mommy be bad, she do like this, Mom—Mom."

In utter shock, and total disbelief, Gabrielle's mother looked over Macy's head, at Hakeem and Tracy, who were watching in silence, as Macy put her tiny hands on her grandmother's neck, and tried to choke her. It was a sight so hard for Hakeem to watch, that he had to turn his head and walk away. Tracy followed him.

"And—And, Mommy hit me on my face real hard, and said her gonna make Fo-Facey die."

It was 7:32 p.m., and the vibe inside of Hakeem's condo was pensive, and even Macy was able to sense that something was wrong. Her mother's absence had her unusually talkative.

Hakeem was the exact opposite. An earlier argument with Gabrielle's mother, still had him extremely upset, because things had been said to him, that had struck some sensitive nerves. Coupled with his anger, Hakeem, like Gabrielle's mother, and Tracy, was finding it impossible not to feel stressed out, and anxious to know what was going on with Gabrielle. In her last text-message, to Hakeem's cell phone, which was an hour earlier, she had told Hakeem that she was deeply sorry, and that if she died, she wanted him and Tracy to adopt Macy, and raise her as their own.

The somber text-messages came across to Hakeem as a dying confession, and because Hakeem knew that things were about to get real cryptic, down in the El-train's tunnel, he was given an intense level of anxiety, that had his mind overcrowded with a lot of deep thoughts.

"Hakeem, what if my dad not even down there?"

With Tracy a few steps behind him, Hakeem twisted the brass handle on the door to his walk-in closet, then walked inside.

"That was almost two weeks ago when Nita saw him down there."

"Take Gabrielle mom, and Macy, to the apartment, Tracy."

"Why?"

"Just do what I said, Tracy," Hakeem retorted, peeling off his clothes, until he stood in only his gray, wool socks, and his white, Polo thermals. He had made up his mind that he was going to go and join Gabrielle and Bill-Bill. "Drive wit' Gabrielle mom, and leave me ya car keys, too. Go get my cell phone, and send a text to Gabrielle and Bill-Bill. It's in there on the bed. Let them know I'm on my way, Tracy."

"Hakeem, why can't'chu just tell them to both walk away?"

"What's goin on in here with ya'll two?"

Hakeem exhaled an impatient sigh when Gabrielle's mother appeared at the doorway of his walk-in closet. Her eyes were still condemning him. Her poignant words from their earlier argument, were still hibernating in his system, and as he chose all-black clothing from his wardrobe, he felt himself sinking deeper and deeper, into a morose state of mind.

"I'm finished my milk n' cookies, Mom-Mom."

At Macy's presence, Hakeem looked at Tracy, and Gabrielle's mother. Like his own, their eyes had become wa-

tery. Hakeem dropped down to his knees when Macy trotted up to him.

"Where you goin', Hakeem?"

"To get Mommy."

"Oh."

Only inches apart, hazel eyes stared into hazel eyes. Both saw trust. One set of eyes saw a daughter that wasn't his by blood. The younger set of eyes saw a father that was hers, by sheer evidence of his actions. Both hazel eyes saw tears.

"I'm comin' right back, okay?"

"'Kay, Hakeem."

Trust.

At 8:08 p.m., an El-train going westbound, blew by the 2nd and Market Street station, without stopping. On cue, on the eastbound side of the train station, at its far end, Gabrielle, Fresh, and Fresh's friend, Amir, all quickly scurried down a metal, step-ladder, that took them from the eastbound train station's platform, down to its tracks. The sight of a rat made Gabrielle catch her breath, and sent her running into the darkness of the tunnel, behind Fresh and Amir.

"Yo, turn ya'll flashlights on, and pull ya'll ratchets out."

Following Amir's whispered-instructions, Gabrielle and Fresh cut on their flashlights, and removed their guns from where they had been hiding them.

"Alright, this how we gon' do this shit. Me 'n Gabrielle gon' go over to the tracks on the other side. Fresh, this ya side. We all gon' walk this fuckin' tunnel, back to Spring Garden, and see if we see ol'head down this mu'—"

"What if some of them transit cops down here?"

"Fresh, man, shut the fuck up, and pay attention, dog."

"What? Nigga, you shut the fuck up. Ain't nobody put'chu in charge of how we gon'—"

"Pussy, I put me in charge. Fuck you talkin' 'bout?"

With his words, Amir raised his gun and pointed it at Fresh's face.

"Now since you got so much to fuckin' say, gimme ya fuckin' ratchet. Matter fact, give that shit to Gabrielle, and take her flashlight."

Moments later, with a gun in each hand, Gabrielle was following her self-elected leader, in absolute fear for her life. Nothing that she had imagined about the El-train's tunnels, came close to what she was seeing with her own two eyes. There was trash and filth everywhere she stepped, and the cold air smelled like piss, human feces, and dead animals. The walls of the tunnel were vandalized with grafitti, and in some places, traces of old blood stains could be seen. Gabrielle felt like she was a tourist in a dungeon. All of the rats and dirty syringes had her walking light, and feeling completely unnerved with each step that she took. She wanted to be home.

"Ay, you said ol' head gotta pit, right?"

Gabrielle nodded her head at Amir, as they both walked side by side, down a catwalk, that was only inches away from the westbound train tracks. It was Fresh who had Gabrielle's attention. He was on the opposite tracks, but he would pause every few steps, and look over his shoulder, as if he heard something, or was seeing something, that warranted him to keep looking over his shoulder.

"Hey?!! Stop right there!! All three of . . . "

Bocka! Bocka! Bocka! Bocka!

Amir had placed his gun so close to Gabrielle's face when he impulsively started shooting at the five transit cops, that one of the ejected shell casings from his gun had hit Gabrielle on the bridge of her nose. The second, third, and fourth shell casing, had all soared over Gabrielle's head, and had found homes down in the garbage, inches from the third rail. Amir was only seventeen, and to label him reckless would be an under statement.

Live and . . .

Let die . . .

Right after Amir's fourth gunshot rang off, a sequence of disruptive events, had caused the fates of eleven people, and one dog, to collide, and explode on contact. The dangerousness of the situation had escalated, quickly blossoming like a black rose of death, as an eastbound train, and a westbound train, came speeding down the tracks from both directions. Also added to the climactic scenario, was the sudden, but calculated introduction, of several pit bulls, along with two fast-moving trails of fire, that were started by Mr. Dave, after he had overheard the shouts, and the shooting.

It was absolutely no doubt in Mr. Dave's mind, that the Philadelphia police had finally discovered where he had been hiding. Being captured alive wasn't in Mr. Dave's plans.

Dying wasn't either.

The fires were to stop the El-trains.

The dogs were for the cops.

Out of everyone, Gabrielle was the only person, whose nerves hadn't become unsettled by the trains, fires, and attacking dogs. With Hakeem's text-message fueling her spirit, and the thoughts of redemption, manipulating her mind, Gabrielle followed her instincts, and threw paranoia and fear to the wind. Gabrielle knew that staying alive, and avoiding prison, meant that she had to move, and move fast, and so that's what she started doing.

"Bitch," Gabrielle cursed to herself, as she pointed the gun in her left hand, at Amir's face, and pulled the trigger. The recoil of the handgun vibrated the entire left side of her body, but it was the results of her homicidal actions, that fed all of the starving demons, that were living in the dark corners of her mind. "You die. You die. You die, pussy."

Gabrielle was granted only a second to look at Amir's lifeless body on the train tracks, because she had the transit cops yelling commands, and shooting at her and Fresh, and in front of her, she had three growling pit bulls headed straight for her. Still, Gabrielle didn't panic. Instead, she did what

she believed Hakeem would do, if he was faced with the imminent danger that she was in, which she assumed would be to first get as far away as possible, from the transit police, and to kill each and every dog that came her way in the process.

Grace.

Under.

Fire.

Outside, Hakeem was frantically clipping away at the fence that surrounded the embankment of the train tracks, with a pair of wire-cutters. Little did Hakeem know, there was already a hole cut out in the fence, big enough for him to fit through, seventeen feet away, to his left, which had been put there by his friend, Bill-Bill, two hours earlier.

The frightening melody of booming gunfire was echoing loudly from the El-train's tunnel. Overhead, speeding motorists were oblivious to the carnage that was going on beneath them. However, while all was calm and appeared normal on the I-95 expressway, all of the passengers on the El-train, that had been traveling westbound, were stampeding their way from the long train's first compartment, back to its last. Following the radioed commands of his supervisor, the train's engineer had brought the train to an emergency stop, just as the El-train was about to enter the mouth of the now smoke-filled tunnel. Passengers on the train's first compartment not only were able to see the fires, but they had also witnessed Mr. Dave, and Bill-Bill, as the two men engaged in a bloody battle with knives, on the fiery train tracks ahead of them.

Several Fire Departments, more transit police, and Philadelphia police, had been notified, and were already enroute to the scene. A helicopter from a local news station was on the way as well.

"Shit," Hakeem growled under his breath, as he ran, tripped, and crawled up the steep embankment, leading to

the train tracks. The loose rocks and gravel made him feel like he was wearing roller skates on a sheet of ice. "Where all that fuckin' smoke comin' from? They stopped shootin'. I should've came—"

Hakeem's thoughts came to an end, and his adrenaline rose to new heights, because just as he was reaching the top of the embankment, and straightening himself up, the panicking passengers on the last compartment of the El-train, were just getting the rear emergency door open. Their shouts and screams started piercing the night air. Others of them, who were stranded on the metal ledges, between the small gaps of each compartment, were beginning to shove, and argue amongst each other, while others took the opportunity to jump down to the train tracks. When more gunshots started echoing from the El-train's smoking tunnel, Hakeem took off running at top speed in that direction. Hakeem quickly found out that getting to where he wanted to go was a fight in itself, because more passengers from the El-trains were starting to use the adjacent doors, between each compartment, as ways to escape all of the hysteria.

Inside of the tunnel, Gabrielle was losing the resolve she had once owned. In only two minutes, and three seconds, Gabrielle had murdered three transit cops, Amir, and Fresh, and two dogs, and now down on her hands, and her knees, crawling through fire and garbage, with Mr. Dave's pit bull, Sammy Davis, locked onto her left ankle. With every move Gabrielle made forward, Sammy Davis was growling, shaking, and yanking her backwards. The pain that was shooting up Gabrielle's left leg was horrendous, and draining what little energy she had left. The thick smoke had her feeling like she was inhaling sand into her lungs, with each and every breath that she was forcing herself to take. When another pit bull joined Sammy Davis and started ripping the leather on the back of her jacket, Gabrielle closed her eyes and stopped struggling. Before losing consciousness, she thought about

the embryo in her stomach. Her guns were empty, and thirty-five feet behind her, amidst fire and garbage.

Again, all of the loud shooting inside of the smoke-filled tunnel went silent. Fate's identity was revealing its true face to Gabrielle's motionless body, and bringing death to her two canine attackers, while fifty feet away, at the mouth of the tunnel, Hakeem was inching sideways by the stalled, El-train, with his gun in his hand. At the same exact moment, Bill-Bill was chasing Mr. Dave out of the tunnel, on the opposite side of the train. Bill-Bill's blood-runner military knife, was sticking out of Mr. Dave's right, eye socket.

"Gabrielle?!!"

"Ay, yo, Hak, we got her down here!!"

"Hak, hurry up!"

Coughing, Hakeem covered his nose and mouth with the collar of his leather jacket, and followed the voices of his two friends, who were part of the five-man group, that had all been disguised as transit cops. Initially, these disguises had seemed like a good idea.

They weren't.

As Hakeem accepted Gabrielle's motionless body into his arms, he looked at his two friends with questions in his eyes.

"She thought we was real transit cops, Hak."

"You gotta hurry up and get her outta here. She still breathin', but all this smoke gon'—"

"Where Lance 'n 'em at?"

"She rocked them niggaz, Hak. She was shootin' at all of us."

"Damn."

Chapter Eighteen

The front page of Tuesday's morning newspaper was a chilling image, that had many people across Philadelphia, feeling deeply concerned about their safety out in public. The headlines on the top of the newspaper read, 'Next Stop: Death'. The picture had been taken by a news reporter, from a helicopter. In the enlargened photo, one was able to see several body bags, that were lined up on the El-train's eastbound tracks, a few feet away from the opening of the tunnel, that led underground. Images of transit police, EMT units, regular police officers, and firemen, could be seen all over the photo. In the top-left corner, on the piece of the I-95 expressway, a roadblock was visible. It was there, where Mr. Dave had carjacked a pregnant, white woman, for her vehicle, and had made his escape. Down at the bottom-right portion of the picture, there were numerous small, and large crowds, of people, who had all been aboard the westbound El-train, before all of the chaos had began.

Share.

My.

Guilt.

"So, what do we do now?"

"Far as what? Us? Or you talkin' 'bout, after what happened last night?"

"Both," Gabrielle answered, watching Hakeem, as he

walked over to the door of their hotel room, and stared silently through its peephole. She wanted to know what his true thoughts were, more than she wanted relief from all of aches and pain in her body. "Hakeem, if we get caught, I'll confess to everything that happened. We can call the cops right now, if you want to. I don't care. From this moment forward, the only thing that matter is, Macy, this baby in my stomach, and your forgiveness. That's it. I'll lay in this bed and say sorry, 'til I lose my voice, Hakeem."

"Gabrielle, I hear all'lat, but—I'm sayin', it ain't like you just crashed one of my cars, or some shit like that. You was somewhere else wit' it."

"I'm not expectin' you to just shrug off what I did, but—"

"What, what'chu askin' me to do, then?" Hakeem asked, turning his back to the hotel door. His body was giving him hints that he was in need for some sleep, but his mind wouldn't allow him to sit down for no longer than five minutes at the most. "Yo, that ain't even what we need to be talkin' about in this fuckin' hotel room anyway. They got Bill-Bill, Gabrielle. That's my fuckin' ol'head. It was ya ass that called him yesterday, and got him caught up in all this bullshit. This ya fault. All this shit is."

"Hakeem?"

"What?"

"Would killin' me make you feel better?"

Giving Gabrielle an angry stare, Hakeem walked over to get his cell phone. It was ringing on top of the TV. Once Hakeem had his cell phone in his hand, he let out a sigh.

"Who that?"

"This Tracy."

"Ask her did my mom come back, yet."

"You ask her. Wake me up in like fifteen minutes."

Hakeem gave Gabrielle his ringing cell phone, then, against his better judgement, he stretched across their hotel bed, and closed his eyes. In just seconds, he was teetering on

the borderline, between sleep, and consciousness, until Gabrielle started shaking him violently, while she was raising the volume on the TV.

"Hakeem, look!"

Just when Hakeem and Gabrielle both believed that things weren't able to get any worse, an unthinkable event began airing on their hotel room's TV, pulling their destinies further down into the darkness of pain, and despair.

While Gabrielle was still pointing the remote control at the TV, and raising its volume, until it was almost deafening, Hakeem was rolling off the other side of the bed, with his index finger poked into his ear, and his cell phone pressed against his other one. To hear what Tracy was trying to tell him, Hakeem walked into the bathroom, and shut the door behind him.

". . . holdin' them hostage."

"What? Tracy, calm down. I can't—"

"Hakeem, she—Oh, my God."

"Tracy, look, stop cryin' and tell me—"

"She at Bayyinah house."

"Who?"

"Gabby mom. That's her on the news."

"What? Tracy, how the fuck she know where Bayyinah live at?"

"From . . . "

Getting angrier with each second, Hakeem switched his cell phone to his left ear, and snatched the bathroom door open. At his return, Gabrielle lowered the volume on the TV, and gave him a look of hopelessness. What she felt, he too was feeling.

". . . registration papers in the glove compartment. Hakeem, the SWAT team about to go in there. Macy in there, Hakeem."

"Tracy, I'ma call you back."

Tracy's voice transformed into a piercing scream, that

sent tiny darts at Hakeem's left eardrum. At that same moment, Hakeem watched as Gabrielle slid off of their hotel bed, and down to the floor. Like Tracy, Gabrielle had started to scream as well. There was no need for Hakeem to ask Gabrielle, or Tracy, what was wrong, because just like them, he was watching as someone's severed head was being tossed from the second-floor window, of a rowhouse, on the television set. Seeing this made Hakeem stagger. When another severed head was tossed out of the same window, in just seconds, after the first one, Hakeem felt a roar of his own, beginning to develop down in the pit of his sickened, stomach. It was when the third severed head came flying out of the window, that Hakeem dropped to his knees, and started to cry, while giving freedom to his pain-laced roar.

The first severed head had belonged to Gabrielle's mother.

The second one was Bayyinah's.

Macy's head was the third.

The live news coverage was happening in South Philadelphia, on 23rd and Morris. Authorities of every kind were on the scene, and sweeping views of the camera, was showing members of the SWAT team, as they moved about in tactical formations, on the rooftops, across from Bayyinah's rowhouse. There were uniformed officers, and plain clothes detectives, up and down the block, and two police helicopters, circling up in the air. Every so often, an aerial view was provided by the news station's own helicopter, showing TV viewers all of the intersections, that had been blocked off by the police department.

As the voice of the news reporter continued to illustrate what was going on, the TV showed as several SWAT officers raced up Bayyinah's front steps, in full riot gear. At the top step, the lead SWAT member started using a battering-device to knock Bayyinah's front door off of its hinges. This only took him eight seconds. Then, one by one, with their as-

sault rifles raised, and their bulletproof shields out in front of them, the pack of SWAT officers began fearlessly advancing into Bayyinah's house. What happened next was an epic act of violence, that transcended all of the assumptions that people had thought would, or should have happened. Inside of Bayyinah's house, there had been two Mexican women, standing at the top of Bayyinah's first flight of stairs, with hand grenades in their hands. The explosion had been so unexpected, and so riveting, that it had brought the mayor of the city, and all of his staff, to their feet, at City Hall.

For Gabrielle's sake, and his own, Hakeem cut off the TV. More than enough had been seen. Hakeem and Gabrielle held each other, and as they both cried uncontrollably, Hakeem's cell phone rung in the background.

"Hakeem, I—I wanna—I wanna go get Macy."

"We can't."

"Why? Why . . . can't we go get my baby, Hakeem? Why?"

Hakeem had so many emotions colliding inside of his chest that he found himself too choked up to give Gabrielle an answer.

"Why not? They—They—Hakeem, they cut off my baby—"

Gabrielle couldn't bring herself to say what she had seen done to her daughter. Her words became loud, ragged sobs, and these sobs began to grown louder, as Hakeem hugged her closer to his chest.

"We gon' get through this, Gabrielle. We gon' get through—"

"They killed Macy, Hakeem. What she ever do to anybody?"

"Nothin . . . Allah gon' punish them for that. Wallahi, He is."

"What made my mom go there? Who was that in Bayyinah house, Hakeem?"

"I don't know."

For half an hour, Hakeem and Gabrielle just held each other, and grieved. It wasn't said in words, but in that mournful, thirty minutes, the issue of distrust, between Hakeem and Gabrielle was put behind them.

"Gabrielle, you sure nobody saw ya face last night?"

Sullenly, Gabrielle nodded her head, as Hakeem helped her up off of the floor, and back onto their hotel bed. Her legs were just as unsteady as her breathing.

"What about the person in the booth, at the El-station?"

"Wasn't . . . nobody . . . in there."

"You kept that wig on the whole time?"

Curling up into a ball, Gabrielle nodded her head again, then closed her eyes. She let out a sob when Hakeem sat down on the edge of the bed beside her. Ironically, the hotel they were at, just so happened to be the same hotel that her parents had stayed in, during their first visit to find Gabrielle. Hakeem had checked into the hotel the prior night, only because it was located blocks away from the melee, back at the El-station. Because Hakeem didn't want to chance him and Gabrielle being pulled over by the cops, in his race from the chaotic scene, he had went straight to the hotel.

"Hakeem, how—How I'm gon' tell my dad this?"

Hakeem answered Gabrielle with a heavy sigh.

"He gon' blame me for everything, watch," Gabrielle sobbed, as she thought about how her father was going to react to hearing the tragic news, about her mother and Macy. Hakeem's consoling hand on her back, did little to stop the anguish that she was feeling. "They ain't have to do that. Who would do somethin' like that to a little girl? Hakeem, she was only a baby. I don't understand why my mother would wanna go to Bayyinah house, anyway. What was she thinkin'?"

"Tracy said she got Bayyinah address from the registration papers in the Acura."

The night before, after learning that Gabrielle was okay,

and with Hakeem, Gabrielle's mother had taken it upon herself to go and confront Bayyinah. Gabrielle's mother had felt that Bayyinah was solely to blame for the problems that Gabrielle and Hakeem were having. Sadly, going to Bayyinah's house had come with a horrible cost. Gabrielle's mother had taken Macy along, for reasons she herself didn't quite understand.

"Who was that in Bayyinah's house, Hakeem?"

"It had to be them Mexican bitches. They—"

"How you know? I thought it was—"

"Bayyinah sent me a text last night," Hakeem interrupted, handing his cell phone to Gabrielle. Guilt caused him to drop his face down into his hands. "I let shit get too outta hand. That night that I rocked Taz, Bayyinah said them Mexican bitches had left a bag of money at her house. She brung it to me when she came to the condo yesterday. I got that text from her when we first got here. I was tryna make sure you was cool, so I ain't never get the chance to get back with her. Then, like, once I knew you was cool, and had talked to ya mom, and talked to Tracy, I tried callin' her back, but she ain't never answer her phone. Then, Alfie 'n them kept callin' me. That's who told me Bill-Bill got caught. I got that last text from her, after I talked to Tracy."

Hakeem's cell phone started ringing in Gabrielle's hand.

"Why would she tell you everything was okay in this last text, if it really wasn't."

As Hakeem accepted his cell phone from her, Gabrielle stared at the teardrops that were rolling down the front of Hakeem's face. It was no doubt in Gabrielle's mind, that at that moment, Hakeem's tears were for Bayyinah, and their unborn child.

"You think she told you that, to keep you from goin' there?"

Hakeem nodded his head tearfully, and answered his cell phone. On the other end of his cell phone, he could hear

173

Tracy crying her heart out. At that second, Hakeem imagined what life must have been like for Bayyinah, Macy, and Gabrielle's mother, during their final moments of being alive, and his mind went on to paint a horrific mural, that set all of his thoughts on fire.

"Hakeem, what hotel ya'll at?"

"The one on 4th and Arch."

"Can I come down there with ya'll?"

"Alright, but come in a cab."

"Okay."

"And I need you to handle somethin' for me, too, before you come."

"Okay."

"As Salaamu Alaykum."

"Wa Laykum As Salaam Wa Rahmatullah."

"Tracy, I'ma text you, and tell you everything I need you to do right now, alright?"

"Alright, Hakeem."

A little over an hour later, at 12:16 p.m., Tracy showed up at Hakeem and Gabrielle's hotel room, with everything that Hakeem had asked for. After a brief discussion with Gabrielle, and Tracy, which left them all in tears, Hakeem left the hotel, to begin a journey that he knew was going to be burdensome, on his heart, and on his soul.

"Pullin' together will keep us from fallin' apart, Gabrielle."

"Really?" Gabrielle asked, shaking her head sadly. From her hotel bed, she watched tearfully, while Tracy began unpacking one of the suitcases she had brought with her. "Tracy, my mom and Macy dead. Dead, Tracy. And not by some drunk driver, or a stray bullet, or some fuckin' hurricane, but behind some retarded stuff I had my hands in. They dead because of me, Tracy. Because of me."

"Gabby, what happened—"

"Tracy, I know it. You know it. And Hakeem sure as hell fuckin' know it. Even Allah know it."

Emotional, and crying herself, Tracy sat down on the hotel bed next to Gabrielle, and wrapped her arms around Gabrielle. Their bodies shook against each other, as the two of them cried.

"What we . . . gon' do now, Tracy? We did all that, and Mr. Dave still got away."

"Gabby, whatever we do next, is goin' to define us for who we are as muslim women. We can either let this break us, or—"

"How we supposed to bury them, if they ain't got no—"

"Gabby, did ya'll pray, before I got here?"

"No."

"Well, look, let's make salat, and then we can figure out what we gon' do about everything, after that, Insha Allah."

"You brung me some overgarments?"

"Yeah, they in the other suitcase."

It took a little bit more prodding, but after a few more minutes of crying, Gabrielle got her emotions together, and got out of the hotel bed. Before losing conciousness, the last thing Gabrielle remembered hearing, as she melted down to the floor, was Macy's voice saying, "Mommy, you not gon' be bad today, 'kay?"

Goodbye.

Wait . . .

Please don't go.

At the corner of 17th and Market, Hakeem stepped out of a cab and answered his cell phone.

"Hello?"

"My secretary gave me your message. Is everything okay?"

"You still in ya office?"

"Well, uh, actually, I'm on my way out of it. I have a

client scheduled to start picking his jury, in about thirty minutes.

Hakeem liked Tobi Russeck, because she was a lawyer, who had a tenacious attitude when it came to defending her clients. In the courtroom, she treated the prosecution as if they were her very own enemies, and treated her clients like they were blood related. Tobi Russeck was one of the prettiest attorneys in Philadelphia, and she knew the law extremely well. If you was prone to get into some kind of legal trouble, you wanted her to defend you.

"Can I meet'chu outside real quick, Tobi?"

"Of my office?"

"I'm right down the street. I'll be there in three minutes."

"Sure."

"Alright."

A slight sense of relief came over Hakeem as he stuffed his cell phone down into the pocket of his jeans. To avoid inconveniencing Tobi, Hakeem quickened his pace. As he walked east on Market Street, he gazed up at the tall, corporate buildings, while rehearsing in his mind what he was going to tell Tobi. Hakeem's deep thinking was interrupted when his cell phone started ringing in his pocket. After switching the suitcase he was carrying, from his right hand, to his left, Hakeem accepted the call he was getting from Tracy, and pressed his cell phone against his ear.

"Tracy, ain't no way ya'll got there that fast."

"Gabby fainted, Hakeem. She okay now, but her, um, her dad keep callin' her cell phone, and I don't know if I should answer it, and tell him what happened."

"Where ya'll at?"

"Still at the hotel."

"They ain't come tell ya'll to leave yet?"

"They called, but I had went down to the desk and had paid for another night, because I ain't wanna chance Gabby passin' out again."

"That was smart. Where Gabrielle at?"

"Layin' down."

"What was wrong wit' 'er?"

"I think it was 'cause she ain't eat nothin'. Then, like, with everything that's goin' on. I just ordered room service, so she can eat."

"How you know that's her dad callin'?"

"His picture keep comin' up on her screen."

"Alright, alright . . . look, I'm meetin' wit the lawyer right now, then I'm goin' to pick up Gabrielle car. Stay at the hotel, 'til I call ya'll."

"What about Gabby dad?"

"I'ma call him as soon as I finish talkin' to the lawyer."

"Okay."

"Make sure she have on her nikab when ya'll leave, Tracy."

"I will. Since we still here, you want me to just throw them clothes she had on yesterday, in one of these hotel trash cans, out in the hallway, while nobody lookin'?"

Hakeem took a moment to think, while walking across Market Street. Gabrielle's clothes were the only thing that could link Gabrielle to what happened down in the El-tunnel. They were items that her and Hakeem had both purchased at a South Philadelphia thrift store, weeks earlier.

"Naw, let's wait 'til we get to Delaware, Tracy. It could be cameras all over that hotel."

"Alright, I'll wait, then."

"Alright, lemme holla at this lawyer real quick."

"Okay, As Salaamu Alaykum."

"Wa Laykum As Salaam."

After returning his cell phone to his pocket, Hakeem forced himself to smile, as he stepped up onto the northwest corner of 16th and Market Street. Tobi was standing there waiting for him, holding a suitcase of her own. She had her black hair, pulled back into a neat ponytail, and her blazer

and knee-length skirt, were both navy blue. To Hakeem, Tobi looked like a much younger version of the pop singer, Fiona Apple. Tobi was very pretty, quick to smile, and she carried herself very seriously.

"What's up, Tobi?"

"Not too much. Walk with me."

Hakeem crossed 16th Street by Tobi's side, and continued walking with her east, down Market Street. The Criminal Justice Center was only two and a half blocks away.

"You look real studious carrying that suitcase, but my intuition tells me that a job interview ain't where you're headed."

"I need you again, Tobi. It's real serious this time, too, "

"Hakeem the last time you and I spoke, you promised me that you was going to be good."

Hakeem and Tobi Russeck stopped walking when they reached the corner of 15th Street and Market. Traffic at the intersection was busy as it always was. When Tobi glanced down at the watch on her right wrist, Hakeem let out a long sigh, then started talking. With City Hall looming behind him, Hakeem handed over his suitcase, which contained fifty thousand dollars in cash, and he told Tobi how he was involved in the publicized drama, that had occurred at the El-station, the previous night. Tobi's eyes grew wider when Hakeem wrapped up his story by telling her that what had just happened at Bayyinah's house, had something to do with him as well.

"Hakeem, you kidding me?"

"I wish I was, Tobi," Hakeem confided, blinking back tears. This admission of his caused a lot of turbulence within his heart. "That was my wife mom, and her daughter. The other girl was my old girlfriend. She was pregnant with my daughter, Tobi. I just want'chu to go check on my ol'head. His name is William Thomas. Tobi, he like a uncle to me. They probably still got him at 8th and Race, as we speak."

"What about your wife?"

"If you hear from us, just show up, Tobi."

"Wow, Hakeem."

"Should I take my suitcase and my problems to another lawyer?"

"Hakeem, you're in the presence of a female attorney, who'll lose sleep, and fight tooth and nail for you. Ain't that why you called me? Haven't I established my worth with you?"

"Yeah, that's why—"

"His name is William Thomas?"

"Yeah."

"I'm all over it."

"Thanks, Tobi."

"I'll call you, and keep you posted."

"Alright."

After a brief, cordial hug, Hakeem and Tobi Russeck, went their separate ways. A light drizzle had begun to fall from the early afternoon sky, and out of no where, several gray clouds had appeared. It was as if the weather was showing Hakeem some consideration, because the moment that he had stepped under the shelter of the Liberty Place's parking garage, the sky had cracked open, and had released a heavy downpour of rain. Hakeem took the elevator up to the third floor of the parking garage. It was here, where Gabrielle had told him that he would find her car. The search only lasted for seven minutes, but once Hakeem was seated behind the steering wheel of Gabrielle's Infiniti, Hakeem found himself faced with yet another pressing, and unavoidable task, which was to tell Gabrielle's father all about what had happened at Bayyinah's house. Tearful, Hakeem raised his ringing cell phone up to his ear, and grudgingly accepted the call from Gabrielle's father. Hakeem's heart was pounding in his chest.

"Basil, As Salaamu Alaykum."

"Wa Laykum As Salaam . . . for a minute there, I thought 'chu wasn't gonna pick up, either. What's up with our women, son-in-law? I just remembered that Gabby might be in school, after I tried reachin' her, but her mom didn't answer her phone last night, or—"

"Somethin' happened, Basil."

Silence.

The scent of weed in Gabrielle's car was so strong, it inspired Hakeem to flip down the lid to Gabrielle's ashtray. Hakeem looked at the half-smoked Dutch, sitting in Gabrielle's ashtray, and shook his head in disappointment.

"Does what happened got anything to do with my calls gettin' ignored?"

"This morning, um, ya—"

"Don't tell me Haleemah found her another husband that fast? She—We had this big fight, and she asked me for a divorce. Then she just hung up and left over here."

"Her and Macy got killed this mornin', Basil."

"Say what, now?"

Hakeem couldn't bring himself to repeat the ill-fated words again.

"Hakeem?!"

Reduced to tears, Hakeem leaned forward and rested his forehead on Gabrielle's steering wheel. As Hakeem proceeded to tell Gabrielle's father about what had happened to Gabrielle's mother, and to Macy, his voice cracked repeatedly. There were times when his voice had lost its volume completely. The entire time, Gabrielle's father just listened in silence. The only noise coming from his side of the cell phone, was violent sounds of furniture being broke, and destroyed. When Gabrielle's father returned back to his cell phone, his breathing was ragged, and it hinted that he was crying.

"Hakeem, you better hope the fuckin' airplane I catch drop in the middle of the ocean, before I get there. What's

goin' on here in Egypt . . . it ain't got shit on what I'm gonna do to ya young ass, once I get to Philly."

"What? Come on, Basil. That ain't for us."

"It is now."

Chapter Nineteen

In Dover, Delaware, Hakeem had an aunt that was quite a character. She was his father's older sister. Everyone called her Mutter, but her government name was, Tynetta Smith. She was the weekend girlfriend of a young, Russian stock-broker, who lived in New York, and she was the every-now-and-then mistress of a famous, music producer, that lived nearby, in Bear, Delaware. Both of the men knew about each other, but had never met. Because of them, Hakeem's aunt was living in a mini-mansion, and driving a white, 2012 CLS Mercedes-Benz.

Hakeem, Gabrielle, and Tracy were forty-five minutes away from Hakeem's aunt's house. She had no idea that they were coming. At the moment, she was hosting a bachelorette party, for a friend of hers, from Maryland, who was getting married in two days.

"Tracy, can you play it one more time, please?"

For the seventh time, Tracy replayed Whitney Houston's song, "Where do broken hearts go?', for Gabrielle. The two of them had been crying, and singing, for the past hour and fifteen minutes. Hakeem was driving ahead of them in Gabrielle's car. Gabrielle and Tracy were in his. It was still raining.

"Gabby, do you think ya dad was serious about what he said to Hakeem?"

"If my dad know what I know, when he get here, he'd act like he got some sense."

"And what if he don't Gabby? I think you should call him back."

"I already tried."

"What happened?"

"It keep goin' straight to voicemail."

"You think he caught a plane already?"

"Only time will tell."

"I think we almost there."

Gabrielle let out a long sigh and sat up. She had been laying across the backseat of Hakeem's Porsche jeep, during the entire trip. Her intentions had been to get some rest, but for most of the ride, she had been replaying her life behind her closed eyelids, sometimes wishing she owned the power to go back in time, to reshape her destiny.

"Tracy, I'm sorry I put you in a position that—"

"Gabby, you don't have to apologize to me about anything. Right now, like, I—Gabby we just gotta trust in Allah. I got this—Gabby, I just keep gettin' a bad feelin' that somethin' else bad about to happen, and it wont go away. It just won't go away."

Clutching her cell phone in her hand, Gabrielle laid back down and closed her eyes. What Tracy had expressed had depleted the last little bit of hope that she had stored in her heart.

"Gabby?"

"Huh?"

"We here. Look at all these—I think Hakeem aunt havin' a party, or somethin', Gabby."

As Tracy brought Hakeem's Porsche SUV to a snail's pace, Gabrielle sat up in the backseat. Her neck swiveled on her shoulders, as she stared through the rain-streaked windows. What she saw was impressing her immediately. Besides the assortment of luxury vehicles, outlining the dark

street, the thing drawing Gabrielle's attention the most, was the odd beauty of Hakeem's aunt's estate. It was awe-inspiring. Attracted to what her eyes were showing her, and desperately wanting to see more, Gabrielle raised her cell phone up to her left ear, and accepted Hakeem's phone call.

"Yes?"

"Yo, tell Tracy to park over there, in front of that Jag."

"Which one?"

"That blue one over there, that's near the driveway, in front of that black, S550."

"Oh."

Gabrielle gave Tracy Hakeem's instructions, while still admiring Hakeem's aunt's house."

"You cool?"

Hakeem's question gave Gabrielle a lot of comfort. His concern for her consoled her heart, and her soul, in a way that was greatly needed.

"I seen better days," Gabrielle admitted, watching the rear of her car, as Hakeem disappeared in it, to find a parking spot down the road. She wished she was in her car beside him. "It's like . . . it's like, I keep tryna make myself believe that my cell phone gon' ring, and it's gon' be my mom, tellin' me that her and Macy just got back to Tracy house. Hakeem, I keep—I keep hearin' Macy voice, tellin' me not to be bad. Hakeem, I started bein' mean to her again. I was bein' mean to Macy, and—Hakeem, Macy died with—With that bein' her last memory of me. That I didn't love her. That's tearin' me apart, Hakeem. I loved Macy."

Bury.

My.

Heart.

At exactly 9:42 p.m., Hakeem called his aunt. He was sitting beside Gabrielle, in the backset of his Porsche jeep. Tracy was still up front, in the driver's seat. Her eyes were watching Hakeem in the rearview mirror. Whitney Hous-

ton's CD was still playing. Gabrielle was still waiting for her mother's phone call.

It was still raining.

"Hello?"

"Aunt Mutter, this Hakeem."

"This who?"

The music coming from the other end of Hakeem's cell phone was so loud, Gabrielle and Tracy could hear the song being played, and were even able to distinguish the lyrics word for word. It went unmentioned, but because the two of them had both assumed that Hakeem's aunt was an older woman, it was surprising Gabrielle and Tracy to hear some of Meek Millz's music, being played at her party.

"Hakeem, Aunt Mutter. Ha—"

"Hold on . . . I can't hear shit you sayin'!"

Hakeem exhaled a sigh of impatience, at his aunt's loud shout over the even louder music, being played inside of her house. Hakeem was frustrated and even a little mad at himself, for not calling his aunt, before making the long trip from Philly, but Hakeem couldn't think of any other safer places for him, Gabrielle, and Tracy, to go to. Seeing that there was a party going on, had him thinking of checking into any nearby hotel, until the next morning. Hakeem and his aunt hadn't spoken in almost a year, and even then, their conversation had been nothing but angry words, which had ended with Hakeem's aunt hanging up on him, after vowing that she would never speak to him for as long as she lived. The two of them had some unresolved issues, that reached back to Hakeem's years as a child.

"Now, this is who?"

"Hakeem, Aunt Mutter."

"My nephew?"

"I'm outside."

While Hakeem talked to his aunt, Gabrielle and Tracy listened to his side of the conversation in silence. It was the first

time that either of them had ever seen Hakeem act vulnerable with anyone. The tears trickling down Hakeem's face inspired their own, because from Hakeem's body language, it was visible that he really didn't want to be at his aunt's house, or ask her for any help.

"Aunt Mutter, I ain't got nowhere else to go. You know I wouldn't've came all the way here, if I did."

After these solemn words, Hakeem lowered his cell phone from his ear and placed it in his lap. For a moment, Hakeem just stared forward, not saying anything. Through his watery eyes, he saw the heads of Bayyinah, Macy, and Gabrielle's mother, being tossed out of Bayyinah's second-floor window. Hakeem could remember squeezing beside Bayyinah to look out of that same window, when they were teenagers. He could remember tossing rocks up at that same window, to wake Bayyinah up at late hours of the night. With much pain, Hakeem lowered his head and brought his hands up to his face.

Gabrielle was first to spot Hakeem's aunt. She was marching across her front lawn like she was royalty, accompanied by two, half-naked, male strippers. The male stripper on her left was holding an umbrella over her head, while the one on her right kept her walking steady, in the highest pair of heels that Gabrielle had ever seen on a woman's feet.

"Yo, I'm tellin' ya'll now, my aunt is extra," Hakeem warned, shaking his head in embarrassment. With a sigh, he elbowed his rear-passenger door open, and swung his right leg outside. "And her tongue ain't got no brakes, so don't take nothin' she say personal. That's just how she talk. She think she a young girl, too."

"She look like one."

"How old is she?"

"And ya'll better not be starin' at these freak ass niggaz, while I'm out here, talkin' to her, either. She fifty-four, and she be gettin' that Botox shit and all'lat other stuff done."

Hakeem stepped out into the pouring rain to greet his aunt. Gabrielle inched over to where Hakeem had been sitting, and looked out through the rain-streaked window, so that she could observe the odd-looking meeting. Gabrielle thought that the male strippers looked absolutely ridiculous.

Tracy did too.

"Gabby, look how Hakeem lookin' at the one holdin' the umbrella."

"Are they strippers?"

"They both got money hangin' outta they G-strings."

"Oh, yup."

"They gotta be freezin'."

"Don't his aunt look like a light skin, Jennifer Hudson?"

"A little."

"She don't look fifty-four to me."

"Right."

"I wouldn't even give her forty."

"You think that's all her hair?"

"We about to find out. Tracy, here she come."

Minutes later, Gabrielle and Tracy, found themselves on opposite sides of Hakeem's aunt, escorting her back across her enormous, front lawn, to her house. The umbrella over their heads was being held by Gabrielle, because Hakeem's aunt had relieved the male strippers of their duties, and had sent them back into her hosue, which was a hilarious sight in itself, because while the male strippers had been running across the lawn, one of them had slipped, and fallen, not once, but three times.

"I'm throwin' one of my friends a bachelorette party, so don't ya'll go and be thinkin', I be havin' this kinda freaky-deaky shit, goin' on in my house every night. Not like I owe ya'll any goddamn explanations, or anything."

"Can I use ya bathroom when we get inside?"

"Which one are you again?"

"Gabby."

"Gabby, the only thing in my house off limits to you, is my dildos, and my nose candy. That goes for you, too. It's Tracy, right?"

Tracy nodded her head, fighting back a smile.

"Now, ya'll both welcome to anything else. Oh, and I don't have any water in my refrigerator, either. I don't drink water, 'cause fish fuck in it."

Gabrielle and Tracy snickered under their face veils. Both of them felt an immediate affection for Hakeem's aunt.

"Ya'll can stay out in the pool house. Okay, now, ya'll might wanna cover ya'll eyes, 'cause some of these strippers in here got dicks long as Washington fuckin' Avenue."

After Hakeem watched Gabrielle and Tracy disappear into his aunt's house, he returned his attention back to unloading their things from his Porsche SUV. His clothes were dripping wet, but the rain wasn't bothering him nearly as much as his deep thoughts were. Earlier, Hakeem had stopped by a known crack house, in South Philadelphia, where he knew he would find Bayyinah's mother. From there, he had visited all of the mothers, and babymothers, of the three friends, who Gabrielle had mistakenly killed. The lies he had to tell them was eating at him. Afterwards, Hakeem had shared a conversation with his lawyer, that hadn't gone so well. At the end of the day, the complexities of each and every last one of these emotional incidents, had drained Hakeem's will power down to an almost empty tank.

"Want some help?"

Hakeem glanced over his shoulder, and was slightly surprised to see that Gabrielle was standing behind him, holding an umbrella in her hand.

"I can carry one of the Louis bags."

"Where Tracy at?"

"Helpin' ya aunt take some linen out to her pool house for us."

"It's a lot of people in there?"

"Well, put it like this . . . count all of these cars parked out here, then just imagine, if four people came in each one."

Hakeem shook his head and cut his eyes at his aunt's mini-mansion, as he handed Gabrielle the leather, Louis Vuitton duffel bag, that he had in his right hand. He had another one just like it, in his left. When Gabrielle started eyeing his drenched clothes, Hakeem shrugged his shoulders and let out a sigh.

"You got everything?"

"Yea," Hakeem answered, after using his foot to close his rear-passenger door. Something from earlier in the day popped in his mind, as he started walking with Gabrielle across his aunt's wet lawn. "When you started smokin' weed again? And don't lie, and say you don't, 'cause I saw the Dutch in ya ashtray."

"That wasn't mine."

"Whose was it, then?"

"Fresh and Amir's. They was smokin' weed in my car, before we went and caught the El."

"So, that's where ya'll met at?"

"I made them meet me in the parkin' garage, 'cause when I was in my car, changin' outta my overgarments 'n stuff, they had called me, and said they was down the street from my school. So, I just told them to meet me at my car."

"Gabrielle, if it wasn't for ya mom, I wasn't gon' even come down there."

"What she say?"

"Just some stuff that I been needin' somebody to tell me for a long time."

"Like what?"

"I'll tell you later on. Plus, we gotta lotta shit we need to talk about, anyway."

"Hakeem, before we go in ya aunt house, I wanna say somethin'," Gabrielle announced sadly, as she followed Hakeem within inches of his aunt's front door. She had some-

thing that she desperately wanted to get off of her chest. "On the way here, I was, um, I was thinkin' about a lot of different stuff. Hakeem, Macy loved you so much. You was her father in my eyes, Hakeem. In hers, too. Like, I know I gave you so many reasons to question my love to you, but I'm willin' to do anything, to prove my love to you. I don't think—I can't get through this without'chu, Hakeem. I can't. Hakeem, I don't want to. I, um, I know you probably wanna get outta the rain, and everything, but I want'chu to know, you really changed me and Macy life. Hakeem, you showed us stuff we never seen before. You danced for us, Hakeem. You rescued us. Hakeem, I'm sorry. I'm the one that messed up every—"

"What the fuck are ya'll some add-water-instant-waterproof niggaz?!"

Hakeem looked over his shoulder at his aunt, then returned his attention back to Gabrielle. She wasn't crying, but she looked like she was on the verge of doing so.

"Hakeem, don't divorce me."

"I'm not."

"Even if they lock me up?"

"Even if they sent'chu to the moon. Gabrielle ,you my baby, man. I love you. I just need you to listen to me sometimes. Just sometimes."

"I will, Hakeem."

"Alright, we good, then."

"Hakeem, you promise?"

"Wallahi."

Going through the first level of his aunt's mini-palace, Hakeem cursed under his breath continuously, and sighed, about a dozen times. By the time him, his aunt, and Gabrielle, had all reached his aunt's rear patio, and were stepping back out into the pouring rain, Hakeem had witnessed seven lap dances, three oral sex performances, and had seen one woman, old enough to be his grandmother, snorting a line of cocaine off of a male stripper's dick.

"Oh, Hakeem fix ya damn face. At least, I don't got them strippers in there sword fighting with they fuckin' dicks."

"See you in the mornin', Aunt Mutter."

"Make that the afternoon. I don't do mornings."

"Alright."

For a moment, after Hakeem's aunt had slid her patio doors shut, Hakeem and Gabrielle just started to follow the limestone path, leading to the pool house. The trail that they were on was spotted with small pools of light, coming from the globe-lights, outlining the long, rain-wet path.

"Ya aunt said she got this pool house built from the ground up."

"She did."

Gabrielle glanced down at the bottom of her garment, as she walked behind Hakeem. She was soaked from her knees on down. Looking back up, Gabrielle gave Hakeem's aunt's backyard a sweeping glance, while continuing to hold the umbrella above her head, that was being pelted with heavy raindrops.

"Hakeem, why you and ya aunt don't get along?"

Hakeem pretended not to hear Gabrielle. He was in a deep, reflective mood, as he stared out into the darkness, at the patch of forest, standing behind his aunt's pool house. It was there, where he had plans on burying the clothes Gabrielle had worn when she had went with Fresh, and Amir, to search for Mr. Dave. This incriminating evidence of hers was inside of the garbage bag that he had clutched in his left hand.

"Hakeem?"

"What?"

"Why you and ya aunt stopped speakin' for so long?"

"'Cause she molested me when I was nine, and every fuckin' time I bring that shit up, she never wanna fuckin' own up to that shit. That's why."

Chapter Twenty

"Please, Aunt Mutter?"

"Hakeem, it's not that I don't wanna help ya'll. I just don't think it's a good idea, because if they catch me in a lie, then what?"

"All you gotta say is, we was out here, since February twenty-ninth, and that's it."

"That's all?"

"That's it, Aunt Mutter."

"And that's ya'll alibi?"

"By now, they know who Gabrielle mom, and her daughter is," Hakeem guessed, as he zipped his burgundy, Young & Reckless hoodie. His appointment to have the staples in his stomach removed was in four hours, and even though he knew that he had more than enough time to make it back to Philly, he still glanced down at his watch, to keep track of the time. "Aunt Mutter, our story is that we was out here, and that her mom was watchin' her daughter for us, while we was gone. Gabrielle gon' say that her mom called her, and that she had asked her, if she knew any muslim sisters, who made overgarments."

"And that'll explain why her mom and daughter went to Bayyinah, I guess?"

Hakeem nodded his head as he cut his eyes at Gabrielle, who came walking into his aunt's kitchen, looking sadder

than she did the night before. Tracy was a few steps behind her.

"Okay, now, what was that you was sayin' about Bayyinah mother earlier?"

"Oh, um, I told her the Mexican Cartel was gon' probably be sendin' somebody after her, too," Hakeem admitted, ashamed of himself for lying to Bayyinah's mother. The guilt was still gnawing at his heart. "She already had it in her head that them two Mexican chicks had somethin' to do wit' Taz bein' missin', so I just went along wit' the idea she already was rockin' wit'. Plus, it ain't no tellin' what the real situation is. Bayyinah ain't fuckin' think them Mexican bitches was comin' back, and look what happened. I gave her some money to go down South Carolina, to chill wit' somebody she said she knew down there. Gabrielle gon' act like she just heard what happened, and she gon' call 8th and Race from here, to make it all seem authentic. Aunt Mutter, we gotta get them to release her mom, and her daughter, bodies to us, so we can give them a janazah."

"Hakeem, I know you not standin' there, tellin' me you just gon' let them people do what the fuck they wanna do with Bayinnah's body?"

"Aunt Mutter, we gon' bury all three of them. You might not even have to get involved, but just in case some cops call you, or some detectives come out here, I just need you to know what to say, that's all."

"Ya'll was here, since the twenty-ninth?"

"And if they start askin' you about anything else, you—"

"Don't know shit."

"Exactly."

"For all of ya'll sake, I really hope this shit work."

"We do, too."

Now that his aunt had agreed to be the anchor to their alibi, Hakeem wanted to go over the details with Gabrielle and Tracy, one more time, before he left. In his absence, Ha-

keem didn't want anything to go wrong, so he led Gabrielle and Tracy out of his aunt's kitchen, and into a room of his aunt's house, that he had always admired, since he had been a child. The room was a handsome library, that had a high ceiling, and walls, that had shelves, and shelves, of books. The shelves were of the same material as the glossy, Italian, hardwood floors. On a white, leather sectional, which faced the only window in his aunt's library, Hakeem took a seat, and let out a long sigh. Gabrielle and Tracy both sat down on opposite sides of him, while their eyes gave his aunt's library a once-over.

"Is it true what Gabby told me, Hakeem?"

"What she—"

"I told her what'chu told me last night, about'cha aunt."

Hakeem frowned his face at Gabrielle.

"She asked me why I was actin' funny when ya aunt came to the pool house this mornin'."

"Why couldn't you just let me tell her?"

"Sorry."

"Yeah, it happened when I was nine, Tracy. It's true."

"And you never told nobody?"

"Naw."

"Why not?"

After Tracy's question, Gabrielle timidly grabbed Hakeem's hand, and laced her fingers in his. She could see that his hazel eyes were becoming stormy.

"My aunt used to fuck wit' this Jamaican dude when I was little," Hakeem explained, while shooting a precautionary glance over his shoulder, at the partially closed door of his aunt's library. He didn't want his aunt to overhear what he was about to tell Gabrielle and Tracy, so he lowered his voice. "His name was Owen. He was my dad and Bill-Bill connect, back in the day. So, like, I don't know, like, how him and my aunt got started, or what kind of situation they had goin' on—All I know is, dude was married, and that every-

time I was out here for the weekend, this nigga would come through. Sometimes, he would stay a night. Then, sometimes, this nigga would chill, and fall back, like the nigga lived in this mu'fucker. He always played my aunt room. I'm talkin' 'bout like, yo, the only time I'a see this nigga, was when he was leavin', or, like, if he was just showin' up. Soon as he'd get here, boom, he'd shoot right to my aunt room. Then, like, when he was here, my aunt wouldn't never let me in her room. I mean, like, for nothin'. Even though I was little, the shit just used to seem weird to me. Lemme show ya'll somethin'."

Gabrielle and Tracy followed Hakeem to the window in his aunt's library, that provided a view of her gigantic backyard.

"Alright, see where the pool house at? Alright, well, that whole area used to be this real big, crazy lookin', vegetable garden, when I was little."

When Hakeem looked over his shoulder at the door, Gabrielle and Tracy did too. The suspense of Hakeem's story, and how Hakeem was being so secretive about it, had both of them anxious to hear more, and wishing that he would hurry up and get to the juicy part.

"My aunt only got that pool house built, 'cause me 'n her buried Owen in the vegetable garden."

Ashes to ashes.

"He had a heart attack, snortin' coke in my aunt room."

Dust to dust.

"I ain't know what the fuck was goin' on," Hakeem admitted, staring blankly out at his aunt's pool house, but seeing it as the vegetable garden, it once was. In one fateful night, his innocence as a child had been stolen from him. "My aunt woke me up outta my sleep, and just, like, just dragged me down the hall to her room. So, she cryin', and she sayin' all this crazy stuff, but keep in mind, I'm only nine, I'm half-sleep, and at first, I'm thinkin', like, she trippin',

'cause earlier that same day, I had broke one of her lamps, out there in the dining room, playin' wit' my football. So, I'm thinkin' she about to whip my ass over that shit. So, when we get to her room, Owen laid out on the floor. Then, she scramble out the room, and leave me wit' this nigga. So, I'm just lookin' at him, waitin' for him to wake up. This nigga had all this coke on his face. And, like, I don't know why, but I was thinkin' he had sugar all around his nose, or somethin' like that."

"Where ya aunt go?"

"I don't know," Hakeem answered, shrugging his shoulders to Tracy's question. There were some details about that night, he didn't even know himself, because over the years, whenever he brought the awkward subject up, his aunt had always refused to talk about it with him. "All I know is, when she came back, she had a fuckin' shovel, and a flashlight. Next thing I know, she handed that shit to me, grabbed Owen by the ankles, then she told me to follow her out to the backyard. Yo, the whole time, while she draggin' this nigga through the spot, I'm still waitin' for this nigga to wake up. Like, I really thought this nigga was sleep. It was the summertime. Yo, I had mosquito bites all over me. I'm talkin' 'bout, like, everywhere. When I started cryin', she—That's when she broke down and told me Owen was dead. I really started cryin' harder, then. 'Cause, now, I ain't tryna touch the nigga. She kept tryna close his eyelids with her fingers, and them jawns kept poppin' open. Yo, the grave she dug wasn't even that deep. Owen was like Mr. Dave size, but he was skinnier, though. She made me take his watch off. She kicked that nigga down into the grave, like he ain't mean shit to her. I'll never forget that shit. When we got back into the house, that's when she started snortin' all this coke in front of me, and made me take my clothes off. She sucked my dick. She kept tellin' me not to cry, and that, if I ever told my mom, or my dad, the cops was gon' lock us both up. She told me, if

I ain't keep her secret, she was gon' make Owen ghost come outta his grave and get me."

Gabrielle was livid, after hearing how Hakeem's aunt had taken advantage of him. She wanted to confront the woman, and give her a piece of her mind.

"Why you ain't say nothin' when you got older?"

"To who? My mom, and my gran'mom died a year after that. Ya'll know I ain't have no rap for my dad. I wasn't gon' tell my gran'pop. I just kept that shit to myself.

"And his wife, or nobody, never wondered what happened to him, or where he was?"

"I was little. I 'on't know who was doin' what."

"That's crazy."

"Yo, I don't even know where that nigga was from."

"So, how you know ya dad and Bill-Bill used to deal with him?"

"Bill-Bill mentioned him before, just on some regular conversation shit one time."

"What he say?"

"Just how him and my dad had this crazy weed connect back in the day, and how the nigga just disappeared on everybody."

"Why you never told Bill-Bill?"

"'Cause I knew he would've told my dad. That shit would've opened up a whole can of worms."

For the next half an hour, Hakeem, Gabrielle, and Tracy, spent their time on talking about the dilemmas they were currently dealing with. The most pressing of them, was the phone call that Gabrielle had to make to the police headquarters in Philly. Hakeem was more anxious about how the conversation was going to go, than Gabrielle was. Tracy, on the other hand, was worried about what Gabrielle's father was going to do, once his airplane landed in Philadelphia. Out of the three of them, surprisingly, Gabrielle was the one

with the most resolve, and she had the heaviest responsibility, resting on her shoulders.

"How the fuck my mom know Tracy car was in Bayyinah name?" Gabrielle wondered, cutting her eyes at Tracy suspiciously, as the two of them walked Hakeem to his aunt's front door. Certain things just didn't make sense to her. "I never told my mom that. I know Hakeem didn't. He ain't have no reason to. Tracy told her that shit. My fuckin' mom ain't figure that shit out on her own. What would make her go check them fuckin' registration papers, if Tracy ain't tell her Bayyinah address was on them? Lyin' bitch. Watch when Hakeem leave."

Chapter Twenty-One

"You okay?"

"Broke a fingernail."

"You don't take no shit, do you?"

"Fuck her. She got everything she deserved."

"She pulled off in Hakeem's Porsche, a few minutes ago."

"So."

"What was that about? Well, I mean, obviously, it had to be somethin' that had you really upset, because you kept on hittin' her, even after she stopped figthin' you back."

When Gabrielle rolled her eyes, Hakeem's aunt rolled her own eyes at the ceiling of the only bathroom, in her pool house, and crossed her arms over her chest. A hint of admiration was reflecting in Hakeem's aunt's eyes, as she stared at Gabrielle, from where she was standing, in the doorway of the bathroom. For her, Gabrielle and Tracy's fight had been nothing but entertainment.

"Any band-aids in here?"

"Should be some in the medicine cabinet."

The earliest memories that Gabrielle had as a foster child were all the kind that Gabrielle had always wished she could forget. Her first few years at the Epps' home had been like an emotional battlefield. In Tracy's mother's absence, which was quite often, because of her rigorous work schedule, Tracy was like the foster sibling from Hell. Tracy was

Gabrielle's first mental abuser. Already dealing with abandonment issues, and having ideas that she was an unwanted child, these beliefs of Gabrielle's were further highlighted, by Tracy telling her on a daily basis, that she shouldn't get comfortable, because she was about to be sent to another family, who probably wouldn't want to keep her either. This mental, and emotional abuse, was only the prelude, to the horrifying acts that Mr. Dave began to take her through, once she had reached puberty, and her body had started to develop. Over those years, Gabrielle had dealt with all of that pain in silence.

The day that Macy was born, Gabrielle had spotted envy hiding behind the happiness in Tracy's eyes. On that same day, Mr. Dave had promised Gabrielle that he would kill her, if she ever told anyone that he was Macy's father.

"Let me call, Hakeem," Gabrielle decided, after wrapping a band-aid around the tip of her right, index finger. Her fight with Tracy still had her heart beating above its normal pace. "She thought somebody was fuckin' stupid. Talkin' 'bout she sorry. Had I not asked her, she would've took that shit to the fuckin' grave with her."

"If you need me for anything, I'll be in the laundry room, washing some clothes."

"Okay."

Gabrielle listened to Hakeem's aunt's footsteps as she walked down the hallway. In her mind, Gabrielle wondered if the eccentric woman ever felt haunted, or even thought about the Jamaican man, who was buried beneath her pool house. After readjusting, and fixing one of the pins in her black, kimar, Gabrielle gave her reflection, in the vanity mirror one final stare, then, with a sigh, she walked out of the bathroom. The sound of her cell phone ringing downstairs made Gabrielle quicken her steps.

Hakeem's aunt's pool house was a terrific edition to her estate. It gave the patch of forest standing in its background,

a less-intimidating presence. Most of the backyard was occupied by a large, in-ground swimming pool. Separating the
pool house, and the swimming pool, was a long ribbon of cement, where there was a line of colorful beach chairs. The
pool house was white, and had stringy-vines, crawling all
over it. Curtains as bright as the beach chairs, could be seen
hanging from all of its windows. On the roof, there was a
huge, satellite dish. The pool house had two levels. There
were two bedrooms, and a bathroom upstairs, and the front
area of the pool house's bottom level, was a family room, that
opened into a small kitchen. The two bedrooms and the family room, were all fully furnished, but because the pool house
was seldom used by any of her house guests, Hakeem's aunt
rarely ever visited it herself. The pool house gave Hakeem's
aunt the chills. To her, the place was her Jamaican lover's
tombstone.

Once Gabrielle made it to her cell phone, and saw who
was calling her, she wasted no time in answering the call.

"Hello?"

"As Salaamu Alaykum."

"Wa Laykum As Salaam."

"Ay, did you make that call, yet?"

"Hakeem, me and Tracy was fightin'."

"What? Gabrielle, come on, man. Didn't we just talk
about'chu lis—"

"Hakeem, she the one that put it in my mom head to go
to Bayyinah house."

"No, she didn't."

"Hakeem, she admitted it to me," Gabrielle argued, as
she walked over to a window, and pulled the curtain aside.
Her eyes rested on Hakeem's aunt's rear patio, while her
heart began singing a sad song for her mother, and for Macy.
"When I asked her, she didn't even deny it. She tried to apologize, and, like, I—I know she probably ain't think about my
mom goin' to Bayyinah house was gon' turn out to be as bad

as it got, but how I'm supposed to not still feel some type of way, Hakeem? Huh? That should've been her that went to Bayyinah house, if she—"

"Yo, man, give her the phone."

"She not here."

"Where she at?"

"She left."

"She left? Where the fuck she go? Man, see, this what—"

"Ya aunt said she took ya jeep."

"So, how the fuck you supposed—Yo, I'ma call you right back."

Gabrielle backed away from the window and jogged back upstairs to the bathroom, after Hakeem abruptly ended their call. Since becoming pregnant, there were times, where the need to empty her bladder seemed to just come about every five minutes. On the toilet, Gabrielle clutched her cell phone, while imagining what Hakeem was saying to Tracy, because that's who she assumed he was calling, after he had hung up on her. Before her Blackberry was able to complete its first ring, Gabrielle accepted the incoming call, and raised it to her ear, as she wiped herself with some wet tissue, and flushed the toilet.

"Hello?"

"She took her stuff with her?"

"No."

"Her phone keep goin' straight to voicemail. Yo, my aunt gon' bring you back to Philly, alright?"

"Alright."

"Look, I'm on my way into the hospital. Text me as soon as you finish talkin' to the cops, alright?"

"Did ya lawyer say anything else about Bill-Bill?"

"I'll tell you what's goin' on when we meet back up later. Ay, you think ya dad'll say somethin' to the cops?"

"I hope not."

"Gabrielle, if he do, we done."

"I know."

"You tried callin' him again?"

"Not today."

"Alright, well, just—Yo, just make that call to the cops first, then tell my aunt to bring you back to Philly. Don't forget to text me and let me know, what—"

"Hakeem, what if when I get to where they got my mom and Macy, they lock me up?"

"Tobi said you cool. They don't know one thing got anything to do with—Gabrielle, they think that was Mr. Dave work. They got that nigga face on the front page of the paper over here. That lady he carjacked was a fuckin' cop wife."

"So, they let Bill-Bill go?"

"They about to. Yo, look, I gotta—"

"Should I try callin' my dad again?"

"I mean, like, yeah. Gabrielle, you know I ain't tryna go through nothin' wit'cha dad, man. We definitely need him to be on our page, 'cause if he get funky on us, we can forget it. By now, they know who ya mom and Macy is."

"How we supposed to give them a janazah, if they bodies all messed up?"

"We gon' have to bury what we have. Whatever they give us, we gotta take and give them they rights, Gabrielle."

"But—"

"Most likely, we ain't gon' be able to wash them. They gon' be in bags when they release they bodies to us. We gon' pray over them, then, like, from there, we gotta take them out to the cemetery."

"And where we supposed—Don't we gotta bury them in three days, or somethin' like that?"

"Yeah, tomorrow gon' be the third day."

"Hakeem, where we gon' do all that at?"

"I know this lady that gotta funeral home in South Philly. I already talked to her. She gon' let us do it there, once— Look, I'm tryna get in, and outta this hospital, 'cause I'm

tryna make it to my man, Lance 'n 'em janazah. Call them people right now, Gabrielle. Do that, then text me."

"I'm doin' it as soon as we hang up."

"Gabrielle, not from ya cell phone."

"I know."

"Alright, As Salaamu Alaykum."

"Wa Laykum As Salaam."

"Yo, if Tracy come back, leave her alone, and tell her to call me."

"Okay."

At exactly 3:11 p.m., Gabrielle's father called Gabrielle's cell phone. Gabrielle let his call go to her voicemail, because she didn't want Hakeem's aunt to bear witness to how much of an emotional storm she actually was. Gabrielle knew that once she heard her father's voice, she was going to fall apart. She was seated in the passenger seat of Hakeem's aunt's Mercedes-Benz. Hakeem's aunt was driving her back to Philly, partially because Tracy had never returned, but mainly because Gabrielle's phone conversation with a detective in Philadelphia had transpired, without any complications, and because she was now expected at the South Philadelphia funeral home, that Hakeem had mentioned to her earlier. Before going there, Gabrielle had to first stop out West Philadelphia, at the Medical Examiner's Office, where she had to officially identify her mother, and daughter's bodies. Since no once had stepped up to claim Bayyinah's body, and only because Hakeem had made a firm point of it, Gabrielle was also assuming responsibility for Bayyinah's remains as well.

The detective that Gabrielle had spoken with had been extremely sympathetic, during their phone call. He had expressed his condolences continuously, and he considered Gabrielle's mother, and Macy, to be unfortunate victims of a heinous crime, who had just happened to be at the wrong place, at the wrong time.

True.

Lies.

The second time that Gabrielle's father tried calling Gabrielle, Gabrielle reluctantly accepted his call.

"Daddy?"

"I'm here."

Gabrielle's hazel eyes watered at the sound of her father's voice. His tone of voice had the markings of stress, pain, and agony, all through it. He was crying. At that moment, more than anything, Gabrielle wanted to be where her father was.

"Daddy, where—"

"Your name was suppose to be Robin. Your mom wanted you to have her middle name, but when she fell asleep, I, um I told the nurses to put Gabrielle on your birth certificate, because I wanted to name you after my mother. I expected your mom to have a fit, so I got outta the hospital as fast as I could. Gabrielle, when I came by to visit both of ya'll that next day, she didn't say anything. Nothin'. She—She loved me through all my fuck-ups. When I messed up all of our futures, she stuck with me. Gabrielle, my gran'baby—This—Baby, tell Hakeem I didn't mean what I—"

"Daddy, where you at?"

"The airport."

"I'm comin' to pick you up, okay? Don't—"

Gabrielle looked at the screen of her Blackberry, after it alerted her that she was receiving another call. A slow-forming frown crept across the features of Gabrielle's face when she saw that her second caller was Tracy.

"Daddy, I'ma be there in like forty-five minutes, okay?"

"I'll be here."

"Okay."

Still frowning, Gabrielle accepted Tracy's call, although she really didn't want to.

"What?"

"Bitch, remove that goddamn attitude outta ya voice."

Silence.

"Yeah, bitch. Un-huh . . . I can hear the piss drippin' down ya fuckin' legs from here."

Gabrielle could feel her heart pounding in her chest, as she turned and stared in open-mouthed shock at Hakeem's aunt. All kinds of ugly thoughts started running through Gabrielle's mind, but one of them was quickly dismissed, after she had heard Tracy release a gut-wrenching scream on the other end of her cell phone, behind Mr. Dave's voice. At that precise moment, it was made horribly clear to Gabrielle that Tracy hadn't become a traitor, but that she had instead, found herself as her father's captive, and this had Gabrielle desperately wanting answers to how things had spiraled to such an unimaginable point.

Clueless to exactly who it was that Gabrielle was talking to, Hakeem's aunt still felt inspired to lower the music in the car. Hakeem's aunt was able to sense that something was wrong from the fearful look on Gabrielle's face, and from the nervous energy that was vibrating from her body. This nervousness made its way to her own body, as she continued to drive down the highway.

"This Mr. Dave," Gabrielle mouthed to Hakeem's aunt, briefly placing her palm over the speaker of her cell phone, as her and Hakeem's aunt shared a momentary stare. When Hakeem's aunt gave her a puzzled look, and returned her attention to the road ahead, she reached over and pressed her cell phone against Hakeem's aunts right ear, so that she could hear what was going on for herself. "That's Tracy screamin'. Her dad got her. That's Mr. Dave. That's who me and Hakeem was tellin' you about."

"He sayin' somethin'."

Wide-eyed, Gabrielle quickly removed her Blackberry from Hakeem's aunt's right ear, and put it back to hers.

". . . lettin' that happen to Macy?! Bitch, all ya'll gon' pay!! All ya'll!! Now, you tell that Cracker Jack nigga of ya'lls, to

stop actin' like a damn coward, and to answer his goddamn phone. Bitch, you tell that chump, God wanna talk to him!"

What goes around . . .

Comes around.

Sometimes.

Although, Philadelphia was experiencing a warm day of beautiful weather, with a temperature that was in the low 70s, Hakeem was in too much of a dismal mood, to enjoy any piece of it. Since leaving the hospital, he had been giving some deep thought to all of the people that had died, in the past six months, starting with the female corrections officer, who Taz had killed, and ending with Bayyinah, Macy, and Gabrielle's mother. The three friends of his, mistakenly killed by Gabrielle, were haunting him with a fresher conviction, because he wasn't able to make it out of the hospital in time to make it to their prayer services, or their burials, out at the cemetery. For almost an hour, Hakeem had been driving aimlessly around his South Philadelphia neighborhood, completely lost in his own thoughts.

At the intersection of 19th and Ellsworth, Hakeem turned off of 19th Street, and made a slow left down Ellsworth Street. After driving a short distance, he pulled Gabrielle's car over and parked, behind a gold, Ford Focus. Next, out of force of habit, Hakeem checked the rearview mirror, both side mirrors, then looked right, down Dorrance Street, and then he shot a sweeping glance into the huge playground he had parked beside, on his left.

"I'm the blame we ain't get to meet, Kareemah," Hakeem whispered, gazing down at the ultrasound photo that Bayyinah had given him. Deep within, he so badly wished that he had the power to exchange his unborn daughter's fate, for his own. "Insha Allah, we gon' get to meet in Janna, if Allah don't send me to—"

Hakeem's private thoughts were interrupted by his cell phone. The thought to not answer it crossed Hakeem's trou-

bled mind, but thinking that it was Tracy calling him again, caused him to consider that maybe it was just time for him to stop ignoring her calls, and simply talk to her. Hakeem's only reason for not answering Tracy's calls an hour, or so earlier, was because he had been far too upset with her, to even say one word to her. With angry eyes, Hakeem reached over to the passenger seat and grabbed his ringing cell phone.

"Yo?"

"Hakeem, Mr. Dave got Tracy."

"What?"

"He got her. Hakeem, he called me from her cell—Her cell phone. Hakeem, he doin' somethin' to Tracy. She was scream—Oh, my God, Hakeem."

Stunned, Hakeem melted so low in the driver's seat of Gabrielle's car, that he could barely see over the dashboard.

"He want'chu to call him, Hakeem. I just got off the phone with him."

Hakeem was so caught off-guard by the recent twist in fate, he couldn't even find his voice to say anything to Gabrielle. He could hear that she was crying. He was beginning to himself. Hakeem could also hear his aunt's voice in the background, but he couldn't make out what she was saying. Not wanting to let any more time escape, Hakeem ended his call with Gabrielle, and called Tracy's cell phone. On the third ring, Mr. Dave picked up.

"Well, well, well . . . looks like the ostrich finally decided to show his head."

"Mr. Dave, Tracy ain't got nothin' to do wit' me and ya beef."

"I beg to differ. See, this bitch here is a traitor of the worst kind. What she did is a crime punishable by death. She gotta die for that. We not gon' discuss her becomin' a goddamn muslim. She learnin' right now, who God is."

"Can I talk to her?"

"Beg me."

"Mr. Dave, kill me instead."

"Say what now?"

"You heard me. Man, fuck all'lat beggin' shit. Let's get right to it."

"Wait a minute . . . so, let me get this straight. You wanna—"

"Let her go, and take me."

When Mr. Dave started laughing, Hakeem listened to see if he could hear Tracy in the background. His love for her was making it easy for him to choose, sacrificing his existence for Tracy's. While the choice was an impulsive one, it was one that Hakeem wholeheartedly wanted to stand by, if Mr. Dave was willing to accept his trade offer.

"If you prove to me that she still alive, I'll come to you right now, Mr. Dave."

Mr. Dave stopped laughing.

Hakeem glanced at the screen of his cell phone to see who he was receiving a second call from, then quickly placed it back to his ear, as he stepped out of Gabrielle's car. Him ignoring Gabrielle's phone call, resulted in her sending him a text-message. Gabrielle's text-message said that she had an idea where Mr. Dave might have Tracy.

"So, what we gon' do, Mr. Dave?"

"We gon' make tonight one to remember, chump. That's what we gon' do."

"Alright, now, let me talk to—"

"Answer ya phone in ten minutes."

After Mr. Dave ended their call, Hakeem quickly called Gabrielle. She answered on the first ring.

"Hakeem, I know where they at!"

"Where?"

"Um, um, didn't you hear gospel music playin' in the background? That's Hakeem, that's—"

"Gabrielle, calm down. Calm down . . . breathe."

"Hakeem, if you heard gospel music playin' in the back-

ground, then they at Tracy aunt house. Hakeem, she live in this big apartment buildin', out West Philly, on, um, on, um 63rd and Chestnut. It's on the driver's side of the block. Tracy aunt in a wheelchair."

"Gabrielle, I told him to kill me instead."

"What?! Hakeem, why? No . . . why would—No, Hakeem. No."

"Gabrielle, I can't let him kill Tracy."

"Hakeem, for all you know, he could've already killed her."

"Look, he callin' me back in ten minutes. Gabrielle, if Tracy still alive in there, I'm tradin' my life for hers."

"Why? No, Hakeem."

The anguish in Gabrielle's voice crucified Hakeem's heart, and brought tears to his eyes. Hakeem sat on the hood of Gabrielle's car and took a deep breath. Not once in his young life, did Hakeem ever imagine that his life would end in such an eerie fashion.

"Hakeem, please don't do this."

"Gabrielle, I'd do it for you."

"Okay, well, we goin' in there together."

"No, we not."

They were.

Gabrielle's father was too.

So was Hakeem's aunt.

Chapter Twenty-Two

West Philadelphia was on fire; literally. A large, apartment complex, on the passenger side of Chestnut Street, between 63rd and 62nd, had a serious fire happening, in one of its fourth-floor units. There were two, fire trucks, and several cop cars on the scene. Tenants that had evacuated the apartment complex were standing on the opposite side of the street, huddled in dozens of small crowds, watching as firemen rushed in, and out of their apartment building. Among the crowd, were people of all ages. Many of them had their cell phones pressed against their ears. Some had babies on their hips.

Up in the dark sky, a half moon was shining like a lamp. It was still seasonably warm outside, indicating that spring was merely weeks away. The smell of smoke was giving the night air a disagreeable odor.

There was a gas station on the corner of 63rd and Chestnut. It was here, where Hakeem, Gabrielle, Hakeem's aunt, and Gabrielle's father, were all standing, and watching what was going on. Hakeem and Gabrielle were holding hands. Hakeem's aunt, and Gabrielle's father, were standing behind them. The thought of Tracy's fate was on all of their minds.

"Who that?"

"Phillipe."

"The doorman?"

Nodding his head, Hakeem gave his ringing iPhone a puzzled look, wondering why the doorman from his condo was calling him.

"Hakeem, see what he want."

Hakeem held Gabrielle's stare as he answered his cell phone, and placed it up to his ear. What the doorman had to say, made Hakeem's eyelids stretch open wide, and sent him running for Gabrielle's car.

"Hakeem, what happened?! What's wrong?!"

"They at the condo!"

"Who?!"

"Tracy and Mr. Dave! Phillipe said they just got on the elevator!"

The sudden flights of Hakeem, Gabrielle, Hakeem's aunt, and Gabrielle's father, attracted a little attention, but not too much. A few people loitering inside of the gas station had turned their heads, but seeing four people running down 63rd Street, wasn't as compelling as the four-alarm blaze, going on down in the middle of Chestnut Street.

Upon reaching Market Street, Hakeem and Gabrielle scrambled into Gabrielle's Infiniti, and hurriedly slammed the doors behind them. Overhead, the loud rumbling of a passing, westbound, El-train, drowned out the sound of Gabrielle's car, as Hakeem brought it to life. Hakeem's aunt, and Gabrielle's father, both had made it to Hakeem's aunt's Mercedes-Benz, just as Hakeem was pulling away from it, with screeching tires. It seemed as if God was sprinkling some of His majestic powers down on 63rd Street, because from Arch Street, all the way down to Lansdowne Avenue, Hakeem had been able to catch all of the green lights. So was his aunt. Unfortunately, the traffic lights going up Lansdowne Avenue wasn't as charitable.

"Gabrielle, put on ya seatbelt!"

"Hakeem watch out!" Gabrielle screamed, when Hakeem suddenly veered right, and raced her car up on the sidewalk.

To brace herself, because her seatbelt wasn't doing her any justice, she planted her feet down in the footwell, and she stiff-armed the dashboard. "The mailbox, Hakeem! Look out for—Turn right!"

Hakeem's aunt was right on the tail of Gabrielle's Infiniti. She was driving her car with the same recklessness as Hakeem was. At times, her Mercedes-Benz reached speeds of 80 mph. By the time her and Hakeem made it to his condo's front parking lot, her Mercedes-Benz had two flat tires, and Gabrielle's car was smoking from beneath its hood. Hakeem and his aunt had violated every traffic law known to man, which was why the police officers in the cop car, pursuing them since Haverford Avenue, had such angry looks on their faces, as the two of them jumped out of their car, unholstering their guns.

"Freeze!!"

"Stop right there!!"

Just when the night appeared to be done with all of its theatrics, it pulled yet one more out of its dark sleeve; thanks to Mr. Dave. From the sky, an elderly woman was falling. She had been tossed from Hakeem's balcony. Her wheelchair was falling with her, but at a faster rate of speed. The woman's screams were like the yelling of fifty tortured souls in Hell.

Hakeem and Gabrielle didn't stick around long enough to see how things were going to end for Tracy's aunt. Had they remained where they had been standing, the two of them would have witnessed Tracy's aunt crash through the windshield of Gabrielle's car. The wheelchair landed behind Hakeem's aunt's Mercedes-Benz, then skidded across the concrete, where it eventually came to a stop a few feet in front of the two angry police officers.

"Hakeem, wait! Slow down!"

"Go back down to the lobby! Gabrielle, go back!"

At the turn of the fourth-floor stairwell, Gabrielle stopped running and put her hands on her knees. Exhaus-

tion had inspired her to lean against a wall. Her lungs were on fire. While gasping for air, Gabrielle listened to Hakeem's still-running, footsteps. It was his idea to take the stairs, and not wait for an elevator, which, given the situation, seemed like the only right thing to do. Tracy had to be saved.

"We ain't got no gun, Hakeem!"

Hearing Gabrielle's warning only gave Hakeem more determination to go on. He was taking the steps in threes; sometimes fours. The muscles in his thighs, and in his calves, were burning just as much as his lungs were, but Hakeem kept digging deeper, willing himself to keep going.

For Tracy's sake.

For his wife.

Stolen moments.

Unspoken tributes.

Hakeem loved Tracy with a deep sense of endearment. Since their marriage, Tracy's loyalty to him had never wavered. She owned the hand that fed his wisdom. There was never a time, where he had to remind her to make prayer. When her menstrual cycle was on, he had witnessed her cry, and was able to see the sadness that it brought her, because it had prevented her from being able to join him in their daily prayers. While Gabrielle had Hakeem's heart, Tracy had ownership of his intellect, and his mind. Hakeem wanted to tell Tracy this. He had to. He wanted her to know that she was the type of woman that his mother would have wanted him to have for a wife.

Once Hakeem made it to the ninth floor, he shoved the metal door open, leading out to the hallway, where his condo was. His condo was around the corner. Breathless, Hakeem paused for just a moment, and after swallowing two gulps of air, he took off running again, and didn't stop, until he reached his condo.

". . . don't do to they fathers, what'chu did to me! I'm ya fuckin' father! You came outta my dick!!"

The sound of Mr. Dave's voice turned Hakeem's blood into molten lava.

"Tracy, that shit was an act of treason! Mutiny, goddamn it!! Mutiny!"

On his second attempt, Hakeem was able to get his front door open, by ramming his shoulder into it. The door, however, only swung inwards, wide enough for Hakeem to fit some of his face, and part of his left shoulder inside. Hakeem's doorman was down on the floor. His unconscious body was preventing the door from opening all the way, but with some of his face inside, Hakeem was able to make eye contact with Tracy, and Mr. Dave.

"Help me, Hakeem!!"

Tracy was kicking and screaming, as her father was dragging her by the ankles, down Hakeem's hallway, headed to Hakeem's bedroom. He was taking her to the balcony.

"Let her go!"

"You better hope this bitch can fly, 'cause her aunt couldn't! Get'cha ass in here. You next!"

After his threat, Mr. Dave disappeared with Tracy into Hakeem's master bedroom. Seconds later, as Hakeem finished squeezing his way through his front door, Tracy suddenly reappeared, crawling frantically on her hands and knees.

"Hakeem, his—His gun not real! It's not real!"

Mr. Dave came walking out of Hakeem's master bedroom with a sly smirk on his face. He was close enough to grab Tracy, but he didn't bother her. In his right hand, he was holding Macy's rabbit by its hind leg. The rabbit was shaking and jerking, trying to free itself.

"That was Macy's rabbit, Mr. Dave."

"Well, maybe Macy want some . . . company."

In telling Mr. Dave that the rabbit had belonged to Macy, Hakeem had thought that this would earn the rabbit some respite. Hakeem was wrong. As he and Tracy watched, Mr.

Dave had twisted, and had popped the rabbit's neck. After dropping the rabbit's lifeless body down at his feet, Mr. Dave had stepped over it, and removed the blood-stained, yellow, handkerchief, that he had been wearing around his head, to hide the injury to his eye. The wound looked gruesome.

Hakeem grabbed Tracy by the arm, and moved her behind him. His heart was in his chest throwing punches. His mind was outthinking; strategizing.

"You gon' be in the Grim Reaper's hands, before the cops get here."

"Go down to the lobby, Tracy. Hurry up."

"Tracy, stay right there. I'm not done with you."

"Tracy, go."

Those were Hakeem's final words, before he charged Mr. Dave with a flying knee, followed by a hammer-fist, and an upwards elbow. The attack was executed with a speed that left no time for Mr. Dave to react. Mixed-Martial Arts was in Hakeem's blood. His father was a black belt, and so were all of his older brothers. Hakeem had learned how to crawl, and had taken his first footsteps on the mats of a Brazilian, Jujitsu school, in South Philadelphia. As he got older, Hakeem had shown little interest for his fighting skills, after the taste of money had wet his tongue.

"Nice move."

"Pussy, get up," Hakeem growled, as he watched Mr. Dave use the doorknob of Macy's door, to help himself back up to his feet. He wanted to humiliate the man, and not only get revenge for his brother, and for Gabrielle, but he had every intention of getting justice for anyone that had ever suffered harm from Mr. Dave's hands. "That was my ol'head that stabbed you in the eye the other night, too."

"You don't say?"

Hakeem nodded his head and slowly circled left, as Mr. Dave stuck his hand under his dirty flannel shirt. With a

blood-stained smile, Mr. Dave withdrew Bill-Bill's military knife.

"So, that means I can hold you responsible for my eyeball. You about to gimme one of yours."

"Watch out, Hakeem. Move outta the way."

Tracy reappeared from Hakeem's living room, holding a gun in her hands. At that moment, a cold and deathly silence blanketed the air. The faint sound of police sirens were creeping into Hakeem's condo, from the balcony in his master bedroom.

"Hakeem, move."

As Hakeem obeyed Tracy, and slowly started walking backwards down his hallway, Mr. Dave grinned devilishly at Hakeem's retreat, then he turned his attention to his daughter.

"Bullets can't kill God, Tracy."

"Shoot him, Tracy. Show his nut ass—"

"I'm fuckin' immortal!!"

"Daddy, shut—Shut up!!"

"I'm God, Tracy!! Look at me!"

"Tracy, shoot him!!"

"I'm ya fuckin' father!"

"Daddy, stop talkin'!"

"Man, Tracy, gimme the fuckin' gun!!"

"No, Hakeem . . . I gotta be the one that do this. It gotta be me. It can't be you, or Gabby. I gotta do this."

"What'chu waitin' for then?!!"

Mr. Dave smiled.

"Tracy, say 'Bismillah', before you squeeze the trigger. Go 'head. Do it, Tracy."

"I'm Allah, Tracy."

"Pussy, you about to find out how Allah work! Tracy, rock that nigga!!"

Tracy nodded her head and took two steps forward. Tears were running down her face, as she stared down the

mirrored-hallway, at her smiling father. The gun in her hand was trembling. Her body was shaking down to her feet.

"I'ma come back to you as a ghost, and haunt'chu for as long as you live, girl. I'ma rape you in ya dreams."

Biting her lower lip, Tracy focused her aim on her father's wounded eye. Slowly, she started pulling her index finger back on the trigger.

"Freeze!!!"

No retreat.

"Hands in the air!! Drop it!!"

No surrender.

"Drop the gun!! Now!! Do it, now!!"

Gabrielle raced off of the elevator just as several police officers were storming into Hakeem's condo. From where she stood, Gabrielle had been able to catch a brief glimpse of Hakeem and Tracy, as the two of them had went running into Hakeem's master bedroom, behind Mr. Dave. A dozen cops were right on their heels. Seconds later, the sound of gunshots brought tears to Gabrielle's eyes, and sent her heart crawling up into her throat. When the shooting ceased, Gabrielle dropped down to her knees, and prostrated her face on the floor. Other tenants that had condos on Hakeem's floor, hesitantly began to poke their faces out of their front doors. Those of them that saw Gabrielle down on the floor, thought that Gabrielle had been shot, but only one of them dared to come out into the hallway to check on her.

The woman was an elderly, white lady, who often rode the elevator with Gabrielle and Macy. Ironically, her son was one of the SWAT members who had entered Bayyinah's house, and had subsequently lost his life.

Chapter Twenty-Three

Police Headquarters: 2:11 a.m.
Interview Room-C

"And where were you exactly, when you realized that the gun your father had used to hold you and your aunt hostage, wasn't real?"

"At my husband's condo."

"Now, was this before, or after your father had thrown your aunt off of the balcony?"

"It was after."

"Speak up."

"After."

"Okay, so let's backtrack for a minute. Start from when you arrived from Delaware, and you received the phone call from your aunt. What did she say exactly, that made you go there?"

"Before you answer my partner's question, would you mind telling us why you left Delaware in the first place? See, I'm finding it interesting that you and your foster sister drove there together, but upon hearing the tragic news about her mother and daughter, you would just leave her in Delaware, knowing she not only needed the ride back here to Philly, but that she had to be extremely grief stricken, over losing her

loved ones. Are the two of you close? Did you know that your father was her daugther's father also? "

"What are you not telling us, Mrs. Epps?"

"You know we'll find out, if you're hiding anything from us. Save us the time."

Tracy wiped a teardrop from her eye.

"We've been doing this a long time, Mrs. Epps."

"Do yourself a favor."

"It's for your own good."

Cutting her eyes from one detective to the other, Tracy wiped away some more teardrops. All of the questions from the detectives were slowly chipping away at her courage, and her pact to Hakeem and Gabrielle.

Seventeen minutes later . . .
Interview Room-A

"So, you never actually met your daugther's foster parents?"

"No."

"And it was your daughter, who told you and your wife, that her foster father was the father of her daughter, you said?"

"Yes, that's what I said. You heard me say it, didn't you?"

"So, why did your wife leave you in Egypt?"

"What the fuck that got to do with—Am I under arrest?! I wanna know why I'm gettin' harrased! Where ya'll got my daughter! I know my fuckin' rights! Call Agent Watkins! We ain't did shit to be gettin' interrogated like this, but ran some mu'fuckin' red lights! Ya'll got my damn file right there! The mother fucker who was in the wrong tonight, did a fuckin' swan-dive off of my son-in-law balcony, before ya'll could catch him! Ya'll chargin' me for his blood landin' on my god-damn gators?! Huh? Yeah, I didn't think so! Now, ya'll goofy mu'fuckers can charge me for somethin' up in this bitch, or

let me and mine the fuck outta here! We gotta bury my wife and my gran'baby, and you need to brush ya mu'fuckin' teeth! Stinkin' ass breath!!"

Five minutes later . . .
Interview Room—D

"Why didn't you pull over for the police officers?"
"Why didn't I—Oh, my mother fuckin' God."
"Is there a problem?"
"It sure the fuck is. How can you be his mother fuckin' partner?"
"Excuse me?"
The two white detectives shot puzzled glances at each other. The one closest to Hakeem's aunt gave her an impatient stare, as he leaned closer, preparing to try to intimidate her with some more questions.
"Child, I swear to fuckin' God, some damn body need to give ya mouth a fuckin' funeral . . . right now. Like, ya tongue, tonsils, and those teeth. Those teeth for goddamn sure. I thought—Are you serious? Wow. Listen, honey, ya entire mouth need an extreme makeover. Ya shit so buck-toothed, you probably can eat a fuckin' apple through a damn tennis racquet."
"Answer the damn question."
"I'm not answerin' a goddamn thing, if you don't back outta my damn face! Smell like you been eatin' donuts made of dog shit!"
The detective backed away from Hakeem's aunt, glaring at her angrily. His partner new that she was telling the truth, but he would never admit to it.
"Mrs. Smith, why didn't you, or your nephew, pull over?"
"Well, to be honest, I thought the cops wanted to race. I can't speak for Hakeem."

"Let me get this straight . . . you thought the cops wanted to race?"

"Ain't that what I just said?"

"Unbelievable."

"No, you wanna know what's unbelievable? That god-damn mouth of yours. And from one mother fuckin' coke sniffer to another, switch suppliers, 'cause that booger sugar you usin' got way too much cut on it. That's why ya nostrils look like you be pickin' ya fuckin' boogies wit' a hot comb."

3:02 a.m.
Interview Room—B

"You think I'm lyin' about somethin'?"

"I think lying is one of your vocational skills. Your eyes say it all."

Gabrielle nodded her head at the detectives insult. He was trying to get under her skin, and Gabrielle knew this. His efforts were useless, but instead of telling the ugly-mouthed detective this, Gabrielle just stuck her index finger under her nose, to block her nostrils from his offensive smelling breath. His partner fought back a chuckle.

"Listen, don't you want the people responsible for what happened to your mother and daughter caught?"

"They committed suicide. What else can be done to them?"

"Mrs. Epps, we can provide you with protection, if that's a concern for you."

"You said that you're pregnant, right?"

"Yeah."

"Think of your child's future."

"We can put you somewhere, where the Cartel will never find you."

"Your foster sister has already told us everything. Make the same smart decision that she made."

Gabrielle felt a fire ignite in her stomach.

"Like my partner just said, think of your child's future, Mrs. Epps."

Fifteen minutes later . . .
Interview Room—E

"Your wives told us everything, Mr. Smith."

"Your doorman did, too."

"Am I under arrest?"

"No."

"Are my wives?"

"No, but all that can change, depending on how you handle this interview, and what you share with us."

"Mr. Smith, we have some pictures, we'd like you to take a look at."

"What'chu say ya name was again?"

"Detective Brady."

"And what's yours?"

"Sullivan . . . Detective Sullivan."

"Check this out," Hakeem spoke, after a momentary staring match with the detective, who was removing several large, photographs, from a manilla envelope. His heart skipped a beat, once all of the photos were laid out on the desk in front of him. "Ya'll doin' all this for nothin'. I ain't got nothin' to tell ya'll."

"Sure you do."

"We picked up Taz's mom this mornin'."

Hakeem felt his heart skip another beat, as his eyes shot a quick glance at the old mugshot of Taz. Directly beside Taz's picture, was one of Bill-Bill. There was a total of eleven photographs, spread out on the large desk, and Hakeem

knew each and every last person, on every single picture. Only three of the people in the photo array were still alive.

"Taz's mother knew everyone in all the pictures, except for him, and these three guys over here."

Hakeem's eyes had followed the detective's index finger, from the photo of Bill-Bill, over to the three photographs of his friends, who Gabrielle had killed by mistake.

"She told us this fella right here was her nephew, and that she knew this guy from seeing him around the neighborhood."

Hakeem stared down at the pictures of Fresh and Amir.

"She also identified these two Mexican women as being friends of Taz's, and she also told us that these two Mexican guys over here, had been to her house once, or twice. She wasn't sure."

Hakeem stared down at the two Mexican guys that had robbed him with Taz, months earlier. Their photos showed both of them with beards, which they didn't have, back on that day.

"Now, Taz's mom brought us a lot of clarity, in our talk with her. She also told us about the advice that you gave her, which was that she should get out of the city, so that these two Mexican fellas right here, and their Cartel, would have no idea where she was hiding."

"Is the information she gave us accurate?"

"How can I answer that, if I don't know everything she told ya'll?"

"Well, let me ask you this. Were you and her son best friends?"

Hakeem stared down at the photograph of Taz, while nodding his head. He felt guilt. Hakeem started to think about Bayyinah.

"And his sister was carrying your child, right? That's what her mother told us."

"Yeah."

"Hakeem, where do you think Taz might be?"

Hakeem shrugged his shoulders. It was there, and then, that he knew that Gabrielle and Tracy, had stood firm. Hakeem's armpits stopped sweating. He could feel the pressure being lifted from his shoulders.

"Have you heard from him?"

"Naw."

"His mother told us that you and him were drug selling partners."

"That true?"

"Yeah, we used to be."

"What happened?"

"I quit."

"Why?"

Hakeem shrugged his shoulders.

"That's not an answer."

"Was it because of the Mexicans?"

"I ain't trust them, so I fell back. Plus, I knew I had a baby on the way, so I was tryna start my life over."

"But Taz didn't want to quit."

Hakeem shrugged his shoulders again.

"His mother believes that those Mexican guys killed him, and that his body might be somewhere in Mexico. What'chu think?"

"How would I know?"

"Give us the name of the Cartel."

"I don't know it."

"What you mean, you don't know it?"

"I never asked them that shit. I ain't care."

"Who were you shootin' at when you got arrested with that gun, a couple months ago, out there in the Northeast?"

"The clouds."

"The clouds?"

"I was drunk."

"Okay, so, why do you think those Mexican girls went nuts like that in Taz's mother's house?"

"Ya'll the cops . . . figure that shit out. Ya'll askin' me like I know."

"Why did you and your wives go to your aunt's house?"

"Was it because of the Cartel?"

"Kinda."

"Were there any other reasons?"

"The main reasons jumped off my balcony."

"David Epps?"

Hakeem nodded his head.

"That was your brother that he killed in front of his house, right?"

"Yeah."

"And you married his fiancé?"

Hakeem nodded his head once more.

"Did you and Taz's cousin, Fresh, stay in touch, after Taz went missing?"

"Naw."

"Why not?"

"Me and him wasn't never cool like that. I ain't have no reason to."

"Did you know he was dead?"

"I heard he was."

"From who?"

"The streets."

"What about this guy right here? Know him?"

Hakeem shook his head when the buck-toothed detective pointed at Bill-Bill's photo.

"How about these guys over here?"

"Don't know them, either," Hakeem lied, as the other detective finger-jabbed the photographs of his three, dead friends. The denial had stung his heart like a wasp. "Look, man, I don't know what they got to do wit' that Cartel, so I can't sit here and act like I do, 'cause I don't. That gun my

wife got caught with tonight was mine. We had that shit, 'cause her fuckin' dad was trippin'. It was under my couch. She went and got that shit when her dad pulled that knife out on me. I'm sayin', like, if ya'll need a conviction that fuckin' bad, charge me wit' that shit, not her."

"Hakeem, I think you and your wives have been through enough this week."

"I'm sayin', 'cause we got this cell phone wit' that nigga sayin' all this crazy shit on her voicemails, 'n all'lat."

"Yeah, she told us."

"You should've called the police, as soon as your doorman told you her father was at your condo, instead of trying to take matters into your own hands. You could've gotten yourself killed tonight."

"I know."

"Okay, well, we're gonna let you get out of here."

"So, ya'll lettin' my peoples go, too?"

"We been released them."

"Oh, alright."

"Hey, that aunt of yours is a piece of work."

Hakeem smiled on the inside. Twenty minutes later, the police headquarter's parking lot, nearest its 7th Street entryway, was buzzing with conversations. A sense of triumph was floating in the night air. Hugs were being given, and some eyes were even wet with tears. Hakeem's aunt had given everyone a high-five.

Tobi Russeck, Hakeem's lawyer, was seated behind the steering wheel of her 5-series BMW, with a smile on her face. Hakeem's friend, Bill-Bill, was to her right, in her passenger's seat.

"So, what do we do now?"

Hakeem broke his three-way hug with Gabrielle and Tracy, to think for a second about Tracy's question.

"I mean, like, after we do the janazahs for Gabrielle mom, Macy, and Bayyinah?"

"Ya'll wanna go visit my dad?"

"Yeah."

"I don't care."

"Alright, well, that's what we gon' do, then. We can figure out what we gon' do next, while we over there."

Yesterday.

Is.

Gone.

Sometimes, an individual will encounter his, or her destiny, on the very path that they actually took to avoid it.

Chapter One

"Brittany, you an ungrateful, little bitch. You know that?"

"I am not! Aunt Tanya, why you just sittin' there, lettin' him talk to me like that? You just gon' sit there and not say nothin'?"

"Me and Marvin was downstairs in your apartment, while you was at work, Brittany. We read one of your diaries.

"What?! Why?!"

"Ay, bitch, look here! Ya aunt ain't gotta do no goddamn explainin' to you about why we did shit up in this mu'fucker! Bitch, don't forget, this . . . whole goddamn buildin' belong . . . to . . . me!!"

Brittany ducked, then shielded the front of her face with her pocketbook, when Marvin, her aunt's boyfriend, shifted his three hundred and forty-three pound body on his couch, and hurled her diary across his living room at her. The lavender pages on the pink diary flapped in the air, until one of the spinning blades on the ceiling fan in his kitchen clipped it, and sent it sky-diving down into his kitchen sink, that was full of sudsy-water and dirty dishes.

"Why—Marvin, why would you do that?!"

"What?! Bitch, you luck that's all I did!"

While Brittany went scrambling through her aunt's boyfriend's kitchen, in her attempt to rescue her book of secrets, her aunt, with an evil expression on her face, rose from

where she had been sitting at the kitchen table. Muttering words that were incoherent, Brittany's aunt raised the chair she had been sitting on up over her head, and went charging at Brittany's back. The things that Brittany had said about her in her diary had hurt her, and had even caused her to cry in her boyfriend's presence.

Brittany's aunt was a plus-sized woman. She outweighed Brittany by one hundred and twenty-two pounds. Due to this, when Brittany's aunt violently struck Brittany on the back of the head with the wooden chair, Brittany immediately lost consciousness, and melted down to the kitchen floor at her aunt's bare feet.

"Tanya, go in her pocketbook, and see if she got some money. I feel like goin' over Atlantic City and doin' some gamblin'."

"This bitch stay with some fuckin' money."

"And get her car keys, too. I gotta stop I wanna make, before we get on the highway."

Brittany's existence had come at the cost of her mother's own. After ten and a half hours of labor, Brittany's mother had died on the delivery table, seconds after pushing Brittany out of her womb. Shortly after that, Brittany's father had gotten into a bloody scuffle with some of the hospital staff, which, then led to his swift arrest, after several packets of crack cocaine, a butterfly knife, and two crack pipes had fallen out of a torn jacket pocket of his, while he had been in the process of cutting Brittany's umbilical cord. Following that chaotic incident, a host of Brittany's family members had shown up to the hospital. However, when the moment had come for someone from amongst them to step forward, and speak to the counselor from Child Services, to claim guardianship of Brittany, only an aunt, who was a younger sister of Brittanys's father, had the moral decency to step up and accept the responsibility.

All of Brittany's childhood, and a majority of her teenage

2

years, had been spent in West Philadelphia. She was raised on Chestnut Street, between the intersection of 63rd and 62nd. Over the past summer, Brittany and her aunt had moved across the city, to live with Brittany's aunt's boyfriend, who had recently inherited a funeral home from his deceased grandfather. The funeral home was located in North Philadelphia. It was on the corner of Franklin and Master, below two apartment units, that were also a part of the three-story, 98-year-old property. The funeral home was currently under foreclosure.

Brittany was twenty-two, gorgeous, and extremely goal-driven. She was passionate about her dream, which was to one day become a national, best-selling author, and she would share her ideas with anyone that was willing to listen to her. Minus the hair, because hers was much darker, and a lot longer, Brittany looked like she could be the younger sister of the CNN news anchor, Soledad O'Brien. Brittany's last boyfriend had gotten killed by an off-duty police officer, after the two men had exchanged stares inside of a West Philadelphia Chinese store. It was a tragedy that Brittany's heart was still trying to heal from.

At a few minutes shy of two in the morning, Brittany blinked her eyes open and let out an agonizing groan. She was surrounded by complete darkness. Aside from the painful fact that she had an excruciating headache, the back of her neck, and right shoulder, was feeling like they both had been the targets of a brick-throwing contest. Pain was inspiring Brittany to remain as still as she possibly could. She was lying on her back. Just as Brittany's eyes were adapting to the darkness, she closed them, and began to think about how she had ended up in the position that she was in. As she slowly began to remember, teardrops started to trickle out of her closed eyelids. There, on her back, Brittany realized her path of mistakes. A car passing by outside gave her a reason to open her eyes again.

"Don't they know I'm the one bitch you don't wanna cross?" Brittany thought, while struggling to bring herself to a sitting position. Her diary was inches away from her hand, to her left, but the darkness was preventing her from seeing it, or the other miscellaneous items from her pocketbook, which had all been dumped on the kitchen floor, in her aunt's haste to find her car keys, and her money. "Watch what happen to them two fat mother fuckers now. Watch . . . watch."

After patting the kitchen floor a few times, Brittany found her cell phone. Tearfully, Brittany called the one and only person who she trusted with her life. That person's cell phone rung six times, before Brittany got an answer.

"Hello?"

"My dad there, Miss Olivia?"

"He right here sleep. Why? You okay? What's wrong?"

Up on her feet, and moving around, Brittany located a light switch in the kitchen, and flipped it up. The sudden flood of light caused her to squint, and increased the intensity of her headache.

"Brittany?"

"Miss Olivia, can you wake him up, and give him the phone please?"

"Okay, baby, hold on."

It was August 18th, 2012. The time was 2:11 a.m. Up above the dark city of Philadelphia, dozens of clouds were releasing a steady downpour of drenching rain. The rain had been falling non-stop, since earlier in the afternoon. In other parts of the United States, in places like Mississippi, rivers were gradually drying up, due to it being a lack of rainful there. Out in the midwest, there were several states suffering from it being a shortage of wet weather as well. It was because of this shortage of wet weather, and dry heat, that was causing a lot of their forest areas to experience wildfires, which, at the moment, were burning out of control.

"Doll baby, what's wrong?"

Brittany let out a sob at the sound of her father's voice. He was a super hero to her; a defender of her name and honor. Inside of her heart, his promises meant more than all of the money in the world.

"You okay?"

"Daddy, they jumped me. They hit me with a chair and knocked me out."

"What? Who?"

"Aunt Tanya and Marvin."

"Tanya and Marvin?"

"Yeah, Daddy. They—They was in my apartment, goin' through my stuff and everything. They was reading my diaries. When I got off work, Aunt Tanya called me, and she—"

"Hold on for a second, Doll baby. Let me get dressed."

"Okay."

Brittany and her father were as close as any parent and child could ever be. Brittany's father's sobriety had glued their hearts together and had put them both on common ground. After promising Brittany, on her thirteenth birthday, that he would never smoke crack again, Brittany's father had stood true to his oath. He had even helped Brittany land her first job.

Brittany was employed at a famous nightclub, in the 'Old City' section of Philadelphia. Brittany's boss' name was Tianna Barnes, and she was one of the most ambitious woman, that Brittany had ever met. At work, Brittany's job description covered a wide range of responsibilities, which, at times, even required that she sometimes watch her boss' 15-month-old, infant son. However, out of all of her duties at work, being her boss' eyes and ears, was really how Brittany earned her pay.

A lot went on at Gossip Alley. It was a nightclub that was always packed to its full capacity, and the home of some of the best parties ever thrown in Philadelphia. Weeknights

5

were crazy, and the weekends were a lot crazier. On the weekends, at the stroke of every midnight, male and female, exotic dancers, became a part of Gossip Alley's night life experience. It was a tradition that had been started, since its grand opening night. Gossip Alley was owned by the husband of Brittany's boss. He was currently incarcerated at a Philadelphia county prison, fighting a murder charge. In his absence, his wife had been keeping his business alive, and thriving. Gossip Alley was so popular, people had to make arrangements to reserve space for their private parties, months in advance. Just recently, Brittany's boss had launched an adult calender, featuring all of the exotic dancers, who were all on the payroll at the club. Over the 2012 summer alone, the adult calender had grossed more than sixty-five thousand dollars. The bulk of those sales had come from Gossip Alley's business website.

"Doll Baby, you still there?"

"Yeah, I'm still here."

"Where that gun I gave you for your birthday."

Brittany walked out of her aunt's boyfriend's bedroom, and went back into the kitchen. Teardrops were still flowing down her face.

"It's in my closet," Brittany answered, after putting all of her things on the kitchen floor back inside of her pocketbook. Noticing that her car keys were missing, she walked over to a nearby window and took a look outside. "Daddy, they took my car. All my money gone, too. I had a little over two thousand dollars."

"They'll replace every dime. Doll baby, right now, I just want'chu to get that gun outta the closet. Use it, only if you have to, okay?"

"Okay."

Innocent.

Sinners.

"Daddy, hurry up."

"Doll Baby, I'm on my way. Stop cryin'. Here talk to Oliv—"

"Daddy, it's gone."

"What's gone?"

"The gun . . . it's not here. It's gone."

"Son of a bitch."

Brittany switched her cell phone to her other ear, as she wiped her face clean of her teardrops. She was beginning to have a bad feeling in the pit of her stomach. Once more, Brittany checked the right pocket of her white, mink vest, hanging in the back of her bedroom closet. Her gun was definitely missing. Brittany spun around and looked around at her bedroom. It was a complete mess. Her bedroom had been ransacked by her aunt, and her aunt's boyfriend. Her entire apartment looked like it had been turned upside down. Out in the living room, everything was in disarray, as was the case in her kitchen, and bathroom.

"They here, Doll baby."

"Who?"

"Tanya and Marvin. They sittin' in ya car, parked behind mine. Olivia, go back in the house."

Brittany stood still when she heard a car door slam on the other end of her cell phone. She suddenly began to feel fearful for her father's safety.

"Daddy, go back in the house, too."

"I wish I would. She might be my sister, but—"

But . . .

The gun that Brittany had been looking for was in the left hand of Brittany's aunt's boyfriend, and being pointed at Brittany's father. The gun's chrome frame was wet from the rain falling from the night sky. The gun was a 9 mm Smith&Wesson.

"Daddy, go back in the house with Miss Olivia."

Brittany's aunt's boyfriend had a cryptic plan of how he was going to unbury his funeral home from the debt it was

in, and rescue it from foreclosure to the bank. His goal was to bring Brittany's entire world crashing down to her feet, by revealing the stories in Brittany's diaries to her family members, friends, and co-workers, starting with some of Brittany's most personal, and juiciest secrets first. Marvin, Brittany's aunt's boyfriend, wanted to have as much leverage against Brittany as he possibly could get. Once he had Brittany backed into a corner, wanting no more, and having no one to turn to, or any place safe to go, he, with Brittany's aunt's help, was then going to force Brittany into starting a bloody, drug war, with some of their neighborhood drug dealers, so that the deadly results of the drug war could help with revitalizing business at his funeral home.

While Marvin's plans were ugly, and methodical, and at least to him, well thought out, Marvin had the slightest idea that Brittany was on the other end of her father's cell phone, listening to what was going on.

"Daddy, please, go back in the house."

"Doll baby, this fat mother fucker gotta nerve to be walkin' up on me wit' the goddamn gun I gave—Ay, Marvin, so, you some gangsta now, nigga? You better watch where you aimin' that . . . "

Brittany flinched and dropped her cell phone when the sudden sound of gunshots exploded on her father's end of the cell phone. It was déjà vu all over again. The gunshots had sounded like there was someone shooting inside her bedroom, standing directly beside her; just like before.

Frantically, Brittany placed her cell phone back to her ear. The gunshots hadn't ended. They seemed endless.

"Daddy?!!"

Brittany's scream came from her gut. Once more, a loved one of hers was being shot on the opposite end of her cell phone, while she could do nothing but listen, with a feeling of complete helplessness, that was almost paralyzing. Crying

hysterically, Brittany released her cell phone yet again, dropped down to her knees, and screamed, until there was no breath left in her lungs. Her only hope was that her father wouldn't meet the same fate as her boyfriend, because if so . . .

Who was going to save her soul now?

Chapter Two

Six days later . . .
Tuesday, 1:56 a.m.

Every so often, a thin patch of clouds would appear in front of the bright, full moon, then casually vanish away into the night. The clouds were being swept by warm winds, coming out of the northwest corner of Chestnut Hill, Pennsylvania. The sky was lit with stars, and as blue, and as beautiful as the waters surrounding the coasts of St. Croix. Even while it was almost two hours past midnight, temperatures still hadn't dropped below the mid-70s, which made the weather nice enough for some people to still enjoy.

In the gigantic backyard, that belonged to Tianna Barnes, the light sound of crickets, was blending in with the soft hum of R&B music, joyful laughter, talking, and the occasional sounds of splashing water, that was coming from Tianna Barnes' large, in-ground, swimming pool. The mood was a lot less jovial inside of Tianna Barnes' master bedroom.

"Brittany, that wasn't just some random misunderstanding," Tia explained, after taking a generous sip of her grape moscato. As she returned her glass of wine back to her nightstand, she looked into her assistant's watery eyes sympathetically. "Brittany, Detective Konn was following your boyfriend that entire night. I know this, because the person

I hired to kill his crooked ass, was on the phone with me the entire time. I heard the gunshots and everything, Brittany. All nine of them. Mind you, this was months before you and I even met. Now, I could've still went ahead, and had Detective Konn killed, like, right then and there, while he was shootin' your boyfriend in that Chinese store, but I let my curiosity get the best of me that night. Brittany, I started thinkin'. I wanted to know who your boyfriend was. What was his beef with Detective Konn. His story. More importantly, though, I wanted to make it my business to find out what he did to cross Detective Konn. And that's exactly what I did. Now, before I tell you what I found out, I want'chu to come with me. I wanna show you somethin'."

Tianna Barnes was twenty-seven, rich, beautiful, and insanely dangerous. Her 15-month-old son was her savior. If not for his existence, death would have been snatched her soul out of her body months ago. Her son's life was keeping her balanced. God had rewritten her destiny more than five times, but the deaths of loved ones, and the intimate betrayals of others, had blinded her from seeing all of the blessings she had to be thankful for. Tia only displayed softness around her son, and when she was in the company of her husband, when she visited him on Mondays, at the Philadelphia county prison. In the presence of her husband and son, Tia was able to let down her guard, and become who she so deeply, and honestly, truly wanted to be.

Herself.

Tia owned gray eyes that were angry on most days, and while she could easily get by as being Hispanic, or some other Latin ethnicity, Tia was actually just a mixture of some Italian, and black DNA. When they were seen together, a lot of people often thought that her assistant was her younger sister, because of their similarities in how they looked. Both of them stood 5'9" tall, had the same complexion, and was of equal beauty. Internally, however, Tia and her assistant

were as opposite as the summer and winter. Few women could compare to Tianna Barnes. Some men didn't even have the heart that she had; or the ambition. Everyone out in her backyard admired her, and knew that she was the alpha-female.

"God, please don't make me regret doin' this," Tia thought, before turning on the lights in her walk-in closet. As her Pomeranian poodle, and her assistant, followed behind her closely, she chewed on her bottom lip with a sense of anxiety, that was soon followed by a feeling of ease, and much-needed comfortability. "Tia, all you have to do is keep trustin' your instincts. The only person that don't like her, is Rhonda. Splash gave her two thumbs up. Sooly love her. Snookums like her. Everybody at work do. So far, she ain't never disappoint you. And not only do she remind you of Camay, but you all she got. She look up to you. What if she turn out to be another Jen, though? Well, here goes nothin'."

Trust.

"Brittany, me and my husband used to kill people for a-Snookums, move."

With her left foot, Tia moved her small dog from in front of the all-glass door, that stood between her and her expensive shoe closet. Her walk-in closet had the length and width of an average-sized bedroom. Walking into it, there was a center path of soft, peach carpet, that came to an end at the rear wall, where there was a window, overlooking Tia's two-laned driveway. Tia's walk-in closet had been renovated into four private spaces. Each area had an all-glass door. There were two on the left of the carpeted aisle, and two on the right.

A feeling of pride and accomplishment swept through Tia's veins as she opened the door to her shoe closet, and walked into it. The cold surface of the hardwood floor chilled the soles of her bare feet, as Tia squatted to pick up her poodle.

"So, like I was sayin' . . . Brittany, step back. Me and my husband used to be professional killers, and we used to make a lot of money doin' what we did."

After pressing the panel beneath the glass shelf, displaying her various styles of Christian Louboutin shoes, and sneakers, Tia quickly took a step back, and stood shoulder to shoulder, beside her assistant. As Tia's wall of shoes slowly began to revolve, Tia's assistant's eyes grew wider and wider.

Brittany had been staying with her boss, since the night her father, and her father's live-in-girlfriend, were murdered. The death of her father had Brittany miserable with grief, and sick to her stomach with depression. All Brittany had motivating her now, was a single promise that her boss had made to her, as the two of them had been going into the Philadelphia police headquarters, six nights earlier.

"Brittany, our lives are a lot alike," Tia spoke, while blinking back a few tears. All sorts of memories began to bombard her mind, as she returned her dog back down to the floor, and walked into her secret, customized-vault. "I've been where you are, more times than I can count. I know disappointment, like I know the back of my hand, Brittany. What I'm about to share with you, is nobody's business at the club. If it ever becomes someone else's business, I'm going to hold you responsible, Brittany. We clear?"

Brittany nodded her head.

"My mom was my dad's mistress. When she got pregnant with me, he bought her this house. He told her to start planning for they wedding. Problem was, he was already married. Brittany, my dad's wife, didn't like the fact that, my, um, that my dad had filed for divorce, or that he was tryna start a new family. She stabbed him to death, while he was asleep. Then, her crazy ass swallowed a bottle of pain pills, got into bed with him, and died right beside him. Retarded, right? The story don't end there, though. It gets better."

"Tia, why you tellin' me this? Why you showin' me this room?"

"Because it's time that we take our trust in each other to another level, Brittany."

"Does this have anything to do with why you told me to lie to the cops, and not tell them who really killed my dad, and Miss Olivia?"

"Part of it does. Sit down."

Sometimes . . .

Revenge solves everything.

"I know what it feel like to get betrayed by an aunt, too, Brittany."

At seeing that her boss' gray eyes were filling up with tears, Brittany lowered her own watery eyes, and stared at the hardwood floors, surrounding her Prada sandals. Brittany didn't want to see her boss cry. However, she was deeply touched to see that her boss was allowing herself to become transparent in her presence, because her boss had never done so before. As Brittany continued to keep her eyes down on the floor, she was feeling entrusted with a piece of her boss' true self, that no one else at work would ever be privileged to witness.

"Way before she even crossed me, my aunt had crossed my mom and dad," Tia confided, while she used the palm of her left hand to catch the teardrops falling from her eyes. Speaking on the skeletons in her family was always an emotional, and psychological hurdle for her. "Her and my dad's wife didn't like each other, and from what I've been told, that's puttin' it nicely. Out of spite, my aunt had hooked my dad up with my mom, who was my aunt's best friend. The whole time, though, my dad was already creepin' with one of my aunt other friends, and my aunt, or my mom, didn't have a clue about it. That's how me and my brother, Malcolm, is related. So, um, yeah, so anyway, my dad and my mom started messin' around, and when she had me, to throw it in

14

my dad's wife's face, my aunt sent her all these pictures of my dad, my mom, and me, when I was first born."

"So, that's why ya dad wife stabbed him up?"

"Yup."

"I guess everybody was mad at'cha aunt, after that, huh?"

"Nobody knew she was the one who sent the pictures, Brittany."

"Not even your mom?"

"Not even my mom," Tia echoed, staring blankly at the cabinet of machine guns, against the wall, behind her assistant. Unconsciously, she touched the gold locket on her necklace, that held a tiny picture of her father. "Would you believe, they had the nerve to bury my dad beside his wife? Brittany, they didn't even let my mom go to the fuckin' funeral. How did that make sense? Bury him beside the woman who put him in his grave, but deny the woman that he wanted to marry, and be with."

"That don't make sense. Not to me, at least."

"My dad side of the family didn't accept me. Just my aunt."

"The one that sent the pictures?"

"Her . . . my mom died, thinkin' my aunt was her best friend, when she was really just her frenemy."

"How ya mom die, Tia?"

"She was in one of the World Trade Centers on nine-eleven, havin' a business meetin'."

"Can I ask you somethin' else?"

"Brittany, when we walk outta here, I want our trust to be beyond where it's at now, like I said earlier. So, how about we do this. You can ask me five questions. I'll answer them all honestly, no matter if I like them, or not."

"So, I can ask you anything I want, and you not gon' get mad at me?"

"I can promise you honesty, Brittany. I can't guarantee that I won't get mad at what you ask me."

"Can you guarantee that I won't lose my job?"

"Brittany, your job is safe."

For a long moment, Brittany looked tentatively at her boss, considering what she wanted to ask her boss first. There were so many things about her boss that she wanted to know. The woman was intriguing. At work, there were whispered-rumors going around, that her boss' husband was in jail for killing her aunt, two of her best friends, and several other people. Feeling a little indecisive, Brittany used a few seconds to look around her boss' hidden room, while her mind slowly began to prioritize her five questions.

As Brittany was thinking, and quietly looking around at the tall, money safes, and all of the machine gun racks, and foot lockers, Tia was casually sitting in her chair, using her feet to play with her poodle. When a ball of dust moved over in the corner, near a pile of her bulletproof vests, Tia was reminded of the last time she had done some cleaning in her secret room. There were so many responsibilities demanding her attention, and pulling her in different directions, that she rarely ever had the time to think, much less relax. Tia never had time for herself. Her infant son was spoiled rotten, which was solely her fault, and from the moment he opened his gray eyes, until the moment he closed them, and went to sleep, he ran her wild. Life as a mother was taxing, but life as a wife, to an incarcerated man, made all of Tia's days uphill battles.

"Okay, I have my first question. Why that cop killed Sean?"

"To prove a point."

"To who?"

"Several people, actually. Brittany, did your boyfriend ever tell you how his mom ended up in that wheelchair?"

"He was little when that happened," Brittany recalled, remembering what her boyfriend had told her. While she knew what she had been told, she sensed that her boss was about

to reveal a different version to the story she was aware of. "His dad started shootin' when the cops was doin' a drug raid on they house, and his mom got caught in the middle of the shootout, right? That's not what happened? His dad, and one of the cops died, and Mrs. Maxine got paralyzed. Sean said he was next door at a neighbor house, Tia."

"Well, maybe, his mom never told him the truth. She could've been tryna protect him, I guess."

Brittany's eyes became watery.

"That was Detective Konn and his partner, Brittany. That wasn't a drug raid. That was Detective Konn."

Brittany's tears became rain.

"Your boyfriend dad got double-crossed by Detective Konn," Tia quietly explained, saddened at the sight of her assistant crying. In a couple of hours, they both would be attending her assistant's father's funeral, and she couldn't help but to feel a little concerned with how her assistant was going to deal with coming face to face, with her aunt, and her aunt's boyfriend. "They had a deal, that your boyfriend's dad was supposed to kill Detective Konn's partner, in exchange for fifty thousand dollars. Your boyfriend's mom knew the whole scoop. She the one that opened the door, and let them in. It was never a drug raid, Brittany. Detective Konn and his partner wasn't even on duty. Now, only ya boyfriend mom know what really went wrong, in that house that day, but as soon as ya boyfriend dad shot Detective Konn's partner in the face, Detective Konn remixed the whole agreement and flipped out. He killed ya boyfriend dad, then he shot ya boyfriend mom, when she tried to jump outta the second floor window."

"And she been keepin' this to herself all this time? Why didn't she tell?"

"Brittany, your guess is as good as mine. You know the lady better than I do. I only seen pictures of her. Brittany, this is what I do know . . . she tried to blackmail Detective

Konn for some money, that I assume she feel like, is still owed to her. Detective Konn killed her son to make a point. She know that wasn't some chance encounter in that fuckin' Chinese store. Trust me, as soon as she found out the name of the cop that shot her son, she knew exactly what the fuck was goin' on, and what it was about."

Tia stopped talking to let out a yawn.

"My other questions can wait, 'til tomorrow, Tia. I'm tired, too."

"Okay, but I wanna make some sense of a few things for you," Tia said, yawning again, and stretching her arms up over her head. She felt exhausted. "My husband in jail, because of Detective Konn. Detective Konn put a body on my husband that I did. I have another brother, and him and Detective Konn are in cahoots together, some kind of way. It's a lot to that story. I'll let you know about all of that tomorrow. More importantly, though, Detective Konn will be dead by Halloween. We're going to get him to come to the club for our Halloween party."

"Are you serious?"

Tia nodded her head, smiling devilishly.

"You gon' kill him at the club?"

"Yup . . . while the party goin' on, and everything. Honey gonna help us get him there."

"Honey?"

"She owes me a huge favor, Brittany."

"She owes everybody, from what I hear."

"True, but here's where things get complicated. I'm gon' need you to move back with your aunt, and her boyfriend, tomorrow."

"What? Why?"

The confusion in Brittany's eyes, and the sudden disappointment that came out with her questions, sliced and diced Tia's heart into quarters.

"Brittany, it's the only way I can fulfill my promise to you."

"But—But I don't understand," Brittany cried, feeling betrayed by the only person she had left to count on. Hurt had her heart in its hands. "How can you—Tia, don't make me go back there. Not there. Anywhere, but there, Tia. Anywhere, but there. You know what they did. They killed—Tia, they murdered my dad and they got away with it. Tia, I didn't tell them cops what I knew, or said anything, 'cause you told me not to."

"Look at this, Brittany."

On the rear, exposed-brick wall, hanging in between a machine gun cabinet, and a cabinet stocked with countless handguns, there was a 22 inch, flat-screen TV. When Tia thumbed the screen of her iPhone, the flat-screen TV lit up, and came to life. For a moment, the flat-screen just showed a blue screen, but in a matter of seconds, it then produced four, split-screen images.

Wiping the tears from her eyes, Brittany stood up, as the familiar images on the flat-screen TV began to slowly register in her head.

"I had cameras put in there the other day, while they was out, "Tia spoke, touching the screen of her cell phone, once more. Doing this, gave the flat-screen TV an audio sound. "I got this app from the security company, that'll let'chu bring up those surveillance cameras, on any TV that'chu near. We gon' download the app to your cell phone tomorrow. Brittany, I gave you my word, and I'm goin' to stand by it. Won't nobody ever get away with hurtin' you, Brittany. I hold grudges for life. Your issues are mine."

Brittany stepped closer to the flat-screen TV with watery eyes that were amazed at what they were seeing. Right there, on the bottom, left corner, of her boss' flat-screen TV, was Marvin, and her aunt, spooning in bed. They were asleep, and snoring like bears.

"We gon' make them pay for what they did to you, Brittany. That wasn't some empty promise I gave you."

Brittany let out a sigh as she looked at her boss. There was conviction in her boss' sentiments.

"Brittany, Marvin gran'father used to be a big trick. He was strung out on heroin, too. That's how his funeral home got into so much debt. He was borrowin' money from any, and everybody. So, anyway, a while back, Detective Konn came to him with this crazy scheme. You see that room right there?"

Brittany cut her eyes to the top, right corner, of the flat-screen TV, where her boss was pointing her finger. Brittany squinted her eyes at what appeared to be some sort of operating room.

"You seen that room in the funeral home before?"

"No."

"It's in there."

"I never been inside of the funeral home. Marvin keep it locked anyway. Since we been stayin' there, I only saw him go in there like once."

"Brittany, Detective Konn, and Marvin gran'father, got this Jamaican guy to get in on they scheme," Tia revealed, suddenly feeling a little unnerved at the creepy story she was narrating. A week earlier, she had experienced a nightmare, because of what she knew. "The Jamaican guy was they bootleg mortician. He used to be in that room, stealin' bones out of dead people, Brittany. He was a fuckin' monster. He was replacin' they bones with rusty pipes, and shit, like fuckin' mop sticks, and crow bars, and . . . whatever he felt like puttin' inside of people, Brittany. And they families never even knew. They still don't, Brittany. Just think about it. Who examine they family members, after they go to the funeral home? We trust them people to cut they hair. Do they makeup. Dress them. All we do is look down on them in a

coffin, and that's about it. Brittany, they was even stealin' dead people skin."

Crying for people she didn't even know, Brittany turned and looked at her boss with eyes that were wide with shock, and disbelief. She was horrified at what she was being told.

"They was sellin' dead people skin to burn victim centers, in places like Brazil, and third world countries."

"Oh, my God. Tia, that's so wrong."

"Blame Detective Konn. It was all his doin'. He master minded the whole operation, Brittany. When people wanted to have they family members cremated, they would give them urns filled with kitty litter, and cement mix."

"I wanna check my dad body tomorrow."

"I would, too."

Brittany shook her head sadly.

Yawning, Tia squatted down and picked up her poodle. This got her a few licks to the face.

"Brittany, I gotta private investigator all over Detective Konn. That's how I know all the shit that I know. I been doin' my homework on him for the past two years. That's how I know all about what happened to ya boyfriend mom. Brittany, that's the real reason why I hired you, and made you my assistant."

"So, it ain't have nothin' to do with my dad, and ya uncle, bein' friends in high school?"

"Brittany, that was just fate smilin' at us. That's how I saw it. I been wantin' to talk to you about all of this for months, but trust is a major, major issue for me. Then, all of this happened. It was just about Detective Konn in the beginning. Now, with what Marvin did to your father, he put himself in the line of fire as well."

"It's like it all just came full circle."

"Karma."

Brittany let out a long sigh.

"Brittany, Marvin called Detective Konn yesterday."

"How you know?"

Tia nodded her head at her flat-screen TV.

"Oh, yeah."

"He tryna start business up at that funeral home again, Brittany."

"How?"

"The same way his gran'father did. His plan is to use you to start up a drug war in that neighborhood, so when they start dyin', they peoples can bring they dead bodies to him. He even thinkin' about tryna get muslims to come there, so they can be doin' they janazah services there."

"But I thought muslims wash they bodies, and—"

"Oh, he don't plan on doin' nothin' wrong with any muslim people, he just tryna bring in money any way that he can. His ass not stupid. I'm just wonderin' how he can do all that other shit in there, without it lookin' suspect."

"What other shit?"

"Brittany, he asked Detective Konn to find that Jamaican mortician, and to set everything up, like his gran'father was doin' before."

Brittany shivered as she placed her eyes back on Marvin's giant, sleeping body. Her aunt's boyfriend was more sadistic, than she had even imagined. She had underestimated his temperament. However, as Brittany stood beside her boss, and continued to stare at Marvin, as he slept, she felt no fear. What Marvin had done to her father, and to her father's girlfriend, had her compulsively wanting redemption.

"From what I heard, Detective Konn is all for goin' into business with Marvin. Ya aunt not. After Marvin left out, she did a lot of cryin', Brittany."

"Fuck her . . . she might as well go along with what he tryna do. It ain't no use in not likin' shit now. You can watch him kill ya brother, but'chu got morals about what's gon' be

done to people you don't know? Fuck her. I want her to get the same thing he got comin'."

"Okay, so, Marvin told Detective Konn all about 'chu, Brittany. He told him he was gon' approach you, after ya dad funeral tomorrow. So, you just gotta go along with whatever he say . . . not so easily, though. Act like you, but—"

"I got this, Tia."

"Brittany, this our opportunity to kill three birds with one stone. We can get revenge for so many people, by doin' this. You just have to be on the inside, for this to work, though."

"Fine by me."

"You sure, Brittany?"

"They killed my dad, Tia. That fuckin' cop killed Sean. I never felt so fuckin' sure about anything in my entire fuckin' life."

"Brittany, this won't be no cake walk."

"Gettin' revenge never is."

About the Author

Khalil Murray was born and raised in Philadelphia, Pennsylvania. Along with being a successful book publisher, and an accomplished, best-selling author, Khalil Murray is also a gifted songwriter, and has a large volume of music available. With each of his novels, from his 10-book series (City of Secrets), there are personal soundtracks for each book. These soundtracks have R&B music, comedy skits, business advertisements, special guest features, and a variety of music from some of your favorite rap artists. Next on Khalil Murray's agenda, is to transition all of his books to screenplays, and straight-to-DVD movies, as well as taking out the time to publish other aspiring writers. The Equal Team Publications is always looking for new bookcover models; both, male and female, as well as graphic designers, music producers, music artists, and film directors.

For previews of upcoming books by Khalil Murray, and more information about The Equal Team Publications, visit:

Twitter/@Khalil Murray_Tet
Instagram/@Khalil Murray
Facebook/Khalil Murray

For online orders, and book deliveries to family members, and loved ones incarcerated, visit: www.weshiptoprisons.com, and enter author's name and book title, or visit Amazon.com

Made in the USA
Middletown, DE
15 February 2022

61255771R00149